"Bet you have a million secrets buried under that beautiful, innocent face."

Beautiful. He thinks I'm beautiful. That was something April could grasp and hold on to while facing his disgust.

"I'm not considered particularly beautiful by the other Fae," she said casually.

Chulah snorted. "Impossible. Harder to believe than the fact you aren't human."

"I'm half human. On my father's side," she said quickly. As if this might make her appear more acceptable and less foreign.

"Why didn't you tell me the truth to start with? I'm a shadow hunter. I've fought supernatural beings most of my life. Hell, I have my own powers."

"I'm well aware of your heightened senses. And your strength." April's eyes roved over his broad shoulders and chest, the lean, muscular biceps of his arms. Her throat went dry remembering how it felt to be wrapped in those solid arms and how much she'd desired his touch over the years.

BAYOU SHADOW PROTECTOR

DEBBIE HERBERT

MILLS & BOON

First Published in Great Britain 2016
By Mills & Boon, an imprint of HarperCollins*Publishers*
1 London Bridge Street, London, SE1 9GF

© 2016 Debbie Herbert

ISBN: 978-0-263-92184-7

89-0916

Debbie Herbert writes paranormal romance novels reflecting her belief that love, like magic, casts its own spell of enchantment. She's always been fascinated by magic, romance and gothic stories. Married and living in Alabama, she roots for the Crimson Tide football team. Her oldest son, like many of her characters, has autism. Her youngest son is in the US Army. A past MAGGIE® Award finalist in both young-adult and paranormal romance, she's a member of the Georgia Romance Writers of America.

Chapter 1

He came in second place to a dead lover. If that wasn't just so typical of his life.

Tallulah placed a hand on his arm. "I'm sorry. Really."

Anger pounded his temples. He didn't want her pity. Chulah shrugged her hand away and took a step back. "Forget about it," he answered curtly, knowing his resentment was ridiculous, but unable to control the emotion.

"I had no idea you felt that way about me," she continued.

Tallulah actually looked surprised. Like he and every other warrior should know that she still thought about Bo, lived for Bo, even when he'd been dead for over a year. Crazy women. He'd never understand them.

"No problem," he lied. He didn't want to hear any more of the words that killed his dreams. Chulah took a deep breath and started for the woods, aware of Tallulah's eyes following him as he made for the tree line. His heightened senses from hunting evil bayou spirits allowed him to feel her focused energy on his rigid back.

I love you as a brother, she'd said. *As much as I do any of my fellow shadow hunters.*

Right.

He should have known better than to reveal his feelings, should have stuck to his code of displaying no vulnerability. Chulah kept his back straight. Eyes ahead. No need for her to realize that the blow had hurt his pride as much as his heart. He was a warrior, damn it. Well, mainly he stuck to the code—with the mistaken exception of this afternoon. But the way she'd stood in the sea breeze—black hair teased by the wind, shirt pressed against her strong, lean form, the leather fringed necklace disappearing into the cleavage of her breasts—he'd lost all reason. She was the epitome of a warrior hunter, the only female hunter in their tight clan. A perfect match. Or so he'd imagined. He'd dared to hope that she must know and return some of his desire.

Wrong.

He'd let his protective barriers down, told her of his secret feelings. Stupid. He deserved the I-Just-Wanna-Be-Friends brush-off.

Marching away, he was so latched on to the eyes-straight-ahead approach and shoulders-back posture that his left foot tangled on something and he stumbled.

His pride took a dive along with his feet and he dared not look back. The old Tallulah would have laughed and teased him; now she must see him as a bumbling idiot or, worse, as a man to be pitied.

Chulah regained his balance and plunged into the woods' underbrush, heedless of the nettles and brambles that tore at his jeans, not caring to follow the easy path. Instead, he strode forward, straight at the black trunks of massive trees, solid, unmoving and forbidding. As unyielding as

Tallulah's words. Words that pierced like poisoned darts. He struck savagely at the parasitic kudzu vines that hung between the trees and underbrush, making his way deeper into the shadows.

Tallulah, even with her heightened hunter senses, couldn't see him now.

He wished he could turn all his senses off. His heart, too. Just off.

His breath grew ragged; his long legs shook with exhaustion. Chulah abruptly stopped and inhaled deeply. The green lushness of pine and moss soothed his battered spirit, even more than the peace his job of repairing motorcycles provided. Fixing motors, his mind and hands were in sync and focused on correcting problems.

In the bayou forest, his trekking abilities kicked in, providing a welcome diversion.

The scent of salt drifted from the Gulf on early autumn breezes and mixed with invigorating pine. His supernatural hearing picked up the lap of the tide, the rustle of leaves, a scampering squirrel and a cawing of crows. Chulah opened his mind to it all, relaxing the barrier he put in place to avoid sensory overload. The forest bathed his battered heart as he drew in the ancient wisdom and energy of the trees, calming his mind.

Chulah worked his way to the path and sat on a large tree stump, resting his tired legs. So he'd finally taken a chance and she'd turned him down, with a swift directness that typified all her actions.

And while he was being honest…he was more relieved than disappointed, now that the initial embarrassment had passed. Tallulah had been, perhaps, a little too convenient. They'd grown up together, had shared similar gifts and had fought alongside each other. Their families were close.

She'd been his secret crush in high school, and with Bo gone, it was only natural he'd drifted to her familiar, comfortable presence.

Now that he'd spilled his guts and she'd rejected him, he could move on.

That was the plan, anyway.

For the past few weeks, he'd grown increasingly restless…bored, even. The last great battle was over, and with it Chulah seemed to have lost his purpose. He spent his days repairing motorcycles, and at night took his Harley out for long, solitary rides. He'd grown lonely.

The future stretched before him…the same old, same old.

A sizzle of energy traveled up his spine. Chulah glanced at the empty woods, wondering where the presence hid. He'd experienced it many times before and yet it had always eluded him. He tried to puzzle it out. It was nothing evil like he would sense with the Ishkitini, birds of the night, or with the few stray will-o'-the-wisps that still eluded the hunters.

This energy was…soothing. And familiar. He often picked up on it alone in the woods and a few times when he had hunted down a wisp and was in danger.

"Who are you?" he asked, searching the shadows. More to the point, "*What* are you?"

No answer.

Whatever that presence was, its silence was getting damned annoying. He stood abruptly and strode for home. "Fine. Don't answer," he said with a shrug, feeling more than a little foolish. Today was a day for acting like a bumbling idiot.

"What I need is a long bike ride," he muttered. Nothing but the roar of his Harley and the land rushing to meet him as he sped down the bayou back roads.

To hell with Tallulah and to hell with trying to communicate with some mysterious spirit that wished to remain unknown.

Now was her chance.

April skittered ahead of Chulah, riding the stiff breeze that blew toward his cabin. Excitement electrified her so much that she worried her Fae form would light up like a luminary beacon. And that wouldn't do at all. She'd promised the fairy queen to warn the shadow hunters of danger and enlist them to fight the dark shadow spirit, Hoklonote. The hitch? She was to accomplish this mission while at the same time providing as little information as possible about their hidden existence. Revealing too many secrets would be a last-ditch effort. A necessary evil to safeguard their world as well as the humans' world.

Plus, she had her own reasons for not revealing too much too soon. And it had everything to do with Chulah Rivers. For eleven years she had silently watched him, invisibly aided him as he fought the bayou's dark shadow spirits. All in an attempt to atone for her Great Mistake. Not that she could ever win absolution, but it helped ease her guilty conscience.

After eleven years, it had grown to more than an attempt to pay for her youthful mistake. At first, his handsome form and bravery garnered her admiration, but his stoic kindness—which often went unnoticed and unappreciated by others—was what most enchanted April.

And today, finally, she'd been given the opportunity to meet him again as a real, flesh-and-blood woman. She'd changed her appearance, yet still worried he'd see through the ruse. She must be very, very careful not to slip up. Chulah could never know what she'd done. He'd hate her, and she couldn't bear that.

April darted behind a huge oak tree in case any human eyes might be around. She bundled her Fae essence until the staurolite crystal, the fairies' cross stone, was positioned at the center of her being.

"Out of the mist I arise," she whispered. "In human form alive. Skin and bone and heart and brain, I now transform to a different plane."

For the second time today, that strange sensation passed through her ethereal body. Transformations that she hadn't experienced since the disaster over a decade ago. Not painful, but a stretching and a heaviness and a gravitational pull to the earth. Wind rustled her hair and teased the skin of her arms, and the texture of cotton brushed against her legs.

It was done.

April ran her fingers through her hair and glanced down at the long flowered skirt, and then to the white sandals housing human feet. She wiggled her toes experimentally and giggled. This was going to be fun. Unlike last time. This time she would do everything right and enjoy every tiny human sensation.

An engine revved across the street and she peeked from behind the wide tree.

Chulah gunned the motor and strapped on a helmet. April startled at the loud beating of her human heart encaged by ribs. It seemed too volatile an organ to pump blood so furiously for an entire human life span, not if it kept up this constant beat.

Clouds of dust streaked behind the motorcycle as he exited the dirt driveway. He had to pass by her to get to the county road.

This was it. With a deep breath, April stepped from behind the tree and stood by the side of the road, waving her arms.

He didn't slow, but sped right by her, and she choked on

the fumes and dust. Not how she'd imagined this momentous occasion. She'd been so positive he wouldn't pass by a damsel in distress.

And then she heard the sound of brakes squealing, loud as a dozen screeching owls. The motorcycle stopped a few yards ahead. Chulah lifted off his helmet and swung one leg over the bike until he stood in the street, facing her.

Hot cinnamon eyes raked her from head to toe. April gulped, her throat suddenly dry. Did she look weird? Was something off in her manifestation? The Fae court had explained that her appearance and clothing would reflect her individual nature, yet be acceptable and appropriate for the human world. And nothing like her last earthly appearance.

So why was he staring at her so intently? The Council had assured her that this current manifestation was unrecognizable from her unapproved earthly sojourn at age sixteen. If he remembered their first meeting, her mission was over before it started.

Shaking off the apprehension, she walked forward and extended her hand. "Hi. My name's April. Thanks for stopping."

His gaze shifted to her outreached hand, but he made no move to extend a return greeting. April dropped her hand by her side and cleared her throat. "Would you mind giving me a lift to town?"

"What the hell is a woman doing alone out here?" he asked incredulously.

"I, um, went for a walk in the woods and got lost."

"Got lost," he repeated, brows drawn together. "Where do you live?"

"I have an apartment above my shop on Main Street. Maybe you've heard of it? It's called Pixie Land."

He shook his head, as if in a daze.

"I'm not surprised. We just opened last week." The Fae

had been hard at work setting up that shop and all her living arrangements. She stuck out a hand again. "My name's April Meadows."

"April, huh?" he asked, eyes narrowed and assessing.

A surge of warmth flowed through her body when he said her name. The name she'd made up by taking the time of year she loved best and combining it with her favorite place. Perhaps he needed proof that she was who she said she was. She remembered the forged paperwork and patted the slender purse across her shoulder. Good. Everything should be in order. She opened the purse and riffled through it. "Here," she said triumphantly. "Want to look at my driver's license? Well, it's not *really* a driver's license. I don't drive. Occasional migraines prevent that. They just come out of nowhere and incapacitate me."

His expression of pained incredulity hadn't changed.

"Anyway, it's a picture identification card if you want to see it."

"I don't want to see your ID."

"Oh, okay, then." April dropped it back in her purse. "About that ride?"

"Don't you know how dangerous it is to walk alone in the woods—especially in the late afternoon? It'll be dark in an hour or so. What if I hadn't come along?"

"But you did." As she knew he would.

Chulah crossed his arms. "I could be a psychopath, for all you know. A serial killer who preys on young, lost women."

April laughed. "You could never be like that."

"And how would you know?"

She tapped her sandals on the red clay dirt. Thinking. "I can just tell. You're a nice man."

"Uh-huh," he grunted. "I bet Ted Bundy's victims thought he was nice when they first met."

She blinked. "Ted Bundy?"

"Seriously? He's probably the most notorious serial killer ever." Chulah shook his head. "You must have been living in a dark hole all your life."

A fairy mound instead of a dark hole, but he was close. April nodded at once, eager to correct her mistake. "Oh, yes, now I remember. Ted. Of course."

Chulah gave her a hard, calculating kind of stare, as if debating the wisdom of letting her hop on his bike.

An idea struck. "Are you afraid *I* might be a killer?"

She should have thought of that before. Quickly, she raised her arms, familiar with police procedures after the fairy council's crash course on human behavior and customs. They'd spent an entire day on what to do should one become embroiled in the legal system or a person suspected of a crime. "You can pat me down if you want to check for weapons."

Chulah snorted or laughed; April wasn't exactly sure which. The sound was rusty, as if infrequently employed, and his lips twitched.

She walked closer, arms still raised, until their bodies were in arm's length of each other. "Really. It's okay to search. I'm completely unarmed."

Not entirely true. She had an inner, secret weapon of casting fairy enchantments, but she'd resolved to employ it only in emergencies. April winced, recalling her disastrous attempt at enchanting Chulah all those years ago. Quickly, she thrust aside thoughts of the past. It was a new day, and she had to focus on the matter at hand.

Enchantments. Chulah had no way of detecting such magic from a pat-down. She frowned, remembering the fairy's cross crystal in the purse. Would he count a stone as a primitive weapon?

He gave an exaggerated sigh and strode back to his bike.

April's mouth dropped open. She'd been so sure he'd give her a ride. "Are you leaving me?"

He unbuckled a side bag from the bike and pulled out a spare helmet. "For crying out loud, just wear this and hop on. I don't know how you're going to manage in that skirt, though."

Not the most gracious invitation, but it would have to do. April eyed the helmet with distaste. How could anyone stand to have their head wrapped in such a tight bubble? "Do I have to wear it?"

"Nobody rides this bike without a helmet. It's the law. Besides, only an idiot would ride without one."

There went her fantasy of the wind blowing his long black hair in her face, covering her like a blanketing caress. And actually, she'd seen him riding around his yard without a helmet, but it might not be prudent to mention that fact. A female member of the Council had taken her aside and explained about the male ego thing. Which was much the same in the fairy realm, so point taken.

She didn't want Chulah to think she was an idiot, so she stuffed the torture device on her head.

It was stifling. Her hot breath steamed the windshield thingy. Chulah lifted the helmet's flap and she sucked air.

"I'm ready," she announced bravely. She was used to flying, the wind fanning her face and hair, free and wild. Had dreamed of a motorcycle ride as a new kind of flying, human style.

His hands were suddenly at her throat and she gasped, taking an involuntary step back.

"Relax. I'm just tightening the straps."

"Oh." She glanced down, mesmerized by the sight of his olive-skinned fingers so close to her pale neck. Fantasies that had nothing to do with motorcycle riding filled her mind, and she shut her eyes. His hands were warm and competent, and a little shiver of pleasure rippled through her as they accidentally brushed against the vulnerable hollow of her throat.

"There. You're good."

Did she imagine his voice had a huskier edge, an undertone of desire? Her eyes flew to his face, but his back already faced her as he straddled the bike, putting on his own helmet. Chulah motioned with his hands. "Let's go."

Now she would get to wrap her arms around his waist. April almost licked her lips. She walked to the bike, assessing it, before lifting her skirt and swinging a leg over the side. The skirt rode up to her butt, but she should be fine. She'd often observed human women exposing much more skin at the beach.

The motorcycle lurched forward, and she wrapped her arms around his trim waist. Damned helmet prevented laying her face between Chulah's broad shoulders. She itched to explore the muscles that she'd seen many a time as he worked outside in his yard. Soon, April promised herself. Very soon.

The roaring of the engine pounded in her ears, and she acclimated to the jerk and shudder of tires hitting small potholes. April liked the ride very much. What it lacked in fairy finesse, it made up for in raw power. No wonder Chulah rode so much when he was troubled. On his Harley, he harnessed that power and focused his attention on the open road.

Pine trees and dirt roads gave way to buildings and pavement. Unease prickled down her spine. She much preferred the woods, but had made periodic, invisible trips to downtown Bayou La Siryna in preparation for this mission.

A mermaid statue came into view and she breathed a sigh of relief at the familiar landmark. "Turn left at the next light," she yelled to Chulah.

He nodded in acknowledgment, and as they turned onto Main Street, she counted the buildings to her left. One, two three, four… "Stop here," she directed.

Chulah expertly swerved into a parking space and shut off the engine. April sat, waiting for him to get off first.

He lifted his helmet, and the hair that had been secured inside it fell loose. A veil of soap-scented warmth enveloped April's neck and shoulders. She again cursed the helmet as it blocked her face from experiencing the same intimate contact. Fumbling with the straps, she took off her own helmet and shook her hair free.

Chulah glanced over his shoulder. "Get off," he commanded.

April hastily complied, throwing one bare leg over the side to dismount. A loud whistle erupted across the street where three young men stared and pointed. Usually a sign of approval, if she remembered correctly.

She looked around, but no one else was close by. Were they whistling at her or Chulah? And for what reason?

Chulah scowled at them and they walked on by, laughing.

"Why were those guys whistling at you?" she asked. "Were they admiring your parking skills, perhaps?"

He arched a brow and studied her curiously. "They were whistling at *you*. Not me."

"Why me?"

"I suspect it was the show of leg," he remarked drily.

But she'd shown less skin than women in bathing suits. Did they constantly whistle while at the beach? Very confusing. The Council had advised covering confusion with diversion. April ran a hand through her hair. "So," she said brightly. "Would you like to come inside for a drink?"

This was a human convention she was sure was appropriate. And her apartment was supposed to be well stocked in all manner of human food and drink.

"No." He turned his back on her and headed for his bike.

"Wait," she called out hurriedly. "Are you sure you don't want a drink? It might be more comfortable to talk about your problem with me than riding your motorcycle all evening."

He slowly turned and confronted her, his face a stone mask. "What makes you think I have a problem? You don't even know me."

Oh, but she did. Only Chulah couldn't know that yet—if ever. That would happen only once he trusted and fell in love with her. Then she could share all her secrets. That was, if he could forgive her. A very big *if.*

"True, I don't know you well," she admitted, scrambling for an explanation. "I just thought you seemed, um, preoccupied and worried."

His jaw clenched. "I'm fine."

She'd inadvertently injured his pride to suggest otherwise. "All right, then." She smiled and shrugged. "Since you've already played my knight in shining armor, maybe you could help me out again."

"What do you want now?"

His response was not promising. How was she to build a relationship with him if he wouldn't even have a drink with her? She couldn't fail. To return to the Fae realm in defeat would be humiliating. She'd been so cocky, so *sure* that Chulah would help them stop Hoklonote.

And she'd been equally certain that he would return her warm feelings could he but meet her in human form. It was what she'd been dreaming of for so many years. That, and restoring the good name of her mother in the fairy realm.

Foolish, foolish Tallulah had rejected his heart. What April wouldn't have given to be in Tallulah's shoes. Hurt and jealousy lanced April inside, a new sensation. Sure, she'd known sadness and disappointment, but not this searing stab in the gut as she'd witnessed Chulah's proposal. Her eyes watered.

"Are you crying?" Chulah asked, surprise written on his face. "Ah, damn…don't do that."

She stiffened. "I am *not* crying," she said with all the dignity she could muster. "If I were, there would be tears running down my face. Which they are not." It didn't count if they were contained behind eyelids; she was pretty sure on that score.

"What the hell," he muttered. "Let's have a drink."

"Really?" She brightened. "You won't regret it. It'll be fun."

"Whatever." He strapped his helmet on the handlebars and motioned for her to hand her own over. She did, and he tossed it in the side bag and buckled it up.

April opened her purse, searching for the store key. In the back room was a staircase leading to her upstairs apartment.

The Pixie Land door swung open and a short man with a red beard beamed at them. "Hey, boss, I've 'bout got all the inventory unpacked and ready to open for business in the morn."

Steven, a fellow fairy helping in the mission, had caught her by surprise. She'd thought he'd have returned to the Fae realm by now. "Th-that's great," she said. "We're going upstairs—"

"No, we're going to a bar," Chulah interrupted. He walked over to Steven and extended a hand. "Chulah Rivers."

"Steven Andrews," he smoothly replied, shaking hands. "Pleasure to meet ya."

Chulah nodded and gestured down the street. "The bar's only a block from here. We can walk."

"Sure."

"Excuse us a moment, will ya?" Steven said to Chulah. "Just need to check with the boss on a small matter."

"Take your time."

Chulah was better mannered around strangers than he was with her, April noted.

Steven pulled her into the shop doorway. "You might be needing this." He pressed a roll of bills into her palm. "A little mad money in case your fellow doesn't pay or you get stranded."

"Good idea." She stuffed the money in her purse. "See you later."

Steven gave a broad wink. "Watched you out there. Excellent job using your feminine wiles on the man. None of us like to see a woman cry."

"I wasn't using my wiles," she sputtered, glancing back at Chulah, who was busy studying the fairy figurines in the shop window.

He gave a maddening little chuckle. "Sure you weren't."

"Oh, for the queen's sake—I'll be back in a bit."

"Take your time. Wrap him around your little finger." The smile left his face. "Don't be like your mother. Your loyalty is to *our* world. Not theirs."

April shut the door in his blathering face, afraid Chulah might overhear and angry at the slur to her mother. She took a deep breath to steady her emotions. "I'm ready." She smiled. "What's the name of this place?"

"Bayou Brandy & Spirits. A friend of mine owns it."

They fell into step, April bubbling with excitement. This officially counted as a date in her book. She'd been courted a few times by her own kind, but they acted as if they were doing her a great favor since her mother was so reviled. Besides, the attentions of the notoriously fickle male of her species held no real charm. In that respect, she was just like her mother. She wanted a forever kind of man.

A man like Chulah.

All she had to do was win his trust, persuade him to help their mutual cause, work with him to defeat Hoklonote, restore her family's name, convince the queen and Council to let her remain in Bayou La Siryna—plus, win his undying love. All while protecting her secret offense against him years ago.

April wasn't daunted a bit.

Chapter 2

Even in the early whisper of evening, stepping into the bar was stepping into night and mystery and a winding-down from the day's work and worries. A dark, velvet smokiness settled on Chulah like a balm.

All heads, mostly male, turned their way. And stayed turned. April's unusual hair color practically glowed like quicksilver in the dim lighting.

They slipped into a booth and Chulah signaled Karlee over. She approached, eyeing April with a jaded once-over stare.

"Hey, sweetie. That's some kind of dye job ya got there." She lifted a thick strand of April's hair and leaned in, squinting. "Blond and silver and lavender. Who'd have guessed that combo worked?" She smiled, not unkindly. "I like it."

"Thanks."

Women and their hair. Chulah stifled a sigh. "I'll have a whiskey double. Neat."

Karlee whistled. "Tough day, huh?"

He recalled the pity in Tallulah's eyes as she said he was like a brother. "You could say that."

"What about you, sweetie?" Karlee asked, turning to April.

"Water?" she said, uncertainly.

Karlee frowned. "That's it? Just plain ole water?"

"What flavors do you have? I prefer floral nectar, but I like orange water, too."

Karlee exchanged a what's-her-deal look with him. Chulah shrugged. "Maybe she means orange juice?"

"Yes, that's it," April said in a rush, pink flushing her cheeks. "Orange juice."

"How about I spike it with brandy?"

April drummed her fingers on the worn tabletop. "I guess. Sure."

Interesting. She wasn't afraid of roaming the woods alone, yet ordering a drink appeared to make her nervous. He needed to know more about this unusual woman. "Where are you from?" he asked. "You're new here or we'd have crossed paths before now."

"I used to live in Tillman's Corner, about thirty miles east of here."

"I know where it is. I have a cousin who grew up there. You know Drew Lattimore?"

She tilted her head to the side and pursed her lips, thinking. "No. The name isn't familiar."

Chulah studied her, a niggling unease prickling his skin. Something about her seemed familiar, but surely he'd remember such an unusual woman if they'd met before. "What brings you to Bayou La Siryna?"

"I'm opening a store. You saw it."

The woman wasn't very forthcoming. Most business owners he knew had a passionate entrepreneurial spirit. She mentioned her store as if it were as exciting as eating a piece of toast. "I know. But why here, why now?"

"Seemed like a good idea." She squirmed in her seat. "What got you interested in repairing motorcycles?"

"How did you know that?"

She blinked. "You mentioned it."

"No."

Her lie didn't sit well with him. He was a man of few words, so it was easy to remember them. And he hadn't said a word about his bike shop.

Karlee returned, setting down their drinks. "Here ya go. Enjoy."

Chulah swallowed a mouthful of stiff whiskey, watching April, trying to figure her out. The woman had a secret.

She took a tentative sip of her drink and licked her full lips, testing it. An unexpected volt of pure sexual desire speared his gut, more potent than the alcohol. She took another, longer sip and nodded her head. "It's good. Strange, though, like a fire going down your throat to your belly."

"About my repair shop—"

"—I want another one." She downed the entire glass and gave him a lopsided grin.

"Whoa. Maybe you should slow down. Pace yourself."

But she was already waving at Karlee and pointing to her empty glass.

Although a complete stranger, Chulah suspected this wasn't her normal behavior. After all, she'd ordered water to start with. Unless she was a recovering alcoholic and he was responsible for tempting her beyond her control. The thought made his skin draw up tight. "Do you drink often?"

"First time." She set her elbow on the table and put her chin in one palm, giggling.

It occurred to him that now would be a good time to press her a bit, discover what made her tick. "So what brings you to this town?" he asked again.

"I'm on a mission." She wagged a finger in front of his face. "And when I make up my mind, I can't be stopped."

"What kind of mission?"

"To save the world."

"From what?"

She stopped smiling. "Evil. There's so much evil."

Didn't he know it. Had battled against it for years with his fellow shadow hunters. But, at least in this corner of the universe, the evil was now contained. They had stopped Nalusa Falaya, the supreme evil being, although a few wisps and other nefarious creatures still remained to be hunted. There would always be some around. Their Choctaw ancestors were testimony to that cold fact.

He leaned in close to April. She smelled like flowers and something...earthy, like moss or a freshly mown lawn. Her face was heart-shaped and her complexion a peachy pale color with dots of freckles sprinkled across her nose, and her full lips were rosy. Her eyes were an impossible purple-blue color. Contacts, perhaps? Altogether, she looked innocent and fresh.

But looks could be deceiving. "What would you know of evil?" he asked softly.

She matched his low tone. "It's out there. Deep in the woods." She raised a slender finger to her lips. "Shhh... it's a secret."

His entire body flushed hot, then chilled. Who was this mysterious woman who appeared out of nowhere and was no stranger to the danger in the woods? She'd deliberately sought him out and knew entirely too much about him.

"I can keep a secret." He pushed the spiked OJ into her hands. "Does this evil have a name?"

April raised the glass to her lips and took a healthy slug. "Mustn't tell." She burped—a tiny effervescent bubble burst that was more charming than vulgar.

"Sure you can. You came to tell me something. Go ahead."

Blue eyes widened and she shook her head. "You are

so smart. And handsome. And kind. Tallulah must be the biggest fool in the world."

He clasped her arm. "How could you possibly—"

"Hey, man, what's up? Who's your new friend?"

Leman Jones kept his gaze on April, even though his words were addressed to Chulah.

Irritation flashed through Chulah as he released April's arm and made the introductions. His old friend had no right to leer at her like that, even if she was the prettiest woman in the place. He shifted his gaze past Leman's shoulder and saw four other males approaching their table.

"You'll have to excuse us—we were just leaving." Chulah slapped a handful of bills on the table to cover the drinks, plus a hefty tip for Karlee.

"But I haven't finished my drink," April complained.

"You heard the lady." Leman grinned at Chulah and turned to April. "If you want to stay and finish your drink, I'll see you home."

Chulah helped a wobbly April to her feet. "Thanks. We're good here."

"Can't blame a guy for trying. She's hot," Leman whispered in his ear.

Chulah guided April past the sea of men with disappointed faces. Outside, the breeze was refreshing. "Doing all right there?" he asked.

She nodded. "A little dizzy, but okay."

"Do two drinks always affect you so much?" he asked, trying to trap her in a lie.

She walked slowly, considering. "I don't know. This is the first time I've had alcohol. I'm not sure it agrees with me."

"I would say not."

Hiccup. April covered her mouth with her hand. "'Scuse me." *Hiccup.*

She momentarily seemed to rise a few inches on the

sidewalk and then lower down. He blinked. Must have been some kind of optical illusion. Chulah inwardly sighed as he took her arm and slowly led her down the sidewalk toward her place. Seemed he was always rescuing women and children. He'd had a spectacularly crappy day and could use a little rescuing himself. At least April was an interesting diversion; he'd grant her that.

In fact, she was so diverting he'd almost forgotten to quiz her about her warning of evil. Chulah straightened his shoulders. He couldn't have questioned her with a flock of men hanging around; much better to get her alone. Yeah, that was the only reason he'd scuttled her out of the bar so quickly. It had nothing to do with jealousy.

At the Pixie Land shop door, April fumbled with the keys. Before Chulah could offer assistance, Steven opened the door.

"What's this?" he asked sharply, nostrils twitching. "You've been drinking?" He whisked April inside and frowned at Chulah.

"Only a little." April's demure response was ruined by a tiny hiccup.

Her face rose from his chin level to eye level. Just as quickly as before, she slipped down again.

Chulah shook his head to clear it. Last time he'd ever order a double dose of whiskey. He faced Steven and held up a hand. "I didn't twist her arm. How was I supposed to know she'd never had alcohol before?"

Steven stuck his nose in the air. "Should have chaperoned the likes of you both." He scowled at April. "I'll fix you a strong herbal brew. Get you right in no time. Where's your head at, missy?"

No need to be so gruff. Chulah stepped between them. "I'll fix her a cup of coffee. Didn't you say earlier you were about to quit work?"

His scowl deepened. "I'm not leaving until I see she's good and sober."

Chulah rubbed his chin. The man seemed entirely too proprietary to be a mere employee. Perhaps a brother? But their coloring and build and mannerisms were so different, that seemed unlikely.

He suppressed his irritation. He barely knew either of them. Yet it didn't sit well to simply leave April in this condition with such an irritable man. "Go on and fix whatever it is you're making. We'll be upstairs."

Steven opened his mouth as if to object.

"We'll be fine," April assured him, patting his shoulder before heading to the back.

Chulah followed, eyeing the myriad glass shelves lined with pastel-colored figurines. There were winged fairies, ballerinas in tutus, mermaids with glistening tails and other magical beings. "You have a sense of whimsy," he noted.

"They are pretty, aren't they?" She stopped and traced her fingers over one of the winged fairy statues. "What do you think of this one?"

The fairy sported silver-and-purple hair, alabaster skin, sort of like April. He examined it closer. There were even… yep, a few tiny freckles on the fairy's nose. "Favors you."

A mysterious smile blossomed on her lips. "I'd like you to have it." She lifted it, and Chulah braced his hand under her unsteady ones, afraid she'd send the delicate figurine crashing to the floor.

Her skin was so soft, so delicate and pale above his calloused, dark hand. A sensual ache coursed through his body. He hadn't felt this way in years about any woman besides Tallulah. He took the sculpture and returned it to the shelf. "We'll talk about the figurine later. Let's get you seated while we wait on Steven to bring your tea or whatever it is he's brewing."

Her full lower lip pouted a bit, which should have irritated him, but instead, he found it adorable.

They climbed a narrow set of stairs and entered her room. The tiny studio apartment was immaculate, but sparse and utilitarian, featuring a bed, a kitchenette, a leather sofa and two chairs with a coffee table between. None of the whimsical shop figures decorated the room. It had a masculine vibe without a trace of feminine softness. It didn't fit her at all.

April plopped on the sofa and patted the spot next to her.

"Doesn't look like you've had time to decorate yet," he said, sitting beside her. "I would have thought you'd have a pink ruffled bedspread at least," he teased.

She gazed about the room, as if seeing it for the first time. "It'll do for now." Her head rested on the back of the sofa and she reached out and placed a hand on his chest.

His heart thundered under her gentle touch. April's mysterious, womanly smile returned, playing on her lips, desire darkening her indigo eyes. Passion crackled and flowed between his heart and her hand. A moment of tension, of inevitability, sparked the air. As if guided by a magnet, his hand reached up and touched the quicksilver hair that charged like velvet lightning between his fingers.

April was fire and ice. Pale coolness on the outside that burned like dry ice and winter's frost upon contact.

But a good burn. A *very* good burn that left him craving more heat. Their lips found their own way to each other, his arms encircled her slim, lithe waist, and his exploring fingers raced up and down her spine.

And he was lost. Nothing existed but skin and heat and the fire of desire that glowed around their fevered bodies like an electrical corona.

Bam bam bam. It took his brain a moment to register

that someone—presumably Steven—was pounding on the door. Chulah drew back from April, wondering if his face reflected the stunned surprise in her own. She licked her lips and he was almost a goner once again. Abruptly, Chulah left the couch and went to the door.

"About time." Steven scowled and held up a steaming mug. "For April."

An herbal scent wafted upward. "I'll take it." He tried to remove the mug from Steven's hand but the little man held fast.

"Can I trust you—or are you the kind of man who would be taking advantage of an innocent woman's compromised condition?"

Warmth flooded his cheeks. Had that been where he was heading with April? He'd never been overly impulsive before, had never let passion override his common sense. Hell, he barely knew the woman.

But that kiss.

That mind-blowing-body-lit-up kiss had completely possessed him.

"Who is it?" April called from the den.

Even the sound of her voice sent blood rushing to his loins. Perhaps some distance was in order. He needed to get away and think on all that had happened, unencumbered by lust. "I was just leaving."

Before he could change his mind, Chulah brushed past Steven and scurried down the stairs, out of the glass menagerie of the shop and into the fresh air outside.

Time for that long motorcycle ride he'd started to take earlier, intending to banish the sting of Tallulah's rejection. But the image of the dark-haired, fierce Tallulah had been replaced by that of a silver-blonde graced with gentle curves and soft lips.

Who knew way too damn much about him.

* * *

Note to self: never, ever drink alcohol again, April thought. Ever. She'd almost blown it tonight. April danced her fingertips over her lips. That kiss…

Steven waved a hand in front of her face. "How's the tea workin'?"

"Like a charm." The delightful, but dangerous, fuzzy feeling had faded, leaving her bemused.

"Good. Now we can talk. Did you tell him you were Fae?"

"No." But she remembered telling him she was on a mission to save the world. She'd also slipped up mentioning Tallulah, something she should know nothing about. She'd think of an excuse for that later. For now, she wanted to relive every moment of their brief kiss.

"Perfect. It's too early. Gradually weave a web of enchantment for a few days until he's besotted with you and willing to do anything you ask."

April sipped more tea. If he took her silence to mean agreement, that was all on him.

"The tea might have reversed the alcohol's effects, but it's clear that this Chulah has affected you much the same as strong drink. Physical contact with a human can be… most pleasant. Especially your first time."

She didn't want to have this conversation. "So I've been told." *Hiccup.*

Her stomach rose to her throat and her body lifted and dropped back down on the sofa.

Steven let out a low whistle. "You just levitated. Must be some glitch in the Fae glamour."

"Is that it? Whenever I drink liquid it makes me hiccup."

"Then be sure not to partake around humans. And don't forget you're only here temporarily," Steven warned. "Take a few days, enthrall the shadow hunter and then warn him of the danger. If we're lucky, he and the other hunters can take care of Hoklonote on their own, without our assistance. If that doesn't work, then petition Chulah to form a mutually beneficial alliance with us to defeat our common enemy."

"I know my duty," she snapped, setting down the mug. April paced the room. It galled her that her own kind cared so little for Chulah or any other human. She didn't want Chulah fighting Hoklonote without help from the Fae. It wasn't right to ask him to fight their battles for them. The Fae saw Chulah and the other shadow hunters only as a means to an end. Whereas she…she wanted Chulah to see the real April Meadows. To come to care for her as she did for him.

But Steven couldn't know that. No one could. It was her own secret wish.

A fairy could dream.

Steven arched a brow. "What's wrong?"

"Nothing," she lied. "Just restless. A little tired."

"And starving, I bet. Have you eaten human food today?"

"No. I forgot."

"I've made a pot of chili. Come downstairs and eat with me. You'll feel lots better. While in human form, you need to consume what they call calories. It fuels your body, gives you energy." He grinned. "Tastes surprisingly good, too."

"If you say so. Let me wash up and I'll be down in a minute."

With a nod, he left. Finally, she was alone. April covered her face in her hands, felt Chulah's lips and hands again on her body. She'd never experienced anything like that from the few Fae kisses she'd stolen from Fae lads while hidden among the lily pads or behind the wild azaleas.

Had it been the same for him? She hoped he found her as desirable as Tallulah. Guilt twisted her gut. When they'd been sitting close together on the sofa, she'd accidentally flung a little fairy pheromone his way.

Okay. So it wasn't entirely accidental. She'd given Chulah the tiniest nudge for him to kiss her. But he'd wanted to, she could tell.

Never again, she vowed. It meant more if he kissed her without the influence of magic.

Curious as to how her human form appeared, April went to the bathroom and stared in the mirror. The Council had told her that this form would manifest her fairy nature, and she saw that truth in the mirror.

Dismay clouded her eyes. She looked nothing like his true love, Tallulah. The white of her skin was the pale of the white bearded iris she slept under. Her eyes were the bluish purple of the wild violets she nibbled on for nourishment, and her hair was moon-bathed in silver, as night was the time she loved to flit about. She slept during the day after a bath in the dew of the early morn. She was thin and lithe as the stalks of sea oats, and the pale purple streaks in her hair were the whisper of eggplant behind a cloud at sunset.

The Council had assured her the human form would be pleasing to the male human species. But April would have traded everything for Tallulah's olive skin, black silky hair and muscular frame. She was like an Amazon warrior of old—the only female shadow hunter in the history of Bayou La Siryna.

No doubt the Council would laugh at her jealousy if they learned of it. "Use your enchantment," they'd advise. "No

man can resist your Fae charm while under your spell."
But April was determined to do this her own way—on
her own terms.

She would succeed where her mother had failed.

Chapter 3

Chulah removed his helmet and sat on his motorcycle, studying the tree line at the point where April had suddenly— mysteriously—appeared from the backwoods. It was possible that some trace, some clue could be tracked down. With luck, he'd follow the signs to the point of origin. At least it would reveal if April had lied about getting lost after a simple hike. One that she claimed to have begun near her apartment. Her story didn't ring true, and even after riding for hours, there was something about her...something disturbing he couldn't quite pinpoint. Compounding his unease was his lack of physical control at her apartment. It was as if she drew him to her magnetically, removing his normal reserve.

Chulah removed a flashlight from his saddlebag and stuffed it in his backpack, which he had weighted down with rocks. His eyes adjusted to the night's dark veil, so he probably didn't need the flashlight, but it never hurt to be prepared. The rocks were for any stray will-o'-the-wisps.

Strapping the backpack across his broad shoulders, he approached the woods. He'd first glimpsed April by the massive oak. The tree had a sharp bend in the trunk, courtesy of Hurricane Katrina years earlier.

The scent of violets and moss teased his nose, the same scent that April bore, one that niggled at his memory. Broken twigs and pine needles marked the ground and he followed the trail.

She'd stayed close to one of the many narrow footpaths that veined the forest and her direction had been true. Never once had she strayed down a different path, or circled back to the one that led to the road and his home. Interesting. You would think somebody new to the area, and supposedly lost, would have strayed at least once, taken a circuitous path or explored a way to exit the woods.

Deeper and deeper, Chulah journeyed to the dark, quiet interior of the bayou forest. Strange that April chose to walk a path so far removed from civilization. An uneasy prickle lifted the hairs on his arms. The scent of violets grew sharper and the trail abruptly ended at the base of an ancient cypress where a large patch of wild violets bloomed— totally out of season. They were spring flowers blossoming in the heart of autumn. Chulah turned from that mystery to another, more pressing question.

Where had April gone from here?

That same April who knew of the bayou's secret, of its evil spirits, who knew things about him she had no logical way of knowing. Whose tracks stopped in the middle of the woods, in a spot that festered with some strange magick he'd never seen. Something was afoot, something he'd never encountered before in all his years of hunting shadows.

He didn't believe in coincidence. This place and that woman were connected. Tomorrow he would visit April and demand an explanation. Had she kissed him to distract his attention from her loose tongue? If so, it wouldn't happen again.

Eerie silence enveloped him like a wool blanket. That was what was different. Not what was there, but the *absence* of what should be there—no insect droning, no underbrush rattles from small animals, no hooting of owls or even the sound of the sea breeze in the treetops. Only silence.

Baffled, Chulah raised his arms, allowing his senses to become totally immersed in the night, seeking out any sign of hidden shadows that secreted the bayou. The sensing was passed down from his Choctaw ancestors, a special line of descendants gifted to detect the evil shadow world. The shadow creatures considered humans intruders and sought to either drive them out or control the ones who stayed.

His family had chosen to stay. And to fight.

They had lived in this south Alabama swampland for hundreds of years, as far back as anyone could remember. Surely they had been here since the beginning of time—same as the shadow beings who didn't want to share the land. Not only that, they wanted to dominate every creature—human, animal and supernatural—that roamed the bayou.

Chulah sent a prayer to his ancestors for guidance. The silence continued, but Chulah's feet directed him to a distance of about ten yards from the tree where April's trail stopped. He looked down. On the side of his right foot, fallen leaves blew and rustled. On his left side, all was still and silent.

Odd.

He followed the divided, splintered land, walking a circle with the cypress tree at its center. Inside the circle, all was silent. Outside the circle, all was normal. Chulah rubbed his chin, puzzling out this new development. Was it possible there was some new manner of creature that he and his fellow hunters had never before witnessed?

Quietly, he withdrew two large rocks and held each in the palms of his hands, ready for attack. He again walked the circle's perimeter, yet found but one set of April's footprints where she had walked from the tree to the road.

It didn't make sense. Something was off.

Chulah halted, allowing the darkness to completely mask him from moonlight, drawing layers of the night's shadow to wrap around his body.

And waited.

His patience was as still as the live oaks that encircled and filled the forest, living sentinels that discouraged most humans from entering deep, and contained the shadows within. A boundary between civilization and the primitive, mysterious evil that had been present since the beginning of time.

As a shadow hunter, he lived in between the two worlds, not fully belonging to either. On full-moon nights, his soul ached to be in the bayou backwoods, a part of the shadows born to shelter mankind from the old spirits who meant them harm and who longed to escape the forest's boundaries.

He continued his watch, attentive to every sound and smell and movement. A gray fox, his namesake, stopped its lonesome prowling and stared at him solemnly before padding away on silent paws. The wily creatures never failed to greet him on his solitary vigils. When he was born, his father had entered the woods and waited for a sign on what to name his son. A fox had wandered close and stared. His father named him *Chulah*, Choctaw for *fox*, to honor his son's appointed animal guide.

An orange glow, the color of citrine lit from within, shone in the distance, a candle in the dark. It wasn't the blue glow of a wisp with a green, throbbing heart at its center. It wasn't swamp gas. And it wasn't a flashlight beam of a fellow hunter. This was something altogether new, the likes of which he'd never observed in all his years of hunting.

It skittered closer, its glow elongated and emitting sparkling cascades of light. He sensed no mischief or ill intent, but then again, shadow beings often cloaked their evil with a display of beauty and purity.

The violet scent intensified and the patch of improbably late-blooming flowers opened their petals and multiplied their blooms. As the orange light drew closer, the violets hummed and shimmered with a fluorescent aura.

The orange luminescence glided to within twenty yards. The closer it came, the more details appeared. Over five feet in height with a thin columnar shape, extensions from the main body occasionally moved like limbs. Although the predominant color was orange, there were also pinks and purples and blues and greens.

Chulah squinted his eyes. Were those *wings* protruding from its back? Could this be some kind of giant, magical insect? Or some creature that feasted on the strange violets that now tinkled with the clean, pure notes of a bell?

Excitement and wonder stirred deep within Chulah. Still, his hands fisted over the rock he held in one hand and a dagger in another. Just in case this was some wisp mutation sent to trick. He knew better than anyone that the swamp held deep, dark secrets. He had lost two hours of his life here one day, two precious hours that had meant the difference between life and death for his father.

Just because something was beautiful didn't mean it wasn't deadly.

The creature stilled, as if realizing it was being observed. In a blink, the light extinguished. Darkness thickened and the flower blooms wilted and died, withdrawing their scent.

The dead flowers bothered him more than the strange creature. Nature's time cycle had warped. How long had he been out here? Had he lost time again, perhaps more than a mere two hours? Chulah scrubbed his face. Tried to rub out the questions that left him disoriented and queasy.

Stumbling, he turned away and ran, clumsy with dread and déjà vu. *Crazy, man. You've lost it again. Crazy, crazy, crazy.* He longed for his cabin, longed to know that no time had mysteriously disappeared and that no one was hurt or dying.

It's happening again, just like before.

No! If someone else died because of him… No, he wouldn't think of it. His blood roared in his ears, combining with the sound of his own strangled breathing. A symphony of terror. It drowned all other noise, as if he were alone in his own private hell.

Thorns sliced at his legs and arms and he welcomed the pain that kept him grounded to the land and reality.

Chulah broke into the clearing near his cabin and ran faster. Just a little farther. Back to normalcy. Everything would be okay.

He hoped.

He took the porch steps two at a time and burst into the cabin, flicking on the light switch. All appeared as he left it. A newspaper lay on the kitchen table alongside his coffee cup. Hands trembling slightly, Chulah picked up the paper and checked the date.

Today's date.

The terror subsided, but still hammered his heart. Quickly, he crossed the room and snatched his cell phone from the charger. Eleven thirty-seven p.m. He pursed his lips, considering. That sounded about right. He'd left about thirty or forty minutes ago. There were no emergency text messages. He checked voice mail... No, there were no messages or missed calls.

Excess adrenaline flushed out of his system in a whoosh. He sank onto the couch and put his head in his hands. Despite his relief, the old sorrow returned. Time had lessened the grief, but the guilt and sadness would be with him forever.

That was close.

April fluttered her wings nervously from the top branches of a sweet gum tree. Damn if she wasn't as careless now as she'd been a decade ago. If he'd seen her in Fae form, she could have blown everything on day one. It was way too early in the game for him to accept that she was a fairy and that her intentions were honorable. First, she needed to establish some measure of trust before asking his help with Hoklonote. Ease into it as much as she could, given the limited time frame. If any of the other fairies had seen her stumbling about, drunk on human kisses, the Council might pull her from this mission.

Fearfully, she gazed around the area and breathed a sigh of relief. No Fae in sight to witness her idiocy.

Home free.

April touched her fingers to her lips, reliving Chulah's kisses. It had been glorious. The best afternoon of her life. No wonder her mother had been so besotted with her human lover. The only surprise was that all the female fairies hadn't defected from the Fae realm. Evidently, they didn't realize what they were missing.

"What the hell were you doing out there?" a voice hissed not a yard from where she sat.

Shock slammed through her essence and she lost her balance, toppling from the tree. A couple of somersaults later,

April righted herself and flew to the ground. Like a cat, she managed to land right side up, unharmed but unnerved.

A thud hit the ground a few yards away. Steven's stony visage flickered into view for a microsecond. Not long enough for human eyes to detect, but plenty long enough for her to see his scolding frown.

"You're supposed to keep me informed of your whereabouts," he said sternly. "I go to check on you and what do I find? An empty bed."

"I'm not used to sleeping in such a confined area," April explained. "It's stifling to be surrounded by four walls with only a small window to see the world outside. I had to get out for a little fly-about. Surely there's no harm in that, is there?"

"Hoklonote might be lurking nearby. It's a dangerous time to be alone in the woods."

Chulah had said much the same thing this afternoon when she'd hitched a ride.

"I'm sorry. I promise to let you know next time."

Steven tugged on his red beard. "I saw that Chulah almost caught you. You need to keep your wits about you. Our lives depend on that."

"I've learned my lesson, and I'm prepared now. It won't happen again."

"See that it doesn't." He tried to keep his voice gruff, but she saw that the worst of the lecture was over.

"I won't get you in trouble," she assured him. As her temporary overseer while on the mission, Steven was as responsible for her mistakes as she was.

"Very well. Let's get back to the apartment. Our human bodies need sleep to function properly."

"I'm going to stay out a little longer."

Steven frowned and she hastened to mollify him. "If it's okay with you," she added meekly. "I want to watch over Chulah as he returns home. He's our best chance to get an in with the shadow hunters. We can't afford to let him get hurt."

He sighed. "You're right. We'll do it together."

Exactly what she *didn't* want. Even though she was invisible to Chulah, April enjoyed flying beside him, as if there was a shared intimacy between them alone in the woods. Steven would definitely be a third wheel.

"No, no, this won't take long. And like you said, we need our sleep. I think my escapade tonight interrupted yours. Why don't you go back to bed?"

He wavered, hands on hips. "I am tired," he admitted.

"I'll be back soon," April said, flying up above him. "See you later?"

"Oh, all right. Just don't do anything foolish."

And she was off before Steven could change his mind. In the rush of the wind, she was behind Chulah. Close enough to almost reach out and touch his shoulder. It was agony and a familiar pleasure to be so close, and yet so far apart. Especially now that she knew the sweet excitement of his mouth and his hands.

In no time, Chulah entered his cottage and shut the door. Still, she was loath to leave him. Instead, she watched through the curtainless window as he settled on the couch and talked on the phone. Was he perhaps calling Tallulah? Inviting her to come over? Begging her to change her mind on his proposal?

Even after he'd hung up the phone, jealousy and curiosity wouldn't let her leave. She'd sleep so much easier if she knew for certain that Tallulah wasn't coming over. Chulah didn't go straight to bed; instead, he opened a book and began to read.

Minutes later, car headlights turned in the driveway and pierced the dark. A man jumped out and ran to the door.

Ah, yes, she recognized his friend Tombi Silver. A smile lit her lips. No reason to stay, other than she couldn't bear to tear her eyes from the lit window and go back to her bare, lonely apartment.

And so she hovered, reluctant to leave.

Chapter 4

"What the hell? A new creature we've never seen?"

Chulah's face warmed at his friend's incredulous stare. "I swear it's true. Saw it with my own eyes. It had wings and…" he stammered, reluctant to share his theory. But their survival depended on total honesty and trust. "If I had to give it a name, I'd say it was a fairy."

Tombi paced the small cabin. "I believe you saw something out there. It's just…*fairies*?" He stopped and stared out the window where shadows lengthened and the woods beckoned with their promise of magic and danger.

"We shouldn't be so surprised," Chulah said. "If there are will-o'-the-wisps, birds of the night, and spirits like Hoklonote and Nalusa Falaya, why not a whole host of other supernatural creatures?"

Tombi shook his head. "You're sure this thing had actual wings?"

That glowed with the light and warmth of a thousand candles. Stunning. Disturbing. But Tombi didn't need to know the effect this mystical creature had on his senses.

His friend pierced him with a hard stare. "Why did it come to you?"

He didn't say it, but he didn't need to. As leader of the shadow hunters, Tombi should have been the human contacted, not him. He was only second-in-command. Actually, he'd been only third-in-command until the traitorous Hanan died in the last great battle.

"I'm not sure why," Chulah said with a shrug.

"Think there's any correlation between your new girl and this vision in the woods? I mean, here's this stranger in town who talks about the shadow spirits. No humans speak of such things. Even our own people regard them as old stories with no truth."

Tombi voiced Chulah's own inner speculations, but hearing it from another set off warning flares. And he hadn't told Tombi that April even knew highly personal things about him, like Tallulah's rejection. He sure as hell wasn't going to bring up that fiasco to Tombi. Too embarrassing. "She's not *my* anything. And we can't be a hundred percent sure that she's a…a fairy or whatever I saw out there tonight."

"I want to meet this April tomorrow morning."

"Yeah, you should meet. I'm sure she'll be at her store."

"I'll take my wife along. Annie has amazing insight."

"Good idea. And I'll go with you," he said quickly, not liking the idea of April being under an inquisition and ganged up on. Three against one was hardly fair. Annie was the epitome of kindness and gentleness, but Tombi could be intimidating and brusque. Chulah frowned, aware that he'd leaped at the chance to shield April. Her feelings should be of no importance in unraveling the mystery.

"Come if you like." Tombi folded his arms and studied Chulah. "Let's hunt. Could you conjure this Fae form to reappear?"

"Haven't got a clue. But I can show you the tree where I saw it. Where sound and movement stop around the base of the trunk."

He nodded. "Stay alert for signs of Hoklonote. Maybe we've grown a little complacent since capturing Nalusa."

Chulah lifted his backpack off the kitchen table, where it was loaded with a slingshot and rocks. The familiar feel of the weapons shifting in the pack made him eager for action. "I've got an extra one if you need it," he offered.

"My backpack's in the car."

"Let's go, then." Chulah wanted Tombi to witness what he had. Over the years since the lost-time episode, no one brought up the subject. Not to his face. Yet Chulah wondered if they secretly mistrusted his sanity. Other than an alcoholic, who the hell lost time? Only him.

"Wait. I want to talk a minute." Tombi hesitated. "I spoke with Tallulah earlier."

Damn. Chulah groaned inwardly. "I'd rather not talk about your sister," he said stiffly, making a show of unzipping the backpack and checking his weapons.

"She's worried about you."

"Right. Tell her I'm fine," he said, avoiding Tombi's eyes.

"Are you really?"

"Yes. Okay? I don't want to have this conversation."

"Might do you good."

Chulah didn't bother with a reply.

Tombi sighed. "Then let me say one thing and we'll never speak of this again."

"If you must."

His friend laid a hand on his shoulder. "The three of us have been friends all our lives and I don't want that to end."

"It won't." Chulah started for the door.

"Hey, buddy," Tombi called from behind.

Chulah stopped but didn't turn around.

"I would have loved it if Tallulah had returned your feelings and we became more like brothers. I've hoped for that ever since Bo's death. But I guess you and my twin are too alike for a romantic relationship."

Chulah slowly faced him. "What's that supposed to mean?"

"You're both stubborn and possessive and set in having your own way."

Chulah opened his mouth to object, then snapped it back shut. He remembered their childhood escapades. Even at that young age, all three of them had argued about taking the lead and how they would spend their day. Being a girl didn't slow Tallulah down a bit. She was a wild tomboy, as fierce and brave and as aggressive as her brother and any of his friends. A real spitfire.

He had always admired that. She was so different from his stepmother and half sister, Brenda, who complained endlessly and depended on him to take care of everything.

"You'd be better off with someone not as much like you," Tombi continued.

His friend never used to say such ridiculous crap. Marriage had softened Tombi. "If you're through playing psychologist, I'll be outside waiting for you to get your stuff." Chulah stepped into the night and breathed deeply.

Maybe Tombi was right. Maybe he and Tallulah would have made a horrible couple, who would spend their lives constantly arguing. Maybe he'd be better off with a different sort of woman. A woman with a gentle, soft nature but an electric touch.

Chulah straightened his shoulders. Enough of such foolish thoughts.

It was like any other autumn night, and they'd hunted the same area hundreds of times. As a child, Chulah enjoyed this season more than any other—the slight chill in the air that annihilated the smothering swamp humidity. But even though winters and autumns were mild, at times the Gulf breeze whipped so fiercely that bits of sand peppered the flesh like BB-gun pellets. It wouldn't kill or cause serious injury, but it hurt like hell.

"Don't expect anything," Chulah warned Tombi as they entered the woods. "I have a feeling I caught the thing by surprise earlier."

Adrenaline coursed through his veins, more than the usual anticipatory hunting mode. He'd never hunted unknown creatures before. Would it appear?

Chulah led the way, sure of his direction. His eyes adjusted to the dark and his senses heightened. He felt the pulse of scrambling squirrels, the splash of fish, the buzz of skeeters, the retreating tide. Somewhere, someone far away had lit a campfire, and he inhaled the smoke of sweet gum and oak, an autumnal scent that brought back childhood memories of Halloween parties and hayrides. A more carefree time.

But as an adult, autumn often felt like the earth dying a little every day. Darkness encroaching on daylight, animals retreating to their dens, foliage dropping lifelessly from the trees. A season when green turned to taupe gray and the sun grew cold.

Unbidden, Chulah again remembered the startling charge of April's touch. The pleasant burn of her lips on his. Now, *there* was light and warmth and all the fire a man needed to fight against the encroaching dark of winter.

They trudged through thickets of saw palmettos, alert for a change in smell or sight, subtle shifts of energy that foretold trouble.

Chulah surveyed the area, frowning. Where was that damn tree?

Tombi tapped his shoulder and lifted both palms upward. *What's going on?*

Chulah shrugged and raised a hand, motioning Tombi to stay put. Slowly, he circled several trees, testing their life force. Nothing but the usual calm, steady wisdom emanated from their roots and the spreading limbs draped in Spanish moss.

He sighed in disgust and returned to Tombi's side, shaking his head. The creature—fairy—had made a fool of him. Chulah was unsure of it reappearing, but he hadn't anticipated trouble locating the tree.

Tombi leaned in and whispered in his ear. "Did you mark it?"

Damn. He shook his head. Now he appeared a double fool. Even a rookie hunter knew that things shifted out here, defied logic and science. What was before might never appear in the same manner again. A new twist in a path, a slight change in the water's course or disappearing rock formations. As if the woods were a living organism with their own laws and ways, unwilling to divulge all their secrets to any one person or species.

Tombi motioned to a fallen log. A place to sit. And observe.

A strategy that didn't often work, but had proved helpful a few times in the past. Like grazing deer, sometimes spirits could be lulled into a false sense of security, never suspecting that a hunter lay in wait.

Patient, silent, at one with the dark stillness. They sat together, absorbing the night and its energy. No hint of anything. An hour passed. Two.

Tombi stood and stretched. "I need to get home and sleep. Long day tomorrow at work."

Chulah followed suit. "Sorry," he mumbled. "I'll mark that tree next time."

"No problem."

They walked the pine-cushioned path in silence, heading back to Chulah's cabin. He pondered the mysterious April, resolving to see her tomorrow.

If she even remained in the bayou.

Foolish humans.

It hurt April's feelings that Chulah had immediately called his friend to hunt her down. Not that they knew it was *her*, but still…it rankled.

She followed them from a safe distance as they left the woods. April had been extra careful and alert, making sure to create an illusion so they wouldn't find the fairy portal tree.

So Chulah and his friends wanted to check her out? She'd keep Steven close by her side to deflect any hard questions so that she wasn't forced to say anything until Chulah was in love with her. The original plan was that once he was, she'd tell him she was a Fae ambassador on a mission to get the shadow hunters' help to fight Hoklonote and save the Fae realm.

And hope he'd buy it without asking too many questions. Although that appeared highly unlikely now.

She heard the Ishkitini before they did. And where the birds of the night cried, will-o'-the-wisps were sure to follow. April picked up a couple of sticks and threw them ahead on their path, alerting the hunters to danger.

"What was that?" Chulah stopped and searched the woods.

A slow smile played on Tombi's mouth. "*Kowi anuskasha.* The forest dwellers."

The Choctaw word for her kind wasn't entirely accurate. The forest was their home, but they could stray from its borders. At least that word was better than—

"Bohpoli," Chulah agreed. "One just threw sticks at us."

As if the fairies could be reduced to a verb...*thrower.* They were more than that, so much more. In the old days, the Choctaw people regarded them as harmless, mischievous beings who threw sticks and stones to scare humans. These days, no one believed in fairies, which suited their need for secrecy just fine.

"April, perhaps?" Tombi asked.

"We don't know that." Chulah appeared unamused. "What do you want?" he demanded, staring into the void.

So frustrating. Could they not hear the birds? She must warn them.

"Wait. I hear something." Chulah raised a finger to his lips and he and Tombi stilled, blending into the shadows. "Ishkitini," he whispered.

Silently, they each withdrew their backpacks and unpacked their slingshots.

About time. The warriors could handle the birds, but the wisps... April flew above the treetops, above the predatory owls with their intent nocturnal eyes and ruffled feathers.

Seven glowing orbs skittered erratically behind the birds. One moment they were a few inches above ground; the next moment they shone in the treetops, only to flit immediately into a tangle of dying kudzu and brambles. Unpredictability, with no pattern in their movements, was part of what made them potentially deadly. That, and their ability to gang up on their human victims. Some of the wisps had more than one pulsing heart at their center, meaning they had entrapped more than one spirit victim.

There were fewer wisps since Nalusa Falaya had been contained in the last battle, but the surviving wisps were more cunning. More powerful. More deadly.

And they wanted Chulah and Tombi. Desperately.

April's heart pinched imagining Chulah reduced to a

green spirit trapped forever in some wisp's miasmic glow. She couldn't let that happen.

But mostly the wisps wanted the shadow hunters' leader, Tombi. None of them realized Chulah's silent determination and superior skill were the bigger threat. Nobody but her. It came from years of watching him. Invisible, unapproachable, unknown.

Forbidden.

Yet she still wanted him. In all his human splendor. His cinnamon-colored skin stretched over taut muscles. His long black hair that lifted in the bayou breeze like a silken armor. His brown eyes that were like a deep well reflecting all that was noble and worthy and vulnerable. His chiseled jaw and strong nose. His large, calloused hands that threw rocks with deadly precision but were so gentle and tender when he tended his vegetable garden or stroked an animal.

Seven against two, not counting the distracting Ishkitini. Not a fair fight. She had to save Chulah. How unfair if he should die now, so soon after she had finally had the opportunity to kiss him as a human girl. To lose him when he still thought she might be the enemy. It broke her heart merely imagining it.

She had to fight.

April flew down, aiming at the back of a wisp lagging a bit behind the others.

The decaying scent of Hoklonote teased her senses. He was behind all this, probably watching this attack from a safe distance. Which made it even more dangerous should he decide to enter the fray once the hunters had been weakened or trapped.

She got close enough to the lone wisp that she could identify the trapped victim inside. The green spirit rippled in agony. His name was Nitushi, Young Bear. At age nine, his spirit was captured, well over a hundred years ago. So young. Forced to suffer an existence of suffocating misery more than ten times that of his human life span.

Help me to help you, Nitushi. She pushed the words at him through the wisp's thin smoke form. Her fairy glow was tiny compared to the wisp's. So far, it hadn't noticed her.

In the green flame, she viewed Nitushi's capture as a human child. He'd disobeyed his parents. Had sneaked deep into the woods at dusk, unafraid and innocent. Convinced that the elders' tales of evil spirits and bogeymen were stories meant to scare children into obedience.

Until Nalusa Falaya stepped onto the path. A man Nitushi had never seen in his small village. A man…yet not a man. The closer Nalusa drew, the more Nitushi grew uneasy. He had arms and legs and a face like other men, but he was too tall. His ears were too pointed, his eyes were too small, his skin a little darker than others in his Nation.

The long black being—Nalusa Falaya? He'd been warned about the dark shadow spirit, like all Choctaw children. Nitushi threw down his small bow and arrow and ran.

But his legs were not full-grown with the length and span of a grown-up's limbs. No way to win this race.

Nitushi darted into the underbrush. His small size could be an advantage. He'd use it to hide. Terrified, he glanced back but the strange man had disappeared. Nitushi panted, his heart pounding like a war drum in his chest. He'd never disobey his parents again. He'd never come alone into the woods at night again, he'd never…

A rustle broke through the din of his drumming heartbeat. Louder, closer, fast as an arrow. He looked down and gasped. The hugest snake he'd ever seen. It slithered S-shaped, rattling and deadly.

Nitushi was mesmerized, paralyzed by the small black eyes in its triangular face. Intelligent eyes. The eyes of

Nalusa. He closed his eyes before the fangs pierced his flesh and poison invaded his veins like a thousand needles pricking his veins. A wisp hovered nearby, ready to claim Nitushi's spirit.

April witnessed it all in an instant.

I will free you, Nitushi. All will be well. She was born for this. For wielding her Fae enchantment to soothe a distressed human soul—or a spirit if need be.

April concentrated, inhaling deeply. She exhaled, releasing a mixture of heat and coolness to penetrate the wisp's orb, a ray of focus that penetrated through the vaporous wisp and to Nitushi.

Fly through the light. Hurry.

He did. The green heart pulsing of his spirit elongated to a thin shaft and he squeezed through the narrow beam of light April provided.

Swoop.

April released her breath. The green light in front of her transformed to a pure white that gleamed like a miniature star in the Alabama bayou. This time, the emanating images were of joy. Nitushi's slender, boyish face alight with a grin. What a handsome lad he had once been.

Find your people, she urged softly. *Your parents have been waiting for you in the After Life for a long, long time.*

He nodded solemnly, and his eyes drifted upward, somewhere private and sacred to him. A place she could not see or enter.

Svshki. My mother. Ak. My father, he breathed.

The wisp shook, darkened. Aware its strength had escaped.

April flew backward, out of reach for its last moment of power. The wisp screeched, a rage-filled rushing of air that sounded like a punctured balloon collapsing. The bayou grew silent again. The other wisps continued on, uncaring that a fellow creature had died. That was the way of their world. A waiting and a battle. A taking or a releasing. Victory or defeat. And always, some form of death in the brew.

Hoklonote's scent grew stronger, but not near enough to cause a panic. The old spirit was far too cunning to confront one fairy. And why should he when his goal was to suppress their entire realm? Besides, Hoklonote was a coward. Anyway, she was far too insignificant to matter.

But Chulah mattered.

April flew to the treetops, determined to help eliminate more of the wisps intent on Chulah's destruction. Nitushi's spirit flashed before her, climbing upward.

Yakoke. Thank you, he whispered. The white ball of light became a pinprick in the heavens.

At least she had helped one soul this evening.

But there was no time for quiet thanksgiving. Not with Chulah's life in danger. Had the birds arrived yet?

April streaked forward. They had probably already dealt with the Ishkitini. Which left six wisps versus two humans. Those odds left her burning with fear. If she was quick enough, maybe she could take out one more before they attacked, even up the humans' chances.

The wisps were almost upon Chulah and Tombi. April flew to the nearest, one with two trapped spirits. Inhale, exhale.

Whoosh.

Two white lights funneled out of the wisp. A brief glimpse of two adolescent girls, shining with hope as they ascended to their Land of the Spirits. Quickly, April rushed back, avoiding the gust of evil energy as the wisp burst and collapsed in on itself.

Five remained.

"Look out," Chulah warned his friend. "Five incoming."

Tombi moved until the men stood back to back. "I've got you covered."

With speed and precision, they dug out rocks and loaded their weapons.

"How did they find us?" Chulah grumbled. "Haven't seen this many at one time in months."

"Me either. The Ishkitini had mostly disappeared, too, after Nalusa's defeat. Until tonight."

Chulah frowned. "If that fairy thing guided them to us…"

The accusation cut deep, but she ignored the pain, concentrating on what must be done. April darted closer and killed one more wisp before quickly flying off. To stay longer meant being unwittingly felled by the shadow hunters as they aimed at the wisps.

Chulah stared directly at her. But was blind. "I smell violets."

She darted away. He needed to concentrate on the wisp attack, not her.

"This is no good. I've got a better plan," Tombi said. He motioned with his hand. "We have time to flush them out. This way."

Chulah ran, following him down the game trail, noiseless and unerring in the feeble sliver of moonlight. Only their supernatural shadow-hunting eyesight made it possible to see in such darkness. They had managed to lose the wisps, but they were still clearly in danger.

Tombi looked back over his shoulder.

"Yeah, I've been hearing the same rustling," Chulah whispered.

Tombi picked up the pace and Chulah guessed at his strategy. The trail ended at a large clearing. Dangerous to cross at night while being hunted.

"The noise has stopped," Chulah said in a low, quiet voice.

Tombi held a finger to his lips and Chulah stood silent, straining to pick up any unusual sound.

It came.

A familiar whooshing of air broke the normal night sounds. The sound of a large flock of Ishkitini flying low. Yet another round of attack. They could outrun and hide from the wisps when outnumbered, but the damn birds could always spot them. And where the birds of the night flew, the wisps were sure to follow. Hoklonote sent them to wear down a hunter mentally and physically so that the wisps could easily finish the job when they arrived.

Chulah called on past experience to determine if they had time to cross the field before the birds, huge horned owls, spotted them. If they miscalculated, they were dead meat to the birds of prey. But if they hurried...

Tombi pointed to a stand of cypresses across the field. "Quick to the trees," he called.

Chulah sprinted side by side with his friend, ever conscious of the approaching birds with their talons of death. Sharp claws that ripped human flesh and feasted on it when possible.

Fifty yards to safety.

Another sound emerged from the generalized whooshing, the flapping of wings and an occasional hoot as the Ishkitini homed in.

Halfway there. The bird noises were so raucous and loud that Chulah's skin stretched taut, expecting the sting of talon at any moment. If they could just reach the tree grove it would help shield them against the attack.

They made it, quickly scrambling behind the gnarled tree trunks. Position reversed and upper hand gained. Now it was the wisps that had to cross open field. Through the tree branches, Chulah counted at least four or five wisp hearts flashing bright blue green. A signal they were preparing to attack.

Expertly, Chulah retrieved his slingshot, a knife and several rocks from his backpack. He gripped the slingshot in his left hand and the knife in his right. In a move born from years of fighting experience, Chulah positioned the knife so that its blade flared out from the underside of his hand, perfect for slashing. This way he could shoot and keep his knife at the ready to kill any predator that came within striking distance.

The droning of owls filled the air and vibrated in his gut. They were upon them.

Two owls flew within a yard of Chulah, their bloody red eyes glowing with fierce intensity. Chulah raised his hand and slashed down. Once, twice. The smell of blood and nasty meat rent the air. Another owl sank its claws into Chulah's left biceps. Chulah slammed the owl against a tree trunk and knocked it unconscious. He circled to the front of the tree, loaded his slingshot and fired at a wisp that had closed within thirty yards.

A high-pitched squeal assaulted his ears as the wisp disintegrated into a puff of smoke that emitted an acrid smell. The teal heart trapped within the wisp transformed to a white spark that spiraled upward to the stars.

But there was no time to admire the lovely sight.

A quick glance to his left and his breath caught. Tombi fired at a wisp, killing it, but he paid a price. He was surrounded by the Ishkitini. The largest owl sank its beak into Tombi's neck.

Damnation.

Chulah rushed over. Tombi slashed the owl that had bit him, but it was too late. Blood streamed from his neck wound and he fell to the ground. At least four owls immediately attacked his prone figure, sinking their talons into his legs and shoulders.

"Help!" Tombi screamed. "You son of a bitch owls. You—"

"I'm here," Chulah panted, stabbing his friend's attackers and kicking at others trying to jump or fly at them.

"Look out!" Tombi warned, rolling to his right. "Incoming."

Blinding strobes of flashing light pulsated in the darkness and Chulah squinted. A cold, foul odor emanated from the nearby wisp and it filled Chulah with an immobilizing dread. No wisp had ever come so close to him. Surprise left him vulnerable. There was no time to mentally shield his mind from the despair the wisps exuded. They fed on human misery. It made them stronger, more lethal.

A rock whizzed by his ear.

"Bingo," Tombi grunted. "I got it."

The flashing light extinguished and the trapped soul escaped, lighting up as instantaneously as a struck match and ascending upward. Joy and peace filled Chulah's heart. The sensation was a hundred times stronger than the wisp's aura of despair.

Incredibly, the Ishkitini arose en masse and left.

Chulah scrambled to his feet and circled Tombi's body, searching for more wisps. "I don't get it," he mumbled, hands on his hips. "I saw at least three other wisps preparing to attack us. Where did they go?"

"We'd be goners if they'd stuck around," Tombi said, his voice so faint that Chulah was instantly drawn to a new dilemma.

He dropped to a knee beside his friend. They'd helped each other many times throughout the years, but this was the closest they had come to almost dying. He'd never forget that Tombi had saved his life with the last-minute rock hit.

Tombi, and some stroke of fortune that scared off the Ishkitini and will-o'-the-wisps. Where had that help come from? A mystery to ponder later.

"We need to get you medical help. Quick." Chulah put one arm under Tombi's knees and the other beneath his back. With a grunt, he lifted Tombi. Somehow, he'd find the strength to carry him to the cabin.

"Put me down," Tombi protested. "I can walk."

Chulah eased him down to his feet and Tombi passed out. Perspiration broke out all over Chulah's body. He was alone in the woods with a man who might be dying.

Just like his father.

And he'd been unable to save him either.

April shivered as an eerie silence split the night, broken only by the faraway screeches of retreating owls. She couldn't stop the flooding waves of panic, even though the danger had passed. The image of Chulah, frozen and vulnerable as the wisp hovered, homing in to claim his soul, would haunt her the rest of her life. Without thinking, she'd attacked another wisp closing in on Chulah from behind, a second before he would have been lost to her forever. The other two wisps had scampered into the safety of the woods, bewildered at the invisible attacks.

Stunned and exhausted, April gazed down at the wreckage.

Chulah's face was grimy and he bent down on one knee to the figure lying prone on the ground. "Tombi? Wake up. Wake up or Annie will never forgive you for leaving her. You hear me?"

The man lay unmoving.

Oh, my queen. Not again. Guilt paralyzed her essence. She'd been responsible the last time when Chulah lost the father he adored. And now his best friend might die, too?

Tombi stirred and groaned. "Give me a minute. I'll be fine."

Chulah let out a low breath and wiped his brow. The same relief almost made April melt, until wistfulness crept in. If only Chulah cared a fraction as much about her as he did his friend.

Okay, she was being unreasonable. He'd never laid eyes on her until recently—at least not that he remembered. Trouble was, she'd been secretly watching him for years. He'd first caught her eye as a young teenager, so brave and strong and dominating the other boys in their fierce stick-ball competitions.

But the first time they'd actually met, she'd ruined his life in the space of a mere two hours. Later, after his father had died, she'd watched him again in Fae form. Around his large family of younger brothers and sister, his face had been stoic. He'd amused the younger kids and comforted the crying girl. For hours. Until he went for a walk.

She had followed. Ashamed for playing a role in the death of the father he loved.

Not having parents, she didn't entirely understand his grief. But as an outcast in the Fae realm, she had made up stories of a mother and father's love. The truth was that her mother had abandoned her for a human lover. April wasn't sure who her real father was or if he cared she existed. Still, she'd fantasized about a parent's love and imagined how she'd feel if one of them had died.

Chulah had stopped and sat on a fallen log, burying his face in his hands. He made no sound, but his shoulders shook. It was awful. It seemed never-ending. A desire to touch him nearly overpowered April. But she couldn't—the Fae taboo was too strong.

Maybe just a little enchantment...enough to give him a

bit of comfort. She hovered closer, planting a kiss on her palm and blowing it toward him on the wind.

He ceased the dreadful shaking and raised his head, bewildered. "Who's there?" he whispered.

April had said nothing.

No human had ever noticed or spoken to her before. Not that she'd done much enchanting, but she'd seen the other Fae cast them. No human had ever questioned who was there and what they were doing.

Concluding she sucked at enchantments, April had drifted farther back into the woods. Chulah arose and brusquely swiped at his face with his T-shirt. "Thank you," he said, thumping his right hand on his chest.

He was talking to *her*!

April hardly dared move as he returned to his family's cabin. She'd probably fallen a little in love with them right there at age sixteen.

A large moan snapped April out of her reverie. Tombi stumbled to his feet, with Chulah supporting his weight on one arm.

"Let's get you home. Annie will have you feeling better in no time."

Tombi laughed ruefully. "The cure will be worse than the pain. I hate to think what bitter concoction she'll brew."

"Whatever it is, you'll drink it and be grateful," Chulah said firmly. "She's saved your ass more than once with her herbs."

They made slow, painful progress. April flew behind, in case there were more surprise attacks.

Chulah suddenly halted, as if he had sensed her presence. He pumped a fist in the air. "Is that you, April? If you had anything to do with tonight, I'll…" He sputtered to a stop, his eyes flashing like lightning and his voice deep and rumbling like thunder.

So he'd guessed and made a connection that she was the creature he'd seen earlier—although he couldn't know for sure. Pain washed over her in waves, drowning her in misery. He was so blind, literally and figuratively.

And maybe…just maybe…he wasn't the man she'd thought him to be. Maybe that young boy she had connected to, the one so moved at his father's death, yet so kind and caring with his family, maybe that boy had died over the hard years of battles and deceits and deaths. Maybe the hardened warrior he'd become had lost the ability to love and sense the beauty that skittered outside his peripheral vision.

If so, that would be the greatest tragedy of all. April slumped to the ground. If only there was someone for her. Someone who cared. Had cared about her her whole life and she just didn't know it.

But there was no one.

She lifted her head, full of resolve. Chulah didn't have to know this pain. This crippling loneliness. She knew that somewhere inside Chulah, the young boy he'd been remained. She just had to find him. Even if he believed the worst of her, even if he learned the truth and condemned her for killing his father, she still loved him.

Chapter 5

Tombi must have been badly hurt.

All day, she'd expected him, his wife and Chulah to show up at the store. She'd even demanded that the irritating Steven stay by her side, sure the trio would try to trip her up with their questions. She couldn't let them discover more about their race or the sacred fairy tree.

But the only thing worse than an inquisition was waiting for one to happen.

To hell with waiting and wondering. Steven had given up on them coming and had gone back to the Fae realm to visit and replenish his shape-shifting form.

April closed the store and rode her bike through the woods to Chulah's cabin. The light shone from his windows, a welcoming beacon in the late-afternoon October chill. She rapped at the heavy wooden door, hoping to catch him alone.

He flung the door open and slumped against the frame. "You," he said flatly.

His face was gray and his hair in wild disarray. He wore only a pair of low-slung jeans, and her mouth went dry at the sight of his bare chest and flat, muscled abs. Sure, she'd seen him bare-chested many times, but within actual touching range, as a human, was so different. It was all she could do not to run a hand down his sleek torso.

"Can I come in?" April peeked past him, relieved no one else was in sight. "You look awful. The wisps got to you last night."

He stiffened. "What do you know about that?"

She couldn't keep her big mouth shut. "I might have been there." She'd been lying in bed in that stark apartment, breathing stale air, longing for the night air. To spread her wings and fly. So she came to the forest, soothing her soul with its life force. But instead of a peaceful interlude, she'd been drawn into battle.

Chulah's eyes narrowed to suspicious slits. "You're the... thing...I saw in the woods, aren't you? Did you send the wisps our way?"

Obstinate, suspicious man. April put her hands on her hips, goaded into spilling her guts. She was tired of all the blame. It was time he learned she was his ally and not his enemy. "Yeah, I was there. And I took out three wisps for you."

So much for waiting until Chulah was in love with her to reveal that she wasn't an ordinary human. He continued to regard her wordlessly.

"You're welcome," she said, bristling. "Now, are you going to let me in or not? We need to talk."

Chulah stepped to the side and waved her in.

April entered and studied the cabin's interior. She'd never seen it before, except that small bit observable through a lit window at night. Not that she hadn't tried. But Chulah and the other hunters placed consecrated sage and salt on all four corners of their dwellings for protection against the shadows. Even though she wasn't one of the *dark* shadow spirits, in Fae form she was a nature spirit, and the salt and sage had effectively prevented her from entering.

Probably a good thing. She'd have been unable to resist being near Chulah as he slept, or even better, showered.

The rooms were as sparse as his words. Minimalistic. The coziness of the log walls contrasted with the modern lines of dark leather sofas and chairs. Bright-colored woven rugs adorned one wall and another enlivened the center of the den. April sat down. Motorcycle magazines, empty soda cans, a wet washcloth and a large bottle of aspirin lay scattered on a glass coffee table.

"Feeling poorly?"

"Like hell. But forget that. I want straight answers from you." He sat across from her. "Who and what are you?"

April chose her words carefully, ones that she'd practiced ever since she'd been called to solicit help from the shadow hunters. "I'm an ambassador of sorts. Sent to warn you that Hoklonote is seeking dominion over the Fae realm—"

"Whoa." He leaned forward, eyes gleaming. "The Fae realm? There really are such things as fairies, then? Is that what you—"

"I'm not a real fairy." *At least not a pure one.*

"You're lying. That was you I saw in the woods." He swiftly lowered his lips to her neck and sniffed. "That's it. That's the scent."

April inched away, dismayed at his heightened sense of smell and at the same time aroused at the intimate contact. "I already told you I was there," she said coolly, hiding the flustered beating of her heart.

"I smelled violets by that tree. It's the way you smell."

"I use a floral perfume," she said, determined to refocus the conversation back to what mattered. "As I was saying, the Fae sent me to warn you and ask your help to defeat

Hoklonote. They aren't the only ones in danger here. If Hoklonote forces the Fae to work with him, he might succeed in unleashing Nalusa."

He gave a low whistle. "You know your stuff. I'll give you that."

"Of course I do. I couldn't solicit your help without knowing the situation."

"An ambassador, huh? What the hell does that mean?"

She ran a hand over her skirt, ignoring the question. "Will you help us—I mean, will you help the Fae?" She sucked at lying.

"I'm not agreeing to a damn thing until you tell me the truth." His eyes burned with anger...and perhaps a touch of fever.

Back off, April. He's not buying what you're selling. She reached across and ran a hand down his heated cheek. More than temper was at play. "You're unwell. I can read it in your eyes and the flush on your face."

"Nothing wrong with me. Just a headache from hell."

Not likely. But she'd help him with that. "And your friend?"

"Worse. But he's in good hands with Annie. She'll fix him something to ease his pain."

"Tia Henrietta's granddaughter? The witch?" All the Fae had heard of Tia, the hoodoo queen of the swamp. Stood to reason that her granddaughter, Annie, was psychically gifted as well.

"Don't call her that," he snapped.

"I didn't mean it as an insult. What does she call herself?"

"A root worker. Says she's into hoodoo."

April couldn't understand the distinction. But whatever. Magic was magic no matter which name humans chose to call it.

A sliver of jealousy clawed her heart. So Chulah stuck up for this woman? While she had been saving him from harm for years, and was viewed with mistrust. She could ease her man's pain, too, with a little Fae enchantment. April discreetly blew out a breath and directed her essence toward Chulah.

The pain lines in his forehead eased and the tension in his shoulders relaxed. He sat up suddenly. "Hey, what are you doing?"

She gave him her most doe-eyed look and shrugged, palms out. "Do you see me holding a fairy wand?"

"No, but…" Confusion knotted his brow. "This…this wave of…calm washed over me."

"Bet this is the best you've felt since last night." His eyes turned cold at the mention, so she hurried to add, "Judging by the look on your face when you opened the door."

He shut his eyes. "I'm not going to fight you over this. I do feel better." He cocked one eye open. "But no more of that fairy stuff. Okay?"

"I'm not a fairy, but agreed." April kicked off her shoes and hugged her knees to her chest, trying to contain her glee. He'd accepted her help! After the fact, without prior permission.

But still. Progress could be measured in the tiniest of increments. There was hope they could help each other with more important matters. Like Hoklonote.

But we might not have time for this, Steven's words whispered in her ears. As if he were sitting beside her. April frowned, but couldn't pick up any sign he was present. She must be paranoid; Steven couldn't slip past the sage and salt any more than she could. Chulah didn't sense something amiss either, or he wouldn't be half-asleep in the chair.

Poor guy probably hadn't slept all night.

"Maybe you should drink some coffee or something,"

she suggested. She'd volunteer to make it for him, but had no clue how to perform domestic chores.

He picked up a can of soda and took a swig. "I'm fine."

The man sure liked those drinks. She wondered what was in it. "Can I have a sip?" she asked impulsively.

Chulah handed her the soda he was drinking and she tilted the can back, downing its contents in a long swallow. Sharp bubbles scalded her tongue and throat. Disgusting. She crinkled her nose.

"Not your taste? I've got—"

Hiccup. Her body jerked upward.

"Aha! You rose again. Just like you did when you drank that brandy. Not a fairy, my ass."

She was so, so sick of the lies between them. At least, in this, she could acquiesce. The man wasn't stupid, and she refused to slowly enchant Chulah in order to force his cooperation. "Liquid seems to have that effect on me," she admitted.

"It was you I saw in the woods."

It wasn't a question.

"Steven claims it's some glitch in the glamour causing the levitation," she continued, all business. As if this were a normal conversation. "Anyway, I came over because I thought we should have a little talk. One-on-one." And not with his friends turning him against her.

Chulah scowled. "Of course you did. The better to influence me, right? I can't believe a thing you say."

"I'm telling the truth now. You know my deep, dark secret." One of them, anyway.

"Yeah, right." He stood and paced. "Bet you have a million secrets buried under that beautiful, innocent face."

Beautiful. He thinks I'm beautiful. That was something she could grasp and hold on to while facing his disgust.

"I'm not considered particularly beautiful by the other

Fae," she said casually. "To them, I'm not even run-of-the-mill pretty. 'A bit plain' is how I'm usually described."

Chulah snorted. "Impossible. Harder to believe than the fact that you aren't human."

"I'm half-human. On my father's side," she said quickly. As if this might make her appear more acceptable and less foreign.

"Why didn't you tell me the truth to start with? I wouldn't have dismissed your claim right off the bat. I'm a shadow hunter. I've fought supernatural beings most of my life. Hell, I have my own powers."

"I'm well aware of your heightened senses. And your strength." April's eyes roved over his broad shoulders and chest, the lean, muscular biceps of his arms. Her throat went dry remembering how it felt to be wrapped in those solid arms.

He stared at her and she sighed. "I'm sorry. Try to see it from my point of view. I was instructed to tell as little as possible."

"You're doing a fine job," he said in a clipped voice. "Try being less of a politician. You'll get a lot further with me that way."

"I will. Promise." Lies of omission didn't count. She kept her chin up and met his stare.

"Very well." Chulah returned to his seat and eyed her wearily. "I tried to find you last night. Turns out I couldn't even locate that tree where you first appeared. You know the one I'm talking about."

April shifted her feet on the pine floor and smoothed her hands over her flowered peasant skirt, debating how much to reveal and how much to keep secret. A balance between telling enough to gain his trust and not saying so much that he could use any knowledge against them. "Sure, I know the tree. It's sacred to us, just as you and your people have sacred spots in the woods."

"Yes, but I bet you know exactly where our spots are and why they're special to us."

"True." No sense lying about something that obvious. "But we can't let humans get too close. You were able to see me in Fae form because I had dropped my guard on my way there." Thinking about his hot kiss.

He didn't need to know that either. Chulah was arrogant enough without further ammunition.

"Why are you so protective of this tree?"

"It's sacred," she said, skirting around the edge of his question. "As you discovered, we protect it mostly by moving it every night. It's never in the exact same place twice."

"Fascinating." His eyes seared her. Was he talking about her or the tree?

The kiss was there between them as if it had happened seconds ago. Which reminded April—she still hadn't conducted an experiment to see if all humans were electric when she touched them. Was it magical between any Fae and any human?

She couldn't speak, couldn't move. Could barely breathe, for that matter. He felt the pull, too. He was still as an oak; only his eyes moved, lowering to her lips, and then lower, focused on the rise and fall of her breasts under the thin cotton shirt.

The silence grew as thick and hot as Alabama humidity in the midst of summer. A fever of longing burned, scorching her with desire. This was not the mischievous kissing game of a fairy lad. This was sensual human desire. All-consuming. All-engulfing.

Exactly what her mother must have felt with her human lover. The one she chose to live with over her own daughter. The dousing reminder cleared her brain. April tore her gaze from his face and stared at her hands in her lap.

Chulah stood abruptly and paced again, bare feet padding the wooden floor, scarcely making a sound. For such a large man, he had the stealth of a bobcat stalking prey. No doubt one of his many hunting skills honed over the years.

"You realize I looked like a fool last night in front of my friend. No tree, no fairy."

Ah, the male pride was injured. "But if he's truly your friend, that shouldn't matter."

He whirled around. "It matters. Where I come from, friendships and family are the foundation of who you are. We are loyal to each other. We are nothing without one another."

April regarded his impassioned face. Chulah was what mattered to her. Exactly as he was. Unencumbered by his needy stepmother and half siblings and his fellow shadow hunters. *You are important for just being you*, she wanted to say. But that would only anger him. And possibly alienate him.

She couldn't bear that. To lose all hope of his returning her love would break her heart. And it would destroy any chance of recruiting his assistance to the Fae cause. It was still important to her that she restore her family's name in fairy. Not for her mother, but to prove to her kind that she was loyal and honorable. That halflings shouldn't be viewed as inferior species. She needed to prove all that to herself as well.

"I understand about loyalty," she assured Chulah. "It's huge in the Fae realm. Maybe even more important than it is for you."

He crossed his arms. "Impossible. The shadow hunters have to trust their brothers in battle. If we don't, we risk being overcome by evil. Which not only would mean our death and eternal entrapment by a wisp, but it would also be disastrous for all humans should the shadow spirits gain enough power to escape Bayou La Siryna."

"And it's extinction for all us fairies if Hoklonote and his spirit shadows aren't restrained," she countered. "We have as much to lose as you do."

His mouth set in a determined line. "How are the Fae threatened by Hoklonote?"

"The shadow spirits want to capture the Fae and trap them in will-o'-the-wisps. They need new, stronger souls to mount a campaign to free Nalusa." She drew a shaky breath. "They'll start with us, and then they'll come after you."

A chilling silence settled between them.

"And if they defeat me and the other shadow hunters, they'll begin to prey on other people. Helpless humans with no power to resist." Chulah dropped into the chair across from her and leaned forward. "It's been so quiet, so peaceful. Why is all this starting now?"

"You think I have something to do with this," she said slowly, remembering his words to Tombi last night. "That I've brought danger to you."

He said nothing, continuing to gaze at her intensely.

"Why would I do that?" April pleaded. "We haven't risked revealing ourselves to a human without good reason."

"Maybe you're, voluntarily or involuntarily, in league with Hoklonote. Maybe you'll lead us to him, all right—right into a trap."

"We mean no harm. Why can't you believe me?"

"A year ago, I might have. But after discovering a betrayer in our own inner circle of shadow hunters last year, I'm a little short on trust these days."

"Hanan," she said with a nod.

Chulah shook his head, evidently bemused. "A bit disconcerting that you know everything about us, and yet we know nothing of you."

She didn't volunteer any Fae information.

Chulah sighed. "Then you also know that because of Hanan, almost all of us were captured and destroyed by Nalusa Falaya."

As if she and other Fae hadn't helped the shadow hunters in their battles. Chulah wouldn't believe her if she told him, though.

A loud knock at the door interrupted the tense air between them. Without waiting for an invitation, Tombi entered the cabin with an exotic woman at his side carrying a small cooler. "Anybody home? We brought you…"

They both came to a sudden halt and stared at her.

"You must be April," the woman said, walking to her with a warm smile.

She stood and nervously straightened her skirt. "And you must be Annie." The healer who was not a witch. The one Chulah was so quick to defend.

The uplifting scent of citrus grounded with a mysterious musk undertone enveloped April as Annie gave her a quick hug. A tiny shock pulsed from the woman's abdomen into her own as they made contact. Not the electrical chemistry she and Chulah shared, but an energetic pulse of a tiny life form.

She was pregnant.

Annie gave a Mona Lisa smile and slightly nodded her head. "No one else knows yet," she whispered. "Not even Tombi."

"What's that? Did I hear my name?" Tombi asked, frowning their way.

"Not everything is about you, dear," Annie admonished. She unzipped the small cooler and withdrew a tumbler filled with bottles of green sludge. "For you," she said, extending the drink toward Chulah.

He reluctantly accepted. "Right. Thanks. I'll put it in the fridge and drink it later."

"You'll drink it now," Annie insisted in a surprisingly firm voice.

"Man up and take your medicine," Tombi said, his face softening as he looked at his wife. "You know she means business."

Chulah accepted the drink and glugged it down stoically. When finished, his mouth pursed, but he didn't utter a single complaint. "Thank you," he murmured.

However begrudgingly Chulah uttered his thanks, it was more than she'd received this morning for helping him over the worst of the owl gashes. Their talons held poison and would have felled anyone but a shadow hunter.

Annie placed the tumbler back in the cooler. "That should help dispel any lingering Ishkitini poison in your system, but you are doing much better this morning, more than I dared hope." She shot a quick sideways glance at April.

Chulah's face flushed. "I have April to thank for that. Should have said that sooner," he added, flicking her a chagrined glance.

She glowed from the faint praise. "My pleasure. I would have come earlier but—"

"And maybe you have this woman to thank for the attacks," Tombi cut in. "We might not have gotten sick if not for her instigating an encounter."

And so the inquisition had begun. She'd run over to Chulah's cabin to explain herself without others around, but now she had to face a group confrontation anyway. Worse, there was no Steven by her side to help answer their questions without giving away too much information. It was a fine line she danced between saving her kind and being an instrument in their destruction.

"I had nothing to do with the attacks," she insisted quietly.

"And why should we trust you?" Tombi asked. His eyes were as harsh as the sharp angles of his face and jaw.

Annie placed a hand on her husband's arm. "Why don't we sit down for this discussion?" she said in a pleasant voice, taking the edge off of Tombi's hostility.

"Good idea." Chulah took April's arm and led her back to the sofa.

She wasn't sure if he meant the gesture to be reassuring, or if this was his way of keeping her trapped into answering all their questions.

"I've been discussing the situation with Chulah. For starters, what do the fairies want from us and what can you do to help capture Hoklonote?" Tombi asked, taking a seat across from her.

"I came to warn you that Hoklonote is alive and growing in strength. You need to stop him before he frees Nalusa. He's a threat to all our lives—Fae and human."

"We—meaning the shadow hunters—take all the risk in capturing Hoklonote?"

He knew how to cut to the heart of the matter. She'd been asked to keep the Fae out of the fighting if possible.

"Isn't that what you do?" she calmly countered. "You've been granted special powers in order to protect everyone from the shadow spirits."

"To protect humans. If there's a threat to the Fae, it's your problem, too. Seems to me the fairies should help in any battle to capture Hoklonote."

"We can cooperate and assist you," April reassured him. That was only fair. The Council would have to accept this reasonable demand.

Chulah cut in. "You've never explained exactly how he threatens your kind."

"The wisps gained knowledge of our secret portals and spells because of an elder councilman who betrayed us, leaving us vulnerable."

"You have a fairy council?" Annie asked. "Fascinating."

"Oh, yes, and a queen, too."

They exchanged an understanding smile.

"We don't care about that stuff," Chulah interrupted. "Can't you just change your portals and spells that were compromised?"

She shook her head. "We have to find and capture our betrayer if we are ever to be safe again. At least your Hanan is dead. We believe our betrayer, Grady, is dead but that his spirit is captured in a wisp. Which serves him right for double-crossing us. You trust the dark side, and that's what can happen to a soul. We want him back."

Chulah frowned. "What do you mean? If he's dead and a spirit, the minute the wisp is killed, his spirit will soar to the After Life. You won't even know which spirit has been released."

"Oh, but we do."

Chulah and Tombi exchanged glances.

"You can identify who the spirit was in their previous human life?" Chulah asked.

She nodded. "Or in their previous Fae life. We can be killed and our spirits captured, the same as humans."

"So if you find the wisp containing your betrayer and see its spirit released, you can know that your kind is safe once more." Chulah rubbed his jaw. "Makes sense."

"No. Once his spirit is released, we can capture it and return him to the Fae realm for eternal punishment."

"But that's—wrong. You shouldn't separate a soul from the After Life."

"It's Fae justice."

Chulah stood. "I would never agree to trap a released spirit. It's wrong and goes against everything I believe in. It would make us as evil as the shadow spirits who trap them."

"You don't have to trap and bind the spirit," she argued. "The Fae will. All I'm asking is your help in finding this wisp. We've not been able to."

"I won't do it." Chulah shook his head. "None of the other hunters will either."

Tombi stood as well. "Absolutely not. And I'm beginning to wonder if there is no danger to us, just the fairies. We'll always continue to hunt for stray wisps and even Hoklonote himself, but he is weak without Nalusa. Not the serious threat you make him out to be."

She was losing ground. April held up a hand. "Okay, let's forget this betrayer a moment. If we can trap Hoklonote, it won't matter anyway."

They could always assign a troop of fairies to follow the hunters and check for Grady each time they killed a wisp. No need to rile the hunters on this point.

Chulah and Tombi remained standing.

"Why should we trust anything you say?" Tombi asked. "For all we know, you're under Hoklonote's control and he sent you to set a trap for us."

It all came down to the same basic question. "What can I do to prove I'm telling the truth?" April turned to Chulah. "I've been following you for ages, helping you in your battles. Doesn't that mean anything?"

"So you say," he answered slowly.

April shut her eyes and rubbed her temples.

"Are you okay?" A soft hand brushed the hair from her face. "I think she's been questioned enough for now," Annie said. "I realize y'all have to consider the worst in others, to be on guard against possible enemies. But what if she *is* telling the truth? This could be an opportunity to stop the shadow spirits once and for all. Don't jeopardize the opportunity."

April stood and faced the group. Tombi looked suspicious as ever, but Chulah nodded.

"You're right, Annie," Chulah conceded. "We should all consider this a bit before making any decisions."

"And with that, we'll take our leave." Annie smiled at April. "Can we give you a lift home? I didn't see a car in the driveway."

The inquisition was over. For now. She took a long, cleansing breath. "I rode my bicycle." And what fun it had been. Still not flying, still not riding with Chulah on his Harley, but at least on the bicycle she could feel the Gulf breeze caressing her face and hair.

"Very well. Chulah, if you need more of my herbal potion, you say the word."

"Um, no, I'm fine, thanks," he said hastily.

"Come see me anytime if you'd like to visit," Annie told her, picking up the cooler.

Warmth lit April's heart. What a kind person Annie was. And to think she'd even momentarily been jealous of the woman.

They turned to leave. Tombi brushed by close to her arm. Without stopping to think, April stuck out an index finger and touched his bare forearm.

Nothing. Not even the faintest sizzle.

Tombi scowled. "What did you poke me for?"

Quickly, she put her hands behind her back. "Nothing."

Chulah arched a brow, a sensuous, knowing grin slowly spreading across his face. He guessed exactly what she was doing.

The moment the door shut behind his guests, Chulah

quirked an eyebrow. "Conducting a little experiment, were you?"

And just like that, the air charged with passion.

"I wasn't sure if it was only you, or if every man I touched would cause a spark," she admitted.

His pupils widened. "Now you know. No need to go touching other men."

That had to mean he cared, even if only a tiny bit. April slowly reached out her hands and lightly touched both sides of his jaw. Tingles shot ripples of pleasure from her fingertips to her toes.

"You feel it, too," she whispered.

"Yes." His voice was raspy and deep.

"With every woman or just me?"

"Just you."

Chulah didn't look pleased at his admission, but at least he was honest. Thank the queen he hadn't felt this way when he touched Tallulah.

April stepped closer into his heat, wrapping her arms around his neck. She laid a cheek against his chest, listening to the pounding rhythm of his heart. His hands pressed into the small of her back and they held each other, unmoving.

There, in his arms, April believed all was possible. The chaotic world ceased to exist. There were only their heartbeats, fast and furious, as they clung to each other.

"Well, hell. Wouldn't you know it?" Chulah pulled away.

"What is it?" she asked, dizzy with desire.

"Trouble, I'm sure."

The crunch of tires on gravel was followed by two car doors slamming shut. Chulah jerked open the front door. Damn. He didn't need this. Not now.

His stepmother marched up the driveway with that air

of desperate determination that meant trouble. Brenda, his half sister, dragged behind with her usual sullen, downcast face. Only sixteen years old, she was the youngest of the Rivers brood, and the only one of his three half siblings who hadn't been in trouble with the law.

Yet.

What fresh new hell did Joanna have in store for him this time? A plumbing emergency? Providing bail for Johnnie or Chris? Or perhaps it was a simple request for more money. He hoped it was the latter.

"What brings you here, Joanna?" he asked, trying to keep his exasperation in check.

She opened her sharp mouth to speak, but stopped short at the sight of April standing beside him on the porch.

"I didn't know you had lady company." Her tone managed to convey disapproval.

Brenda, sporting dark lipstick and a boatload of mascara, snickered and rolled her eyes. "Lady company."

Inwardly sighing, Chulah made quick introductions. "Is there something I can do for y'all?" Best to get it over with.

"Well…" She cast a pointed look at April. "It's actually a private, family matter."

I bet it is.

"No problem. I was leaving," April said. She quickly went down the porch steps and over to a pink bicycle leaning against the cabin wall.

"Hey—cool hair!" Brenda's expression—for the first time in forever—was downright warm. Friendly, even. "How'd ya do that streaky stuff?"

"I didn't do anything," April protested. "It's…" She glanced at him and broke off.

Brenda snorted. "Right. C'mon, tell me. I want to bleach my hair like yours."

"Don't be ridiculous," Joanna snapped. "All your makeup

is bad enough without adding bleached hair to the mix. I won't allow you to do that. It looks trashy."

An awkward beat of silence descended.

Brenda kicked at the gravel. "Mooommm. You are, like, so rude."

Joanna lifted her chin. Bayou La Siryna would have a snowstorm in August before that woman apologized for anything.

"April's hair is beautiful." He surprised even himself with the words. It felt good to goad Joanna. "Unique. It fits her."

His stepmother's chin lifted another inch. "So you say. But I didn't come all the way out to the edge of the wilderness to talk about some woman's hair."

Double barb. It irked her that he refused to live close by in town where he could be more at her beck and call. And then there was the subtle put-down of April by calling her *some woman.*

"See y'all later," April said, cheerily. If she caught the insult, she refused to acknowledge it. She waved at Brenda. "Come by and see me anytime for girl talk about hair and such. I love your long black hair. I'd exchange with you if I could."

April reached up on her tiptoes and whispered in his ear. "Meet me at midnight in the woods."

Before he could respond, April had flitted away. Chulah watched as she hitched up her skirt and mounted the bike. Her bare legs glistened in the fading light and his throat went dry. She waved and pedaled off, silver hair streaming behind her.

It was as if April took all the sunshine with her when she left.

"Chulah? Are you listening to me?"

He jerked his head back to Joanna. "You've got my attention. Go on."

"My power's been shut off. I need you to go to the electric company and take care of it."

His temples throbbed and he resisted the urge to rub the pain away. "I gave you money to pay the bills last month. What happened?"

"You didn't give me enough, obviously."

His teeth ground together. At this rate, by the time he was an old man, the enamel would wear down to nothing. Joanna would still be hounding him for more, more, more, sucking his soul dry.

As always, Chulah swallowed his anger. Thick, unspoken recriminations burned the back of his throat and made his stomach churn—get a job, live within your means, leave me alone, not my problem.

Except, it was. His family, his problem. He had promised Dad to take care of them. A deathbed promise that he vowed to keep. Of course, at age fifteen, he didn't fully realize the enormity of that commitment. Still, Joanna had kept a roof over his head and provided food until he left at age eighteen and struck out on his own.

Not to mention, his dad's death was his fault. He sighed. "I'll take care of it. Don't I always?"

The bigger question was what to do with April. First, he would meet her tonight to see what she wanted. After that, he knew where to seek a final answer.

Chapter 6

The moon was a mere crescent sliver, but bright enough. Chulah trudged down the woodland path, alert for a sign of April. How typical of her that she provided no details on an exact time or place. Or even if she would appear as human or fairy.

For all he knew, this was a wild-goose chase.

Or a trap. Just in case, Chulah clutched a rock and slingshot in his right hand.

Tombi would chastise him as a fool for agreeing to meet her alone in the bayou after her lies.

Too bad.

In spite of everything, April intrigued him. He sensed a goodness in her. Normally, he trusted his instincts. But he had to remember he was dealing with a magical creature who most likely had the ability to manipulate his mind and heart.

A whiff of violets teased his nose, and Chulah stilled. She was near.

Off to the east, an orange glow—too small to be the sun—flashed as beautiful as a Himalayan salt lamp. It drifted closer. Closer.

He dared not breathe for fear of scaring it away. As before, the details grew crisp as the light drew near, coalescing into a distinguishable figure with a halo of hair that rippled in the breeze. A female with silver-and-purple hair and skin as pale as snow. On her back, a pair of wings fluttered like a mammoth butterfly.

His breath caught and the rock and slingshot fell from numbed fingers, thudding harmlessly to the pine-cushioned ground. Chulah was mesmerized at the vision.

It was April, and yet it wasn't April.

Her form wasn't solid; it shimmered and sparkled, emitting enough light to illuminate most of the forest. She wore a white dress that rippled like the break of a wave over the sea. And those wings... Yet it was undeniably her. The hair, the eyes, the body.

She stared straight at him. Chulah glanced down, saw that her light had stripped away the shadows he'd gathered around his body like a cloak to hide from the spirits. He stepped toward April. *Never show fear.* "We meet again."

The glow died instantly—as if it were a candle extinguished by a blast of wind. Chulah blinked. April took a tentative step his way, eyes wide and frightened.

He'd known it the first second he'd seen her waving at him by the side of the road. The woman was capital-*T* trouble. "So it's true. You really aren't human," he said roughly.

She flinched, but her gaze didn't waver from his face. "I told you I was sent to warn you. You and your hunters are in grave danger."

He folded his arms. "From what? A...pack of fairies?" Now he'd said the *F* word, curiosity overcame him. "How many of you are there?"

"Not important." Her eyes shifted to the left and right, as if she were afraid of being discovered.

He shouldn't be surprised; he'd seen all manner of strange

beings out here in the woods. But amazement clouded his mind. "I want to know," he insisted.

"Of course there's lots more. I don't exist in a vacuum." Again, she glanced around, twirling a lock of purple hair. "But that's our secret, okay?"

"No. I can't promise that. The other shadow hunters need to know. We share everything. There are no secrets among us."

April hurried to him and placed a hand on his chest.

The same electric current that flowed between them returned with such force that his knees buckled an inch. Was this a seduction meant to ensnare him? Chulah straightened. He grabbed her wrist and thrust it aside. "What kind of magic is this?" he asked through a clenched jaw.

She ignored the question. "Listen to me. Maybe seeing me like this will drive the point home. You're in danger. Hoklonote grows stronger and is plotting against you and your kind."

He raised an eyebrow, deliberately raking his eyes over April, from her toes to the top of her head. How could he trust this creature so different from his own flesh-and-blood roots?

"I'll prove it to you." April raised her right arm.

From the north, a faint odor of decay and mold carried on the wind. His blood stirred at the familiar scent, one he hadn't smelled since the great battle when Nalusa Falaya had been defeated and his spirit contained within the Choctaw Nation's sacred tree. The lesser shadow spirit, Hoklonote, had been there, assisting the greater spirit power, Nalusa. But when he realized the end was near, Hoklonote had scurried away from the scene and disappeared into the woods, like a coward.

No one had seen him since that night.

Foolishly, he'd hoped the little man had permanently disappeared. Should have known better.

Chulah frowned, unable to stop the cynical bent of his mind. Hoklonote reappeared the same time the mysterious April arrived? Highly suspicious. Beneath the beautiful fairy appearance might lurk a soul of evil. He hardened his heart. His people depended on him. "How do I know this scent isn't some kind of illusion? For all I know, *you* could be Hoklonote in disguise."

This was not going well.

Ridiculous tears burned the backs of April's eyeballs. She'd expected way too much, had dared to hope this man could have feelings for her so soon. "Please, listen to me," she pleaded, peeking past his large, muscular form. Had she been observed by any of her kind?

Nervous, she glanced over her shoulder. Should they catch wind of this, the Council would chastise her for revealing her Fae form to a human.

"Are you looking for someone?" Chulah asked, frowning.

"N-nobody," she lied, crossing two fingers behind her back. If any fairies were nearby, she'd die of shame. She'd been given a task. And she was failing. Spectacularly.

"It's hard to believe anything you say."

April didn't think it possible, but her spirits further bottomed out. *Enchant him*, the Council would advise. *You're just like your mother,* the queen would proclaim, *a besotted fool. Loser,* the rest of the fairies would sneer.

"Please. This is no illusion. Hoklonote is gathering what wisps remain and what birds of the night are left."

Chulah shrugged. "We've contained Nalusa. After what happened last night, we know to stay together in large groups. That way, Hoklonote isn't much of a threat."

"You're wrong. He'll still come after you and force the hunters to release Nalusa Falaya so they can rule together."

"Any of us would face death rather than free Nalusa."

"Are you so sure?" At his stone-faced expression, April sighed. "And I bet you thought Hanan felt the same. Until he betrayed you."

His face remained stoic. "How do you know about Hanan?"

"Because we watch you and help from our plane of existence when we are able." At least, she did. Most of the time, the other fairies couldn't be bothered. She reached a hand out to touch him, but let it drop to her side. Chulah would think the contact merely a ploy to trick him. "Haven't you ever felt a presence by your side in battle?" April held her breath. For years now she'd been by his side, tripping his foes as much as possible, helping in every subtle way within her means—pinching the enemy, distracting the Ishkitini in flight, directing the wind his way to better pick up scents.

And through it all, she'd come to admire Chulah—his quiet strength and confidence. His loyalty and dedication to the other shadow hunters and their cause. Surely he'd been able to pick up on some of her strong feelings and constant help?

He hesitated. "Maybe," he conceded. "During the last battle with Nalusa—were you there with me?"

Whew. "Yes," she breathed.

"Is that the only time you've been alongside me?"

"Mostly," she hedged.

In the past, she'd broken every fairy law by being with him even when it wasn't necessary. She'd followed him because he fascinated her, enchanted her in his own human way. And she owed him a huge debt, one she could never repay. A dangerous undertaking to be near him so much.

Remember what happened to your mother. Yet April was unable, or unwilling, to stop.

"It isn't, is it? You've been following me around everywhere." His voice dropped dangerously low, a sure sign he was irritated.

It was the same tone he used with his stepmother. April gulped.

"Eavesdropping," he continued. "No wonder you knew so much about me." His words were clipped, cutting her heart with each syllable.

This wasn't what she'd imagined. In her dreams, she materialized and Chulah recognized something of her essence that had been with him through dangerous times. He'd be profoundly touched and grateful. And he would never remember their first encounter. He'd take her warning and together they would work to defeat a common enemy, thus restoring her reputation in the fairy realm and leaving her free to love whom she pleased. Which was Chulah.

"I'm sorry. If only—"

"Save it," he interrupted. "At the next full moon, I and the rest of the hunters will search for Hoklonote. Consider your mission accomplished."

"But we can work together. That way—"

But he'd left. April stared at his back, stomach tightening in distress. She'd been so sure she could reach him without resorting to enchantments.

Maybe human love at first sight was a fairy tale after all.

Chulah ignored the rumbling in his gut. Three days without food would not kill him. He needed an answer. True, he hadn't gone on a spirit quest for over a year, but he'd survived such a journey nearly a dozen times.

Which didn't mean the hunger pangs wouldn't make him wish he were dead. But by the evening of the second day, his body would make the adjustment and his mind would sharpen, become more receptive to any messages or signs from the Other Side.

He slowed his pace and eyed the small clearing in the midst of massive oaks. This would do. Chulah pitched his pup tent and set up camp. Not that a fire would serve any useful purpose since he wouldn't be cooking or need its light to see at night or even its warmth in the early autumn. But often gazing into its blue core and in the flicker of ashes drifting skyward, a thought or image of significance to his problem would flash in his mind like a comet streaking through the heavens.

Plus, it was something to do.

He gathered large stones that he set in a circle, then collected twigs and large sticks to feed the flames. Carefully, he arranged the wood and pulled a pack of matches from his backpack. He was into camping and the traditional spirit retreat of his people, but not the primitive ways of old. Modern suited him fine when it came to starting a fire.

A flare of light, a whiff of sulfur, and the montage of twigs and sticks exploded to orange. Its own kind of magic. He rubbed his jaw and concentrated on the problem.

April.

April with her sparkling caresses and violet scent and otherworldly hair. The woman—fairy—who claimed to have watched him for years and been by his side. Her charming naïveté on human customs. Hell, even her intoxication at the local pub was sweet and cute as she smiled and proclaimed her mission to save the world. He held her image in his mind until every detail of her face was etched so clearly he could almost reach out and touch her.

Wait. Maybe he could.

He glanced around the gathering darkness, listening and searching with every supernatural cell of his being. Noth-

ing. He was surprisingly disappointed. He'd told her his
plans and the need to be alone to think over her request.
She'd respected his need for solitude.

Chulah adjusted the blanket beneath his legs and took
a long, cool swallow of water from the canteen. His belly
clawed for solid food, but water helped sate its clamor.

Deep breaths, in and out, and noticing the tiny pause in
between. Calming, sinking into solitude and focus, allowing his mind to drift where it willed, trusting the spirits
to direct his thoughts where his attention needed to focus.

Peace flowed from scalp to toes in a slow-moving stream.
For this moment, at this space and time, all was well and
as it should be. The sensation was familiar and welcome.
Many times in the past he had done such a request or retreat.

Always, a message would be given. Either through a
planted thought from an ancestor spirit, or by an encounter
with an animal or bird. Signs available to anyone if they
took the time to be alone with themselves and with nature
and study its ways.

With time and patience, he would emerge from his quest
with a decision reached on some vexing problem, or with
renewed energy and peace to take care of all the demands
on his time: family, employees, and his sacred mission to
hunt the shadows and keep evil at bay.

If it took longer than three days to decide if the Fae should
be trusted and given assistance, then he would wait as long
as it took for his answer. Because he had to get this right.
If April and her kind were trying to trick the shadow hunters, it could be disastrous for his fellow hunters. But if her
warning was true and Hoklonote was a threat, the hunters
had to help. They were born to do so, to protect the world
from the shadows, to keep a balance in the bayou.

There would always be evil, as there would always be

goodness and light. A shadow hunter existed to ensure balance.

And so he waited for a sign.

Bells tinkled at the front door. Finally, Steven had returned. He'd promised to round up several fairies to watch over Chulah in the woods. Far enough away so that Chulah couldn't detect them, but close enough that they could intervene should there be a shadow attack.

She hurried from the back of the store. "Is Chulah okay? Is everything…?"

Oh, hell, it wasn't Steven.

"So you must be April." Tallulah pinned her with a hard stare. Her sharp, angular features and stony eyes were even more intimidating than her brother's haughty bearing. Easy to see that she and Tombi were twins. They were both born to lead and to assert their will.

Face-to-face, the fierce charisma of Tallulah was a potent force. She was not a woman that any man could ignore. Even if she wasn't classically beautiful—her jaw was a fraction too dominant, her nose slightly long and sharp. But she had cheekbones to die for, a long curtain of black shiny hair and a female warrior body that was toned and chiseled. And she showed it to advantage, too, with tight jeans and colorful tops that featured plunging necklines. Tallulah was tall and exuded confidence. She proudly showed her heritage with a turquoise beaded necklace and bracelets and a leather belt with a large turquoise-and-coral buckle. Altogether, a look that proclaimed, "Here I am. Take notice."

As if Tallulah didn't have all *that* going for her, there was the heavy knowledge in April's heart that this was the woman Chulah loved. The woman he'd proposed to mere days ago.

April wiped her suddenly sweaty palms on her floral

skirt, spirits plummeting. Next to Tallulah, she appeared like a ghostly sissy. A piece of cotton-candy fluff next to steel wool.

"And you must be Tallulah." She lifted her chin and offered a tentative smile.

Her unwelcome visitor didn't soften for a second. Instead, her eyes narrowed. "You don't look like a fairy. Where are your wings?"

April stiffened. "They don't appear when I'm in human form."

"Sorry if I have trouble believing that. You appear ordinary enough to me. Show me one of your tricks if you're really a fairy. Fly around the room or do some abracadabra with a fairy wand."

If she had a wand, she'd zap Tallulah into the nether land and smack that smirk off her face. "Tricks?" April licked her lips. "I don't have any."

"Then how can you prove you're a fairy? I think you're a liar."

Anger flushed her cheeks. "I don't have to prove anything to you. Chulah believes me."

"Chulah's a dear friend. His only fault is that he's too kind, too trusting. A real sucker for helping out others."

April snapped at the insult to Chulah. He was intelligent and cautious. So he had a blind spot in his heart for his stepmother and half siblings. That didn't make him a sucker. "And you would know. Right? You've strung him along ever since Bo's death, let him think he had a chance with you when all the while you were sleeping with Hanan."

Tallulah drew an indignant breath and put her hands on her hips. "I didn't string Chulah along! How the hell would you know anything about it, anyway?"

"Because I've watched you. That's right. I've seen your lingering glances, the way you've touched him—a heartbeat longer than necessary. Yeah, you led him on, gave him just enough encouragement for him to think you would turn to him after you finished grieving for Bo and your brief fling with Hanan. Must have really stroked your ego to have a fine man like Chulah desiring you."

Tallulah stood immobile, as if shock had rendered her frozen. "Th-that's not true."

"It *is* true. Admit it."

She vehemently shook her head, black hair rolling and shimmering like a dark sea wave. "No. At least…not intentionally."

"Only because it suited you not to take a hard look at your behavior."

Tallulah's lips pursed. "Enough."

"No." She could take whatever insult Tallulah wanted to fling at her, but not when it came to the way she mistreated Chulah. "It's time someone stood up to you besides your brother."

"You know nothing about me," Tallulah said with a growl.

"I know more about you than you do me, yet you come into *my* place and insult me." April delivered her deathblow punch. "At least I don't sleep with people that are traitors to my own kind, like you did with Hanan."

"It's none of your damn business who I slept with."

"Right. Except while you were sleeping with Hanan, you could have had a good man like Chulah. But you were too stupid to realize it."

Tallulah's hands fisted at her sides and her eyes narrowed, her whole posture tensed, like a cat ready to pounce. "You're jealous. You've only known him a few days, yet I take it you think you're in love with Chulah."

"Of course I love him. What's not to love? He's handsome and kind and strong and brave." April stared at her adversary. Tallulah had all the same qualities as Chulah—minus the kindness.

"You only met him days ago. I've known him all my life."

"I've watched him for years, been by his side whether he realized it or not."

She gave a sardonic laugh. "Little good that did you."

That truth made her eyes water, but April refused to cry. Tallulah would love it too much if she did. "Why do you care? You turned him down."

Tallulah's brows arched. "He told you that?"

She smiled enigmatically. Let Tallulah think Chulah confided everything to her. The woman's ego could use a little shake-up.

Tallulah drew up even taller, taking a deep breath. "The past is over. What matters now is the future. Don't think you can lead Chulah on with some crazy airy-fairy tales."

"Why would I do that?"

"Maybe you're in league with Hoklonote. Maybe, if there really are such things as fairies, the entire lot of you want human blood for some evil purpose."

"Human blood?" April snorted. "We're not vampires." Although Tallulah was like a vampire...or a succubus... sucking a man's soul for sheer sport. Bleeding his heart dry just to stroke her inflated ego.

Tallulah walked over to her. Slowly, her eyes full of scorn and menace. Not stopping until she stood a mere six inches from April. "If you *are* tricking Chulah, it won't do you any good. Tombi and I won't join him if he comes back from his spirit quest with the decision to help the Fae. *If* there is such a thing."

Dread chilled April's spine. This wasn't something she'd considered. "I thought all the shadow hunters stuck together."

Tallulah grinned at April's discomfort. "We usually do—but not always. You want us to help you, you'll have to prove yourself."

"How do you expect me to do that?"

Tallulah shrugged. "That's your problem to figure out. Not mine."

Witch. "You're doing this out of spite, aren't you? You'd rather take a chance that I'm lying about the danger of Hoklonote just so you can get rid of me and keep stringing Chulah along for yourself."

"If I wanted Chulah, I would have agreed to marry him."

"You don't want or love him, but you damn sure don't want anyone else to have him, do you?" April complained bitterly.

"Not true."

"Is too."

"Are you two fighting about my brother?"

Tallulah whirled around and April took a step backward. Of all people, it had to be Chulah's sister.

"Eavesdropping?" Tallulah asked, frowning at the newcomer.

Brenda rolled her eyes and tossed her hair. "Hardly. Y'all were so loud you didn't hear me come in."

April's shoulders sagged. Part relief, part embarrassment. "How much did you hear?"

"Enough to know you both want him."

"I don't want— Oh, never mind. You're too young to understand," Tallulah said dismissively.

"Am not." Brenda glared at Tallulah. "You're always so mean."

Tallulah laid a hand over her heart. "You've hurt me deeply," she said. Turning to April, she lifted her nose. "Don't know why you went to all the bother of setting this store up.

If I were you, I'd hightail it out of Bayou La Siryna now. Cut your losses."

"I'm telling Chulah how mean you are to April. He won't like that."

Bless her heart, Brenda was sticking up for her. April couldn't help being delighted to have a human champion. Any champion, for that matter.

"Tattletale. Nobody likes them, Brenda."

"Leave her out of it," April said to Tallulah.

"Whatever. I was on my way out. I think I made my point." Tallulah walked slowly toward the door with exaggerated insouciance.

The bells tinkled as Tallulah slammed the door behind her. April relaxed and drew in a deep breath. "Thanks for sticking up for me. I'm afraid I wasn't being very nice either."

"Yeah, well, you're a whole lot nicer than Tallulah. She's stuck-up."

April was in full agreement but didn't want to be a bad influence on the young girl. Besides, she didn't want to dwell on the encounter. "I'm glad you came. What brings you here?"

Brenda touched a lavender lock of April's hair. "You were going to show me how you got those streaks."

Joanna would have a fit if she were responsible for Brenda attempting a dye job. "Why don't you tell me how you get your hair so silky and soft. I'd love to have your hair."

"Trade you if I could," Brenda said glumly.

"Yours is much prettier than mine." Inspiration hit. "Let's go upstairs. I want you to show me how you plait those gorgeous braids."

Brenda patted her hair. "These ole things?"

"I'd like to do something with mine other than have it

hanging loose all the time. C'mon up to my apartment and help me out."

Brenda's face lit. The girl appeared much friendlier without her surly mom present. "Sure. Thanks."

"Follow me." April led her past the rows and rows of glass shelves.

"It's like a fairyland in here," Brenda breathed.

April turned, catching the rapt look on the girl's face. "Pick something out to take home."

"Really?"

"Sure."

Brenda slowly walked up and down the aisles, only to keep returning to a large statue of a sleeping woodland sprite laying her head on a sphere of polished orange citrine as if it were a pillow. At last, she selected a small, delicate copper statue of a fairy on a swing and held it out. "This one."

"It's pretty, but not the one you truly want." April strolled to the sprite statue and lifted it off the shelf with both hands. "This was made for you."

Brenda shook her head. "I couldn't. It's too much. My mom would kill me."

"Why?"

"She'd say it's too fancy. Too expensive. That I don't deserve it."

"Your mom doesn't have to know the cost."

"Well…"

"Tell her it was a gift for you working in the store this afternoon."

"You mean…lie?"

Oh, dear. What was she doing? "No, of course not. Forget—"

"Awesome idea. Thank you." Brenda carefully gathered the statue and cradled it in her arms like a beloved baby doll.

"Leave it on the counter and I'll find the box for it before you go."

Gently, Brenda set it down, a smile of wonder on her face.

Upstairs, Brenda plopped on the couch beside her and pointed to April's hair. "What did you use?"

April had researched and was ready. "Hair bleach. But that's not important. Your hair is beautiful like it is. I want you to show me how you had it braided the other day."

"Why would you want your hair like mine?"

April laughed. "We all want hair we don't have. If it's curly, we want straight. If it's blond, we want black. So accept what you have. Now. Braid my hair."

April sat still as Brenda delicately twisted strands of hair until it was up off her neck. She strode to the mirror and preened. "I love it!" And it was awesome to have the thick hair off the back of her neck. Long hair was fine flying in the evening sea breeze but not so much fun during the heat of the day.

"Are you in love with Chulah?" Brenda asked suddenly.

April slowly turned to face his sister. "Yes."

"Does he love you?"

"Not yet."

"You think he will? He seems so…hard. He doesn't much like my mom and me. Or my brothers either."

"I'm sure he must. Doesn't he do things for you?"

"Yeah, but he ain't happy about it."

"But the point is…he's there for you."

She shrugged. "I guess."

"And he's not so hard. Tell him how much you appreciate him sometime. It would mean so much to Chulah. You're his family."

"Maybe."

April didn't push it. Best to plant the seed and let it germinate. She went to the window and looked outside. Her apartment was high enough that the distant woods were visible. Somewhere out there, Chulah was alone and deciding their fate.

A great longing welled deep within, stronger than all the years of loving Chulah while he knew nothing of her. Here she was in human form, and yet they remained apart. Impatience made her squirm like a five-year-old on Christmas Eve. She touched her fingers to her lips, remembering their electric kisses. Removing her fingers, April cupped her hands and blew on them slightly, sending her love across the miles.

The third night was much like the first and second for Chulah. Only now he had more focus. The hunger pangs were gone. He took in the slightest nuances of sound and the textures of the wind on his skin, the gritty ground beneath his feet, the rough scratch of bark on the trees, the crunch of dried fallen leaves as he slowly walked near camp. Each step a meditation, a prayer for guidance.

His legs tired and he started a fire and sat on his blanket, one that was woven by his great-grandmother. Tonight, the answer would come; he was sure of it. At twilight, he'd heard the rustling of a nearby fox, although the animal hadn't yet appeared directly.

Soon.

Prickles of awareness ran like a current up and down his spine. The wind picked up speed and he strained to discern patterns. A familiar baritone underpinned the whoosh of air. The regular pulse of a drum methodically vibrated. Its notes rumbled in his gut as if a nearby train sped by.

The rhythm increased tempo, louder than the rush of air. Closer and closer.

"Father," Chulah whispered, eyes closed. Past experience had taught him that the voice of his father was clearer with closed eyes. "I am here."

The wind ceased its movement.

"My son."

The words filled him with utter contentment. His mother had died before his memory was born, and so it had always been him and his dad. The one person in his life who was steadfast and true.

"You seek guidance," his father stated, going straight to the point. The visions never lasted long. "Guidance on whether or not to assist the Fae in the war against the shadow spirits."

"I do."

"There is precedent. Before the dawn of human memory, the Fae and the shadow hunters worked together to fight the creatures of the night."

Wonder and hope lightened his heart.

"But I must warn you. The Fae are not entirely trustworthy."

Chulah bit down on the inside of his mouth until the metallic taste of blood pooled. There was always a "but."

"Why? What happened to the alliance?"

"The Fae grew greedy. They craved some of the power that was not rightfully theirs. While the shadow creatures are evil, and the shadow hunters fight for the good, the Fae beings are in between the dual forces. They fight to preserve their own realm, to keep their nature hidden from man."

He could hardly blame them for not wanting humans to know of their existence. Such awareness could very well result in their extinction. An image of April's golden aura filled his mind. Such beauty was not meant for mankind, who would either covet their glory or destroy that which they could not understand.

"Every species seeks to preserve their life. That's a law of nature."

"To a point," his father cautioned. "Problem is, the Fae will form secret alliances with either side as it suits their purpose."

"And so our people considered them too risky and broke ties," Chulah guessed. His father wouldn't be able to say, but Chulah asked anyway, long shot or not. "What about April? Should I trust her?"

"You know I cannot answer that for you," he said, resigned. "I can only provide light on what has been. You are the future and must forge your own path." A tinge of sadness crept into his voice. "I am but a shadow of what has passed and never will be again."

The wind crept up, rustling the limbs above and the leaves below. His father's time was short.

"Thank you, Father," Chulah said, the words a benediction and farewell. Who knew when or if the spirits would ever grant them communion again?

"I raised you well, my son."

He strained to hear the words. His father's voice was fading fast, growing distant.

"I have faith in you, Chulah. You will make the right decision."

If only he could be as sure.

Chapter 7

The promise of dawn etched the sky, and the internal debate had not ceased. No easy answer was to be found. He wanted stark, crisp facts edged with concrete borders marked *wise* or *foolish*. Yet even April's Fae essence defied precise definition. Her human side was lovely, sparkly and electric while her Fae side was a glow that burned hot at the center and dissipated outward into an ethereal aura.

Chulah tried to keep faith as the hint of the morning's rays shone on the eastern horizon. Time was almost up.

Send me a sign. Right now.

Awareness prickled his scalp and the nape of his neck—familiar and comforting. The unseen presence that had been a childhood invisible friend that never left.

It grew stronger, gentle as a mother tracing her newborn baby's face, an instinctive bond sealed with the wild, ancient scent of violets and oak moss.

"April," he commanded. "Show yourself."

He held his breath. If she appeared, would it be as the

female vixen with the touch that sent shock waves through his body, or as the glowing, winged fairy he could only admire from a distance? The day poised between dawn and dusk, shadows and light, magic and mundane.

She stepped from behind a tree, silver hair of moonlight, blue-purple eyes framed by opal skin—milk-white flesh that reflected specks of purple, pink, blue and silver. April glided toward him, not quite a walk, but not flying either.

Chulah stood and held out a hand. In an instant she was by him—solid and oh so very real. His April of the Meadows, who shook the foundation of his ordered world. She extended both her hands, too exquisite and ethereal to be solidly human.

A ray of sunlight splintered through the treetops and April's form grew solid. He clasped her hands in his own and tingles spread from his palms to the soles of his feet.

"I want to trust you. But I've been warned about the Fae and their selfish motives." He released her hands, taking a step backward. He needed to think clearly, unencumbered by her electric touch. "Do you really want to work with the hunters to capture Hoklonote? Is he actually a threat to us and other humans?"

"He's dangerous for both our kind. I—that is, *we*—can help. We have in the past, although it's been so long ago that humans have forgotten."

"So I've been told. But again, why should I trust you? Do you have a hidden motive for seeking me out?"

She hesitated, so brief he might have imagined it.

"I chose to seek you over the other hunters because I've watched you over the years. You are a good, honorable man."

"Hardly."

Chulah almost laughed. Sure, he did all the right things, performed his duty by his family and the other hunters. But deep inside, he did so with a grudging spirit. There was no joy in dealing with the cold Joanna and his troublesome half siblings. Tombi and the other shadow hunters were his friends and he'd die for them, but all the responsibilities weighed on him, oppressed his spirits.

The only times he was truly happy was when he was immersed in repairing motorcycles, or riding alone on one through the back roads of the bayou. Chulah longed to be wild, free, unencumbered by duty.

"Why do you say that? You've financially taken care of your family since you were a teenager. And you are the best trekker of all the hunters. Without you, Nalusa would never have been captured."

"You give me too much credit." It was disconcerting to realize just how much she knew about his past. And although she'd seen his outside actions, she couldn't know that inside he was dead—a hollowed-out shell of a man. Especially since he'd made a fool of himself proposing to Tallulah.

"No, I don't. Why can't—"

He cleared his throat. "Stop. Are you trying to flatter me so I'll agree to help you? The real question here, again, is why should I trust you?"

"Why would I lie? What would be the point?"

"Maybe only your fairy world is in danger and you want to use me, use all of us. Maybe you're working with Hoklonote to draw us into a compromising position so that you can defeat us for good."

"It's not true. Is there anything I can do to prove I'm telling the truth?"

"No."

He studied her anxious face, the way she twisted her hands in front of her body. "Guess it all comes down to a matter of trust."

"Guess so. Unless…" Her face lit up and she gave a broad smile. "Perhaps there is a way."

"What did you have in mind?"

"What if I could prove I was a true friend to you—or, at least, that I always cared about you? Could you trust me then?"

"I…suppose." He was instantly on the defensive, wanting to believe her, but prepared to catch her in a lie. Apparently, that was their nature.

"Excellent."

She stared at him and he was mesmerized by the blue-purple pupils. So vivid, he felt as if he could step into an indigo-tinted world. A sense of calm, comfort and peace rushed over his body in wave after wave of pleasure. All was well. All was easy and effortless.

The constant tension Chulah held in the middle of his back released, his brow smoothed, and he breathed deeply. The scent of decomposing leaves and salt and pine underpinned by April's violet-and-vanilla-and-moss fragrance. All his muscles loosened and his bones became weighted in a delightful lethargy. Better, his heart was full of appreciation for being alive on this October morning.

"Feeling good?" she breathed. "Relaxed and happy?"

"How do you do it? Must be some kind of fairy magic." He should be angry at the manipulation, but he couldn't summon the energy or desire.

"It's called an *enchantment*," April explained. "And there's varying degrees of it. Can you recall a time in your life when you really needed this and peace mysteriously appeared in the midst of anguish?"

Chulah inhaled sharply. Of course. "After my father died. You were there…in the woods." Heat spread down his neck. He'd broken down the day his dad died and he'd left the house to be alone in the woods with his grief. It was the first and only time in his life he'd ever shed tears. And April had witnessed this.

"I couldn't bear to see you so unhappy. I sent you the strongest enchantment I could."

"It worked." Not that he hadn't been sad, but he'd gathered enough emotional support to handle all the funeral arrangements and take care of his houseful of half siblings and stepmother, who depended on him as the new man in the house. "Thank you," he ground out grudgingly.

April stroked his cheeks and lips with a gentleness he'd never experienced.

He'd better watch it with this one. She knew him too well. Knew what he craved at the same instant he did. Knew how to soothe him—and inflame him with desire.

But April had performed a kindness without an apparent ulterior motive and his mind was settled.

At least temporarily.

"I've never turned my back on a challenge and I won't now," Chulah declared. "I'm giving you the benefit of the doubt."

"So you'll help me—I mean, you'll help the Fae?" She hurried to add, "And it's in your own interest as well."

"I will do what I can."

She clasped her hands in front of her. "Wait until I tell Steven and the others!"

Ah, so the short dude was one of *them*. "Steven's a fairy. Should have known."

"He's my guardian fairy while I'm in human form."

"Why do you need a guardian?"

"To help me in case I give a clue about the fairy realm. He set up the shop and the apartment so that I would have a reason to fit in Bayou La Siryna."

"I could tell the shop meant nothing to you. And your apartment was downright bleak."

April shrugged. "The figurines were pretty enough, but I prefer real flowers and real creatures. Not some fake imitation."

"I need to go home and eat and strategize." Chulah kicked dirt on the smoldering coals.

"Will you call Tombi and the others to your cabin today?"

He nodded, taking down the tent poles. "Better hope they trust us enough to agree to work with the Fae."

"But if you do, surely they will?"

"Probably." Hard to imagine Tombi wouldn't trust his judgment in the matter. They had always worked as a team. All the shadow hunters cooperated with one another, even if they split off separately to hunt shadows when the full moon reigned over the forest.

"Can I be with you when you talk to them?"

"Okay. But don't try to pull any of that enchantment stuff on my friends. They'll see it as manipulation."

"I wouldn't do that." Her long eyelashes lowered. "You're the only man I've ever enchanted."

Chulah frowned at the words. They made him sound weak, a slave to a Fae spell. "Because I let you," he said curtly. "To-night, anyway. If I want to stop it, I can."

He hoped. Best not to let April think she could put the whammy on him whenever she wanted to get her way. He was the one in charge here.

"Of course you can," she purred.

He kicked more dirt on the smoldering sticks.

"I'll take care of this while you pack up your tent." April waved a hand over his campfire, and the hot gray sticks cooled at once and the tendrils of smoke ceased spiraling upward in the dawn air.

"Nice trick," he said drily. Did she have the ability to wiggle her nose and take care of everything like Samantha on the old TV show *Bewitched*? If so, she probably secretly laughed at him performing mundane human chores.

Chulah couldn't blame her if she did.

"You're doing *what*?" Tombi roared.

The other shadow hunters glanced at one another uneasily. This was why he'd decided April shouldn't be present when he broke the news. It would only antagonize the men more. Chulah dug his heels in and raised his chin. "I've committed to help April and the Fae. They need us, and we need them if Hoklonote has plans to release Nalusa Falaya."

"*If*. A mighty big *if*."

"A possibility we can't ignore," Chulah insisted. "I caught the barest whiff of Hoklonote when I saw April in the woods. Being around a fairy heightens my hunting senses even more than usual. It gives us an edge we've never had before. Plus, they can kill wisps like us. It's more dangerous for them, though, because they have to be closer to their target than us."

"Or it could be April tricked you into imagining you smelled Ole Hokie," Tombi argued. Chulah recognized the obstinate expression on Tombi's face. Fine—he could be equally stubborn.

This was not going well. And he hadn't even told them the worst yet.

"There's something else all of you should know," he began, grudgingly. Tombi had already heard it, but now everyone needed the same information. "The Fae seek the soul of an elder in their Council that's trapped by a will-o'-the-wisp. This elder is revealing information that jeopardizes their secret world."

"We can't identify the individual spirit that's released, like they can, when a wisp is killed," Tombi said, brow furrowed. "Well, Annie did once with Bo, but that was an exception."

Chulah's gaze involuntarily darted toward Tallulah where she stood in a corner, arms folded across her chest, full lips tugged down in a frown. This must be gut-wrenching for her. Bo, as he'd painfully discovered, was still the love of her life.

"True. We can't, but the Fae can. Which could also prove useful for us," Chulah argued. How he hated bringing up the next point. "But there is one hitch." He paused, took a deep breath and rushed on. "When they find the elder's spirit, they intend to bind it."

"No way—"

"Oh, hell no—"

"It's wrong—"

Tombi spoke up over the roar of disapproval. "Told you that would be the reaction. Released spirits are sacred. We have no right to judge them or keep them from the After Life. It's not our place."

Chulah held up a hand. "I've thought about this long and hard. Look at it this way. Is it any different than us trapping Nalusa in our sacred tree? We did what had to be done in order to protect our world from his evil. The Fae are doing the same. This elder betrayed them to Hoklonote and they have to silence him to save their own world."

Silence settled in the room as the men weighed his words.

"I don't like it. Especially helping them catch a spirit in order to kill it," Poloma broke in.

Chulah's hopes sank. Poloma was influential and usually reflected what his fellow hunters believed. "Bind it," he corrected, "not kill."

"Why the rush to help the Fae?" Poloma continued. "You

could have waited until we all had time to investigate the woman's claims."

Murmurs of agreement greeted the hunter's words among the dozen hunters crammed in Tombi's cabin.

Chulah pinched his lips together, refusing to repeat himself about the danger from Hoklonote. He'd anticipated a bit of resistance, but not to this degree.

"This April must have some special means of persuasion," Shikoba, a fellow hunter, said drily. "Don't let your dick rule your head."

Tombi patted him on the back. "Understandable that she turned your head. April's a beautiful woman...or fairy... or whatever the hell she calls herself. Just tell her we all need time before we agree to jump into a possible trap."

"I've already promised my assistance. You don't have to join me."

"I'm not saying we will or we won't," Tombi said. "I'm saying we need time to study the situation."

"Study all you want. I begin the hunt with her tonight."

"C'mon, dude. Don't be that way," Poloma murmured. "We're like family."

The others would back Tombi all the way. Chulah tamped down the bubble of hurt clogging his chest. What had he expected? He'd never been more than second- or third-in-command. He was alone and on the outside.

Tallulah pushed her way to the front of the group and Chulah stiffened. Judging from the fire in her eyes, she'd be piling onto the other's objections.

"I spoke to your April at her shop. There's another side to her you haven't seen. She may be all sweetness and light around you, but she showed her ass to me. The bitch... wrongfully accused me of some hard things."

That was a surprise. "Like what?" he asked.

"Not important."

"Yes. It is. You put her down in front of everyone and then refuse to go into the details?"

"April is jealous of me. Okay?"

The buzz in the room stilled and Chulah was conscious of everyone listening and watching. Could it get any more embarrassing?

"Seems she overheard your proposal and—"

Yep, question answered. It could definitely get more embarrassing.

"Enough," he interrupted quickly. "Female emotions have nothing to do with our decision on a Fae alliance."

"That's the most sexist, outrageous..." Tallulah sputtered to a stop, hands on hips.

Damn if she didn't act like a spoiled younger sister. A romance between them would never work. He accepted that now.

Chulah looked past Tallulah to the faces of his closest friends. Friends who shared his supernatural gifts. Friends he had joined in battle and he'd known all his life. Friends who were closer to him than family.

He knew the risk he took. That his way of life hinged in the moment like a fragile piece of crystal on the edge of a table with a twitchy-tailed cat on the prowl. He had never broken from the tribe before, had always followed the majority-rules principle. Known as a man of few words who solidly backed Tombi and their friends. A way of existing where he'd been, if not joyous, comfortable and mostly contented. Doing his duty, doing the right thing. Good Ole Chulah, who could always be depended upon.

To hell with that.

"Do what you have to do," he said stiffly. "And I'll do as I believe right. If you change your minds, you know where to find me."

Jaws slackened, eyes widened, and the hunters eyed one another with raised brows.

Except Tallulah. Her face still held its familiar scowl, but her eyes had softened and he could sense her respect, if not approval.

Chulah turned his back on the lot of them.

"Wait. Where are you going?"

He recognized Tombi's voice but kept walking. Why couldn't they—this once—trust *his* judgment? Follow *his* lead?

If April was a mere trickster, he'd discover it for himself—and pay the price.

He chose me over his friends. Me!

April couldn't stop stealing sideways glances at the tall warrior by her side. He packed camping supplies—rope, canteen, food and tent—efficiently and with clipped, precise movements.

"Are you sure you aren't upset with me?"

"Stop asking. I told you I wasn't."

He lied. His face was stoic and the suspicion in his eyes was more intense than ever. Heck, she didn't even have to look in his eyes to see the resentment; it radiated from every cell in his body.

"I'm sorry."

"Stop apologizing. You've done nothing wrong." He paused from the tent-folding and stared her way, brown eyes with copper flecks glinting with intensity. "Have you?"

"No."

The Fae *did* need his help to capture Hoklonote. The elder *was* captured. And if working with Chulah suited her own secret agenda to restore her name and find true love, so much the better.

"I can't believe none of your friends would come with us. Not even one."

"We'll do what we can together."

She should be disappointed that he was the only hunter willing to help them. Steven and the Council hadn't been pleased a bit at the news. "It's a start," she had told them. Secretly, she was pleased. No—ecstatic. She would be alone with the man she loved. It couldn't have worked out any better. With time and close proximity, he would grow to love her, too. Soon, she hoped. April fought her impatience. She'd known him for years; he'd known her for only a week.

"April? Did you hear me?"

"Huh? What?" she asked.

He gave a lopsided grin. "Stupid question. Do you want a tent for tonight? I have an extra."

"I was hoping to share your tent."

Chulah's eyes darkened. "That would work," he drawled slowly.

His words sounded thick, as if his tongue were swollen in his mouth. Her own throat went dry and she licked her lips. Everything was right here, right now, within her grasp. All the lonely, outcast, invisible years were history.

She nodded her head toward the back porch. "Let's go." She almost winced at the eagerness in her voice. Would he think she was…immoral? A loose woman?

Together they left his cabin and entered the woods.

Inhabiting a human body was strange. In the Fae kingdom, she flew or glided from flower to flower without much thought. But here, her body felt plodding, heavy— leaving footprints in sandy soil, evidence that she had trod this land. The solidity of human weight, tied to the earth by gravity, left April feeling powerful instead of cumbersome.

"Why do you keep looking at the ground?"

April started at the sound of his voice. "Watching my footprints," she admitted sheepishly.

His brow furrowed and then cleared. "I take it you've never shifted to human form before."

"Not much," she hedged, tamping down the memory of the disaster of her youth. "I like having a human body. Especially when you kiss me."

"I imagine you have something similar in your…um… other form?"

"Nothing that compares to naked human touch," she assured him.

Leaves crunched as they proceeded deeper into the woods. April thrilled at the sound her feet produced.

"Tell me," Chulah said at last, "what's it like in your fairyland? I imagine it's all sweetness and light. All of you flitting about like tiny glowworms without many cares."

"It's no paradise. The other fairies don't trust me."

Chulah raised a brow and she sighed.

"Long story short—my mother committed the ultimate sin in forsaking the Fae realm for a human lover."

"Doesn't sound like such a big deal."

"That's because you don't understand their—I mean *our*—vanity. They consider themselves superior in every way to land-tied humans."

"I take it you don't share that opinion."

If she did, she wouldn't be in love with Earthbound ones. "I don't."

Chulah pointed to a log. "Rest your legs."

Gratefully, she hurried to the log and sat, Chulah seating himself beside her, his thigh brushing against hers. April's pulse accelerated, the way it always did at his touch.

"So you're an outcast of sorts," he said, direct as always.

Not for long. Not if she got him or the other shadow

hunters to take care of Hoklonote. "I am. I've always envied the closeness of you and your friends."

Chulah's face tightened and she bit her lip. Way to remind him of his friends' refusal to cooperate in the hunt. She rushed to divert his attention. "My own kind look down on me."

"Then why did they send you on a mission to save their world?"

Unease rumbled in her stomach. "I begged them. And they were aware how much I watched humans—particularly you. They figured their best success lay with me."

He appeared doubtful and April couldn't blame him. She'd been so excited to be chosen, she hadn't examined the Fae reasoning too closely. It had to have been her desperation that made them conclude she was the right one for the job.

"We should stop talking," he said, surveying the darkness. "If we don't, we'll have no luck spotting anything. The sound will warn them of our presence."

"There's an easier way. We don't have to wait for them to come to us."

His gaze locked on hers. "Go on."

"I can revert to Fae form and sing. That'll draw the wisps close."

"We don't want too many at once."

"Of course. I can find a stray loner and shepherd it to you."

He nodded. "I can see how the Fae and the hunters were once powerful allies. Our skills complement each other."

April stood and withdrew, touching the fairy cross crystal pendant at her throat.

By air, at night.

My wings take flight.

A whirring dizziness cycloned through her brain, and

the ponderous heaviness of bone and muscle dissolved to a glowing lightness of being.

Chulah shook his head, as if stunned. "Not sure I'll ever get used to that."

"Later," she called as she drifted upward, light as a child's balloon. A song tingled in her lungs, bubbling up through her mouth. An old, old ditty passed down through the generations, one that lured the wisps like a siren's song at sea.

Which meant one was nearby.

April held the notes in her mouth and chest. She had to ensure there wasn't a cluster of them. Her lungs were near bursting by the time she spotted it.

Cobalt blue flames licked the night air. The green heart of the trapped soul flickered and glowed in time to its beating pulse. Bright, dim, dim, bright.

April opened her mouth and let the musical notes escape. Fairy bell–clear, they chimed in the Gulf breeze. The orb of light bent in her direction, as if the wind pushed it toward the music. She hovered midflight, wings flapping. The wisp slowly stretched and strained, moving toward her.

She guided it to Chulah, who was alert and prepared to strike, slingshot at the ready. His eyes widened as he spotted the wisp behind her. Quickly, April flew up and out of the path of the rock.

Bull's-eye.

High-pitched wailing filled the darkness like a banshee. The wisp's light collapsed in upon itself and extinguished, sending wisps of smoke upward in spirals.

The green heart transformed to a pure white light. It skittered like a five-year-old jumping out of sheer joy and pleasure.

An image of an elder chieftain washed through her mind—a wrinkled, dignified face framed with feathers in his hair. An old soul at last free to cross over to the After Life.

A tinge of disappointment gnawed at April. How nice it would have been if the soul happened to be the councilman the Fae sought. Ha. As if her luck would ever amount to that.

"You there, April?"

She touched the crystal at her throat and drifted down, solid, human legs touching ground. "Here. We make a great team, don't we?"

"So far, so good."

Gaining his complete trust wasn't going to be easy. But she was up for the challenge, and the hardest part was won.

April crossed her fingers behind her back for luck.

Chapter 8

April frowned and tapped a foot impatiently. There had been no sharing of Chulah's tent last night. Which freaking disappointed the hell out of her. For a whole week, she'd been careful not to touch or tempt him, to prove that she wasn't casting enchantments. And still he'd made no move to reach out to her first.

"What's got you all twitchy this morning?" Steven asked with a wry smile. He picked up a dust rag and swiped the countertop for the millionth time.

"You know, at some point we're going to have to actually open this damn place to the public." She flinched as he tossed her the rag, grabbing it awkwardly a millisecond before it slapped her in the face.

"Until then act busy, in case someone wanders in," he warned. "We have to maintain appearances and behave like we have a credible reason for being in Bayou La Siryna."

Not really, not now that Chulah had agreed to help them. But unfortunately, she had nothing better to do this morning. Lazily, she walked up and down the aisles. Not how she envisioned this morning. She had thought to spend the day lying in Chulah's tent—or at least his bed in the cabin. But no, he claimed to need a few hours' sleep before working at his motorcycle shop.

The fate of the world was at stake and he wanted to work. She could hardly expect him to drop the entire routine of his life for a woman he'd met a week ago. Not even a real woman either.

A fairy.

"Bet you haven't had breakfast," Steven observed. "Saw you came in at the wee light of dawn. But I knew you were out hunting with Chulah again, so I didn't worry about you last night."

Irritation flared in her gut. She could take care of herself without his snooping around and watching her. No doubt reporting everything to the Council.

"As long as you're in human form," he continued, "you need to do certain things like eat and sleep or your frail body will collapse."

"How do you know so much about it?" she asked, trying to keep her patience.

"I've been around," he answered vaguely. "There's a pot of grits on the stove and milk in the fridge. Maybe with a full belly, you'll stop your grousing."

She reckoned it couldn't hurt. April entered the break room with its small kitchenette and dutifully served up a bowl of grits and poured a glass of tap water. She took a large swallow.

"Bleh." How could water taste so bad? It had a coppery, chemical tang with no nectar sweetness. She banged the glass on the table. Maybe the grits would be better. She scooped a spoonful and ate. Double bleh. Felt like a mouthful of sand.

"You've much to learn about human cuisine." Steven

barged in and bustled about the kitchenette. He placed a dollop of butter in her bowl. "Now try the grits."

April frowned but determinedly forced another spoonful down her throat. "Whoa. This is a million times better."

"Wash it down with fresh milk," he said, setting a glass by her bowl.

Dutifully, she took a sip. "It's better than the water."

"Hold on." He rummaged in a cupboard and returned with a box, spooning out brown powder and stirring it in her glass. "Now try."

She took a delicate sip. What. The. Fairy. April closed her eyes, savoring the sweet goodness. "What was that brown stuff?"

"Powdered chocolate."

"I want to put it on everything from here on out."

"It doesn't go with everything," he cautioned.

April regarded him suspiciously. "You lie."

Steven threw back his head and laughed. "Try it for yourself."

April's mood improved, a result of Steven's companionship and a side effect of sugar goodness. "Seriously. How did you get picked for this job? Most fairies want as little to do with the human world as possible. Yet I can tell you're accustomed to their realm, that you've spent a fair amount of time here."

Steven sat across from her and nibbled on a cookie. "I'm almost as much at home with humans as fairies. Not surprising."

"It is to me. I've never known anyone else like you."

"Why shouldn't I be comfortable between the worlds? My father is human and my mother Fae. Just like yours. As halflings, we're the best suited for this mission."

"Is that the only reason we were chosen?" she asked

wistfully. It would be nice to have been picked for her brains or her abilities.

Steven put down the cookie and swallowed a bit of her chocolate milk. "I thought you knew."

She shook her head and sighed. His words only confirmed what she'd guessed.

Steven scraped back a chair and stared. "The pure Fae are unable to live in flesh and blood for more than a day or two."

"And to think I went before the Council and queen and begged them for the chance to come here."

"Oh, no. There was never any doubt that you would be the one chosen to be in the world."

She blushed to think of how she'd practically lain prostrate at the Council members' feet, desperate to be granted human form and contact Chulah. How they must have laughed behind their sleeves the whole time she pleaded for the opportunity.

He covered her hands with his own. "You are special. Don't let them destroy your spirit. I know how you feel. All my life, they've made me feel inferior for my halfling heritage."

"Halfling." She gave a bitter laugh and pulled her hands from his. His pity was worse than his gruffness. "I'm so sick of that word."

"It doesn't matter." His voice lowered, turned coaxing. "C'mon, April. They're ignorant. We can't help who we are. We had no say in the matter."

Impure. Halflings. They didn't belong in either world. Humans didn't believe in their existence and the Fae only regarded them as creatures to be used.

"How many others are like us?" she asked curiously. She'd never known another besides herself.

"Only a handful. Some have renounced the Fae realm

and pass for human in their land. But if the Fae catch you trying to do it, you could be in a lot of trouble."

"Is that what you've done? Renounced your Fae nature?"

"Not totally. As long as I provide them a valuable service, the Fae begrudgingly allow me to pass between the worlds at my own risk."

The meal settled heavy in her stomach and she pushed away the plate, reliving all the old memories. Her mother didn't want her, had deserted her infant daughter in the Fae realm knowing that they would never accept a halfling. Maybe her mother scorned her, too. Her biological father might not even be aware of her existence.

Other, more insidious thoughts wormed around her brain. Maybe she was destined to be like her mother. No wonder she'd been drawn to Chulah. Half of her biological body craved physical contact with a male human, and her spirit longed, like a human's, for a loving, accepting mate. Chulah had only happened to be in the right place at the right time, and she'd fixated on the man.

In the end, he would reject her like everyone else.

"I've been a fool," April said, twisting the words past the cramping pain in her throat. "I was so sure I could find my mother, win the love of Chulah, and gain the admiration of the Fae and the shadow hunters."

Steven smiled wryly. "Hardly realistic."

"So what can I *realistically* hope for? Can Chulah eventually convince the other hunters to help my—" she ground out a barking laugh, had started to say *my kind* but realized she didn't have *a kind* "—that is, to help the Fae against a common enemy?" April scraped the chair back from the table and paced the claustrophobic room, seething. It was so clear now. No matter what she did, the Fae would never accept her. "And if we succeed at defeating Hoklonote…

what then? Stay in the Fae realm and be treated like trash? That's no life."

"It's not so bad. You get used to it." Steven bent his head, gazed at his clasped fingers. "They mostly ignore me, and I come and go as I please."

April pulled out a chair and sat next to him. "But are you truly happy?"

"I'm…content. Most of the time."

"Sounds lonely to me."

He lifted his head, settled his smoky gray eyes upon hers. "There's always hope. I have my dreams."

April waited. "What are your dreams?" she finally prompted.

His fingers drummed the table and still she waited for an answer. She wouldn't ask again.

"Like anyone, I'd love to find a mate," he said slowly.

"You should." April nodded vigorously. "Absolutely. Surely there's someone for everyone. Another halfling, perhaps?"

He said nothing, but sorrow and longing pinched his features. Steven stared at her like she was the essence of nectar in an unearthly beautiful flower.

Oh, no. So that was how it was for him.

He stroked her hand, his thumb tracing circles inside her palm. His touch glided upward, past her forearm and up her shoulder, at last cupping the side of her neck. It wasn't the thunderbolt touch of Chulah, but it was warm and sweet.

"What are you doing?" April asked weakly.

Steven pulled back. "I've spoken too soon. You still imagine you love Chulah."

"I do—" April stopped. What did she really know of love? Only that she wanted it. She rubbed her forehead, sighing. "I'm confused."

"Of course you are." He stood and patted her shoulder.

"I've bumbled my way this morning, blurting out things you weren't ready to hear. Forgive me."

"There's nothing to forgive. Don't apologize for speaking the truth." She bit her lip, sorry she couldn't offer Steven more comfort. A bit of hope. If only she could learn to love him…

It would be the perfect solution to their mutual loneliness. A little love would be better than none at all. But she could muster no enthusiasm at the prospect. April shut her eyes, remembering Chulah's kiss, the feel of his arms wrapped around her body.

No one else could ever do.

Her lips trembled and she firmly clamped them shut, fought back the rise of tears. Steven didn't deserve to see her cry over another man.

But when she opened her eyes, Steven had vanished.

Chulah dropped a wrench on his big toe. "Son of a—"

"Whoa, boss."

Chulah slid out on the mechanical creeper board and glared at J.B. "As if I don't hear you cussin' like that a thousand times a day."

"Yeah, but I ain't the Man." J.B. hooked his thumbs in his overalls and winked, the fat folds of his triple chin wobbling with mirth. "Must be lack of sleep got ya grumpy. Hear tell you been busy most nights with that new chick in town. A hot blonde."

Chulah's annoyance deepened. "Maybe you should pay more attention to your own business, Slim."

"Mine ain't near as interestin' as yours, though." J.B.'s grin grew broader.

They'd known each other since they were knee-high to a possum and Chulah had never seen him get riled. He always reacted to any barb with a good-natured grin.

J.B. held out a cold water bottle. "Figured you might have worked up a righteous thirst, hard as you been at it today."

"Thanks, man." Chulah gulped down half the bottle, swiping his mouth as he came up for air.

"Seriously, boss. Why don't you knock off early this afternoon? We're all caught up round here. I'll finish up Linc's Honda Shadow here for ya. Go home and catch up on some shut-eye."

An excellent idea. Chulah rubbed the back of his neck where he'd kept a lack-of-sleep headache. Hunting nights with April and then working all day at the shop were getting to him. It had been almost a week and there was still no sign of Hoklonote.

Just as worrisome, a change had come over April. She'd grown distant. They'd worked together, finding the occasional wisp and releasing its spirit. But in all their nights together, she hadn't once tempted him to kiss her by touching his arm or bestowing on him her innocent-yet-sexy smiles.

Why should she? April got what she wanted. He'd gone out on a limb and helped her. There was no more need for seduction and pretense to persuade him to get her way.

He should be glad.

They each had a job to do. A fling would only interrupt their concentration.

Chulah left the shop with its smell of brake fluid and grease and hopped on his motorcycle. As he sped down the road, the crisp air invigorated his weary mind and body. Somewhere along the familiar path toward home, he took a detour and found himself downtown by the Pixie Land store.

Chagrined, he parked the bike and headed to the door. *Can't leave well enough alone, can you? If April's upset about something, that's her own business.*

Right.

Bells tinkled a warning as he entered. Damn if the place didn't smell of violets. And what the hell was the matter with him? Since when had he ever been so enamored with the scent of flowers?

Like never.

Chulah straightened his shoulders. He was here to discover what was wrong with April. It was only for the good of their partnership. Maybe there was some crucial element about their mission that she was withholding for fear of losing his cooperation.

A flash of red beard shone in the mirrored shelves, fragmented and bright. Steven emerged from the back of the room. "Oh, it's you," he said flatly, halting momentarily before walking behind the cash register.

"Good to see you, too." So much for the small talk. "April home?"

"No." Steven opened an account ledger and promptly ignored him.

"Mind if I take a look for myself?" Without waiting for an answer, Chulah walked past him and bounded up the stairs.

"Suit yourself," Steven called to his retreating figure.

Chulah rapped on her apartment door. "April?" Knocked again, louder.

But there was no response and no noise to indicate she was home. So Steven had told the truth. Chulah trod back down to the main floor and stood in front of the counter. "Any idea where she went?"

The man refused to look up from his ledger. "Not a clue."

Chulah closed the book and Steven at last raised his face. "Have you got a problem with me?"

His face turned almost as red as his beard. "No."

"So you're just rude to every potential customer who walks in the store?"

His mouth twisted. "Only the ones who run around with April at all hours of the night doing who knows what."

"She always let you know where she's going and when to expect her back," Chulah said sharply. "Kinda ballsy of you to make that comment."

Steven drew himself up stiffly, although he was still a good foot shorter than Chulah. "I'm supposed to be her guardian while she's here."

More like the Fae's spy on April, he suspected. "Even so, her private life is none of your business. Unless…" Chulah stopped short. "You've got a thing for April, don't you?"

"And that is none of *your* business."

Aha. No wonder he was such an ass at their first meeting. A frisson of doubt niggled at Chulah. April claimed to have loved and watched him for years, but maybe she had feelings for this strange little dude as well. "How long have you known April?"

Steven crossed his arms. "Long enough."

Chulah nodded at the stone Steven wore around his neck, identical to the one April wore. "Are all the Fae as annoying as you?"

"Don't call me Fae. I'm a halfling. Like April. Only difference between us is that she actually cares that the rest of the Fae look down on her. As for me, I'm content to go my own way."

He lied. Of course he cared, but Chulah didn't call him out on it. "Women are more sensitive than we are. Guess that holds true for humans as well as fairies."

Steven nodded and some of the hostility melted from his sharp eyes and stubborn chin. "She's been moody all week. I kinda made her face some hard truths on why she's even here in the first place. She deluded herself into believing the Council had picked her special for this mission. She'd secretly hoped to win you and the other shadow hunters' allegiance and then climb her way into acceptance with the Fae." He snorted. "A foolish dream."

Chulah schooled his features to stay neutral. "I see."

Boy, did he ever. April had flattered him just to get him to do her bidding. Tombi and the others were right. She wasn't to be trusted. A white-hot anger burned his brain, cleansing and purifying his clouded emotions, allowing him to see her as she really was: a lying, manipulating fairy. That was why she'd been so down all week. Her dream had been shattered. And to think he'd been worried about her.

Still, Chulah maintained his outward composure. He'd pump information from Steven as much as possible, because he sure as hell wouldn't get it from April. "Why do the Fae look down on halflings?"

"Because we aren't pure. They can never forgive our half-human nature. They see flesh as disgusting."

Chulah tried to digest the thought. Was that why she'd been so withdrawn? Did she find contact with humans disgusting? A yawning abyss seemed to open between their worlds.

Not that it mattered.

Chulah went in for the kill. "Is that why you love April? Because you're both outcasts and you're lonely?"

"I'm not… I don't…" Steven glared at him. "Think you're so smart, do ya?"

"No, actually I'm feeling pretty stupid right about now."

What secrets did April harbor behind that innocent facade? He'd been so taken in by her looks and her charms that he'd lost his senses.

And yet, to be fair, he'd sought and found confirmation with his father during his spirit quest. At least helping the Fae *in general* was the right thing to do. But as far as April herself—he could never trust her motives again.

"Ah, we Fae are the secretive sort. I'm sure April has all kinds of hidden dreams she's never told a soul."

"There's nothing wrong with dreams," Chulah said hastily. "I've got a few of my own. But it's wrong when you use someone else to get your way."

Steven shrugged his shoulders delicately.

"You don't agree?"

"Depends."

Chulah scowled. "There's right and there's wrong."

"So you say."

Really, this guy was maddening. "We'll have to agree to disagree," he gritted through his teeth.

"Suits me. But with my way, I can accept April as she is."

Chulah straightened. "Meaning I can't."

"Meaning you won't."

Chulah crossed his arms and fought to keep his temper. "What you're really saying is that as a human, I'm an unacceptable match." His neck warmed. "Not that it matters."

"As a Fae halfling, I understand April far better than you ever could. We have similar backgrounds and values and are familiar with each other's worlds."

"And I'm the outsider. Gotcha." Chulah walked briskly to the door and shoved it open. The tiny bells jangled a mad tune. He slammed the door shut, surprised the front windowpanes didn't explode from the force.

Chulah reopened the door. "And you can have her. May you both be miserable together."

This time when he slammed the door, he left for good,

hitting the accelerator on his Harley as he sped out of town. *Forget about her. Learn your lesson now. She's untrustworthy, and you live in two different worlds. It can never be.*

Chapter 9

The bayou twilight cast touches of silver on the tips of dark shadows, as if beckoning the world to delve into its secret magic. But April was immune to its charms tonight.

Don't give up on my brother, Brenda had pleaded. *You're special to him. I can tell by the way he looks at you when he thinks no one is watching.*

A slight smile played on April's lips. Her only hope came down to the words of a sixteen-year-old who admittedly had a rocky relationship with her half brother. They had spent the day together going to lunch and the movies. April had reassured Brenda that as long as she was—*ahem*—in Bayou La Siryna, they could be friends outside of her relationship with Chulah.

The glow from Chulah's cabin pinched her heart. She'd gladly trade the silver-patterned shadows of the forest for the cozy warmth of his home. To be a part of his world, safe and loved and protected from evil spirits while alone together inside the cabin.

Heaven.

She paused at the path to his door, imagining a different sort of welcome than what she'd received the past week. This time, as her hand was poised to knock, Chulah would open the door, so eager to see her that he'd been waiting impatiently at the window for her approach. A slow, sexy smile would soften the sharp angles of his jaw and face. And the topaz rays of his deep brown eyes would glow like banked embers of a fire.

Her heart skittered just to think of such a reception.

Maybe he would be more loving if she acted more loving. Just because her own kind rejected her didn't mean there was no hope for love, in spite of what Steven had said.

April breathed deeply and rang the doorbell. Again and again. At last, Chulah jerked opened the door.

"I wondered if you'd show up tonight. Should have known you would. Anything to help you look better to the other fairies. Right?"

What was he talking about?

"Don't play dumb," he continued. "Steven let it slip that you dragged me into this just so you can be a hero and look good to the rest of your kind."

A chill crept up her spine, followed by a heated flush on her face and neck. "He d-did?"

"I take it you haven't been home all day." His eyes narrowed. "What have you been doing? Hunting other hunters for your cause, I bet. Casting your spell."

"It's not a spell. I'm a fairy, not a witch."

"What the hell's the difference?"

"An enchantment is just allowing my Fae charm to be... appreciated...by a human."

"Appreciated." Chulah snorted. "Kind of like using sex to get your way?"

"Is that what human girls do?" A lick of jealousy burned

her throat at the thought of Chulah with someone else. "Like Tallulah?"

"Tallulah is none of your damn business."

His heated defense confirmed her worst fear. The two had been intimate and he still wasn't over her. She wanted to scream or at least shake some sense into Chulah. What did he see in that sullen woman?

Maybe she was terrific in bed.

April turned from the doorway, refusing to let him see the hot tears burning her eyes. Why couldn't she be more like Tallulah? Bet that coldhearted woman never shed tears. She forced a hard edge in her voice. "Are you coming with me to hunt Hoklonote? Because if you aren't, I'll go by myself."

"You're bluffing."

Only one way to prove him wrong. Even though her legs felt heavy, April began walking. Oh, she would show him. She'd show everybody—human and Fae alike. She'd capture Hoklonote all by herself. She needed no one. And wouldn't they be surprised and sorry they'd underestimated April Meadows. Why she—

"Damn it, woman, wait up."

A door slammed but she didn't look back. *Crunch crackle snap.* On she stalked, murdering dried leaves and pine straw in her wake. "Go away," she called over her shoulder. "I don't need you."

"Like hell you don't."

A heavy, strong hand weighed down her right shoulder. "Stop."

April shrugged out of his grasp. She didn't care if it was childish. She was past caring. He thought the worst of her anyway. On she plunged, the nip of the Gulf breeze whipping her hair about her face like leather cords. She welcomed the sting and the cold. It reminded her that she was alive, in the flesh-and-blood way of humans. Along with thrilling electric touches and delightful ambrosia drinks that made her dizzy with smiles, there was also pain. All worlds had a dark side.

Chulah followed behind. Unlike her own angry tread, his trod the path lightly. So noiseless that if she didn't sense his energy she wouldn't be aware of his presence. But whether as Fae or as human, April suspected she would always feel connected to Chulah.

A pelting rain erupted. April stopped and tilted her face to the moon. The cool drops coating her skin was a novel experience, one she wasn't sure if she liked or not. In fairy form, rain merely passed through her aura with no sensation. She stared, marveling at the wet rivulets running down her forearm. She rather liked it.

"What are you doing?"

Chulah was beside her, staring at her as if she were daft.

The smile flirting with the corners of her lips flattened out. April dropped her arm and lifted her chin. "Nothing," she replied airily, refusing to look at him. "Go away."

He didn't.

April stomped ahead.

"You know, it wouldn't kill us to miss a night hunting. We're not having much luck anyway. Might as well go home and stay dry."

Ahead she plunged.

"Catch up on sleep," he added.

April walked faster.

"You know, with all the noise you're making, we aren't going to scare up any will-o'-the-wisps, much less Hoklonote."

"If you stopped jabbering I could," she shot back.

"Touché."

April turned. "This isn't working. Not tonight or any other night. Just forget the whole thing."

"What do you mean?"

"I mean that the two of us can't do it alone."

He frowned. "Is this your way of goading me to get the other hunters to come along? I already did. They're not sure that's wise."

So now he was going to question everything she said or did. Lovely. Wait until she got ahold of Steven. He had no right to ruin her delicate relationship with Chulah. April shrugged. "You tried. You can absolve your conscience and go home."

His mouth settled in a grim line. "What about you? Have you convinced all the fairies to join in? Or are they happy to throw you to the wolves and stay out of it?"

He hit the mark with that gibe. Her life meant nothing to her own kind.

"Bet you haven't even tried to get them to rally and fight. You're too busy playing their savior."

"I'm not anybody's savior. I can't even save myself."

"What's that supposed to mean?" Chulah held her by both arms and frowned down at her. "Are you in some kind of trouble?"

Energy crackled between their bodies. His long hair was plastered against his wet skin, emphasizing his high cheekbones and angular jaw. Dark brown eyes stared at her with an intensity that took her breath. No one else had ever looked at her this way, as if he wanted to devour her—body and soul.

She licked her lips, wanting nothing more than to feel the heat of his body against her chilled skin, to be drawn into his strong arms. His eyes lowered to her lips.

Chulah wanted the same thing.

His mouth was on her, his hands pressed against the

small of her back. A wild joy sparked, and she ached to be filled by him, to be his woman in every sense of the word. To belong to him, to be consumed by him, even if it was for only one evening. She arched her hips against Chulah, felt the proof of his desire straining against his jeans.

He moaned. Or was that sound emanating from her own throat? It didn't matter. Chulah lifted her off the ground and his hands cupped her ass, pressing her core against his sex. His heart thudded against her breasts. She was suspended in the air, but anchored by his strength.

The rain grew heavier, matching the intensity of their need. April didn't care. It could be hailing golf ball–sized ice clumps and she wouldn't willingly part from Chulah's embrace.

"I want you," she groaned against him.

His breath was ragged and hot against her ear.

She did this to him. Made him as crazy with desire as she was. April wanted nothing more than to have him capture her body against one of the massive oaks and take her as the rain fell on their fevered bodies. She imagined rough tree bark grazing her back as Chulah stroked into her core from the front. Trapped between two hard forces of nature—and never wanting to escape the sweet torment.

Chulah set her on the ground and rested his forehead against hers. "This is crazy," he breathed. "We're outside in the middle of a storm."

Their hot, jagged breaths joined together. April bit the inside of her mouth to keep from moaning in frustration. He was right, of course, but she was loath to let go of Chulah.

And so they remained. Holding on to each other, breathing the same air. Gradually, the frenzied need racing within April calmed to a dull ache.

"We can forget hunting for one night," Chulah said at

last, looking up at the drenched heavens. "Let's get out of the rain."

He took her hand and they ran down the path. The soil sucked at their shoes, making a speedy exit to shelter impossible. By the time she stumbled into his cabin, April was soaked.

Inside, Chulah looked at her and stilled. His eyes traveled down the front of her cotton shirt.

April glanced down. The sheer fabric clung to the curve of her breasts, and her nipples were hardened from cold. So that was why human females wore bras. Still, April doubted she could force herself to wear the torture device all day every day.

A slam of a car door sounded outside.

Chulah groaned. "It's got to be Joanna."

Of course it was. That miserable woman snuffed out Chulah's happiness like a starved bloodhound, determined to chomp it down.

Quickly, he ran to his room and emerged with a red flannel shirt. "Put this on."

April shrugged into it. The warmth of the fabric was cozy, and it smelled as earthy and sexy as Chulah. Like peat moss and pheromones and pine. She held up an arm and inhaled deeply.

"This is probably for the best," he said.

She lifted her head. "What do you mean?"

"I mean this." He pointed between the two of them. "We aren't meant to be together."

"I say we are."

"No. Think about it. We're from different worlds."

"It doesn't matter, not to me. If only—"

He held up a hand. "Stop. This can only end badly. For both of us."

Harsh rapping sounded at the door and he turned away.

"Wait," she said desperately. She had to change his mind.

Chulah faced her. How easy it would be to enchant him. To use the powerful attraction between them and breathe a little fairy dust into the mixture. Surely a little magic never hurt anyone? April took a deep breath, concentrating on Chulah's love, and exhaled, sending a bit of magic his way.

His eyes narrowed. "Stop it. I know what you're doing. How can I ever trust you when you do crap like that?"

Her face flushed and she bit her lip. "I—I'm sorry."

He scowled and stalked to the door. April looked down at the hardwood floor and blinked back hot tears. She was used to disappointment and was willing to take a risk for true love. But if Chulah got hurt in the process…well, that was quite another matter.

Everything she did turned out wrong. The harder she tried, and the longer she stayed outside of the Fae realm, the more damage she could inflict. Her kind had chosen the wrong person for the job.

She'd have to fix their mistake.

"Where's your little girlfriend?"

Chulah sighed as his stepmother followed him into the cabin. "She's…"

The den was empty. Had April retreated to the bedroom to avoid Joanna? A flash of silver shone from the den window. He walked over and looked outside, in time to see April vanish into the woods.

Go after her. The pull was strong. He took a step to the back door and stopped. What was the point? If he chased after her, she'd think he'd changed his mind.

What if she gets sick from the cold and the rain? Again, Chulah took a step and stopped. It wasn't like April wasn't used to being outdoors in the elements. Once in the woods, she'd change to fairy form and be fine.

"You sure are acting strange tonight," Joanna said with her customary tartness. "Stranger than usual."

Chulah couldn't help the sardonic smile at her barb. She always found a way to slip one in every conversation.

He sat down on the leather sofa and motioned to a chair. "Have a seat and tell me what brings you out so late tonight."

Joanna carefully perched on the sofa, as if afraid it contained cooties. She crossed her skinny legs and folded her hands in her lap. The wedding ring, worn now on her right hand, picked up the lamplight and the prisms in it glowed.

A reminder of his father's marriage and his promise to look after Joanna.

"It's Chris." She looked down into her lap. "He was caught driving under the influence."

"Again? What's this—like his third offense?"

Her head snapped up. "It's only his second."

The outrage in her voice ate at him. No matter who got into trouble, no matter whether or not they were clearly in the wrong, Joanna found a way to defend her spoiled brood and excuse their behavior.

But he said nothing, refusing to give her ammunition for more anger. Because whatever he said, it would be wrong.

She shifted uncomfortably in her chair. "Anyway." Joanna cleared her throat. "They've got him locked up in the county jail. If we hurry, we can get him out before the bond shop closes for the night."

"We?"

Her thin lips pursed so hard that white lined the edges of her mouth. "I can't afford bail on my own."

"Have you ever considered that it might do him good to suffer the consequence for his actions?"

"You know nothing about it. Stop being such a cheapskate."

"It has nothing to do with money."

"Don't you dare sit there and act so righteous with me. I'm his mother and I know what's best for him. Being locked up overnight with hardened criminals isn't what he needs."

That was exactly what the would-be con needed. "He'll never change as long as we keep bailing him out."

"Everyone deserves a second chance." Her voice cracked. "Unlike you, he didn't have a father to raise him. Your father died when he was only six years old."

That was right. Hit him by bringing up Dad's name. Chulah sighed. "How much is Chris's latest escapade going to set me back?"

The tears clouding Joanna's eyes cleared immediately. With businesslike efficiency and precision, she produced a document from her purse and handed it over.

Chulah surveyed the paper and gave a low whistle. So much for the new equipment he'd planned on buying for the shop.

"I'll do it," he muttered. "But this is the last time."

"Of course," she quickly agreed. "I'm sure he's learned his lesson."

Yeah, right. Chulah scrubbed a weary hand over his face. If it wasn't Chris, it would be Johnnie. Or the plumbing needed fixing. It was always something.

And to think if Joanna hadn't knocked on the door when she did, he'd no doubt have April in his bed, making love to her in every possible way. Instead, the lonely night stretched before him.

Chulah wasn't sure if he should be grateful or angry with Joanna for that fact.

April slogged through the rain and the cold until she came upon the Fae portal by the cypress tree. A momentary glance behind to make sure she hadn't been followed, and

April touched the fairy crystal pendant. The stone was cold as ice, as if the black cross fault at its center were rimed with frost. She gripped it and whispered an incantation.

Flesh and bone give way to vapor and mist.

From grounded to airborne, I am fairy-kissed.

A lightness of being lifted her from gravity's force, transporting her to the Fae realm. It could have been day, instead of night, for all the twinkling of light. The tips of every tree branch glittered silver and green. Pale pink moonbeams, pixelated into fragments, settled on the trees and ground like a frosting of snow. Green crystals glimmered on saw palmettos like peridot sprinkles.

She was in the same bayou woods, only in a different dimension.

In a matter of moments, she would be noticed. April took in her sickly yellow aura, so different from her usual spring green. They would know immediately that something was wrong.

Let them.

She'd come to resign anyway.

Hundreds of Fae gathered around her with their usual twitters and words spoken behind hands covering their mouths. Which meant they weren't saying anything flattering. April continued forward and the fairies split a path before her that became a carpet of rose petals. The Council were near.

The Council members' auras were larger, brighter than other Fae. The twelve of them, male and female, formed a horseshoe pattern with the fairy queen in the center position. She was dark and shadows, bedecked with smoky quartz jewelry and an obsidian tiara. As royalty, she rarely deigned to speak directly with anyone except the Council members. April didn't dare face the queen directly.

April braced herself and stepped into the middle of the Council.

"What's the problem?" asked an older, matronly fairy.

"I quit. That is," she hastily amended, remembering her manners, "I wish to quit." They had the power to banish her from their realm. Then where would she go? "With your permission, of course," she added for good measure.

"Why?" the same councilwoman probed. "Because you have successfully completed your duty?"

"In part," April hedged. "The most skilled of the shadow hunters, Chulah Rivers, is helping locate and kill Hoklonote."

"This we already know," an elder male interrupted impatiently. "What about the rest of them?"

"So far they refuse." She paused, collecting her confidence. "Which is why I think you should send someone else in my place. Someone more skilled than me."

The Council members exchanged glances. Even the queen's remote expression flashed a frisson of concern.

"But we chose *you*," one of the younger councilwomen remarked.

"And I appreciate the honor." Her throat tightened on the lie. She had been honored at first, until Steven told her the real reason she was chosen.

She was expendable.

"You cannot quit until we say you can," the older matron snapped. "Go back."

Okay, so they had the power to banish her. But they needed her, too. As a halfling, she was suited for long periods of time in the human world. A feat none of them could manage.

"I have tried and failed," April repeated. "Perhaps there is another halfling who could take my place?"

Silence settled like a deep sleep.

She waited.

No answers or objections. She would take their silence to mean she could take her leave while they considered the matter. April took a step back and bowed her head, preparing to leave.

"Wait. You don't have permission to leave." The eldest male glared at her, his eyes flashing red like fresh pools of blood. "As it happens, we don't have another halfling available. You're it."

"There's Steven," she pointed out.

"That won't work. He's male."

"So what?" April gasped at her blunder. "I mean, why should it matter?"

"Because the shadow hunters are men and you have the power to enchant them. Steven does not."

Not that again. She couldn't—wouldn't—resort to enchantments for Chulah's cooperation and love.

"But there is a female shadow hunter. Tallulah." Even saying the name of Chulah's love hurt April's heart.

"There's one female and dozens of males. The chances are greater that you can succeed."

"But…I don't want to enchant Chulah," she admitted softly.

He slapped a hand down on the table. "We don't care what you want. You have your orders. Now do it."

"Besides, there are other hunters." The youngest councilwoman spoke up with a voice sweet as cotton candy and a dazzling smile. "You don't have to stick to one male. Forget Chulah."

Forget Chulah? Impossible.

"Please," she begged. "Just let me quit. I've failed you."

A loud murmur arose from their audience.

She had failed to live up to their Fae expectations. She had failed to win Chulah's love. And she had failed in her secret dream of connecting with her long-lost mother. Every woman she met in the human world, she wondered if she was her biological mother. Every trapped spirit released, she'd secretly hoped it was her mother and not Grady, the betrayer that the Fae sought.

"Failure's not an option," one of the Council members ordered above the din. "You're our best hope for capturing the traitor and stopping Hoklonote from destroying our kingdom."

April shook her head. "No—"

The queen stood and the world hushed. "Go back. And don't come back until you have better news."

April nodded slowly and touched her fairy cross stone, prepared to leave. If the fate of the Fae depended on her, they were all doomed.

Chapter 10

Chulah padded across the hardwood floor in the darkness and stared out his bedroom window. The moon shone on the wet grass. It was cold enough it might turn to frost by morning. The temperature had dropped rapidly all night. He cracked open the window and breathed in the crisp air.

Was April okay? Did she make it back to her apartment safely? What the hell was the matter with him—he should have given her a ride home. He blamed his atrocious lack of manners on his sex-addled hormones, coupled with the chilling effect of Joanna reappearing with yet another problem.

The image of her long hair plastered against her wet clothes reproached Chulah. Could a fairy catch a cold? Surely it was dangerous for her in human form. And she didn't have the good sense, due to lack of experience, to know to come out of the rain.

And he didn't have the human decency to make sure a young woman left his cabin and was safely chaperoned home. His father would be highly displeased to witness such a glaring lack of kindness.

Did she even have a phone number? He needed to remember to ask her next time they met.

With a sigh, Chulah pulled on a pair of jeans and a flannel shirt. Nothing would ease his conscience but to drive downtown and make sure she was safe. When Chulah pulled up outside the Pixie Land shop in his truck, he saw that no light shone in the windows. He braved the cold and got out of the truck and pressed the doorbell. Would she even hear it upstairs? For the hundredth time, Chulah chastised himself for not getting a phone number.

He waited several minutes and turned away to go back to his truck, more uneasy than when he'd arrived.

"What are you doing here?"

Chulah snapped around. Steven stood in the doorway, his red curls spiked one side of his delicate face, lying flat on the other. He rubbed his face, obviously roused from sleep.

Irritation spiked up and down his spine. "I should ask what *you're* doing at April's place."

Steven folded his hands across his chest and yawned. "Sleeping on the sofa in the break room. Busy day here yesterday."

"Yeah, right. Cut the act. We both know you're here as some sort of official fairy guardian, so just tell me. Did she get home safely last night?"

Steven jerked to attention, his body tensed. "She didn't spend the night with you?"

Holy crap. Chulah strode past him. "Asleep on the job, huh? I'm going to check her room."

He sprinted up the stairs, and his stomach bottomed out at the sight of April's unmade bed. "Where would she go?" he asked. "Back to her own realm?" The thought made his head spin. It might be for the best, but he hated to think he'd been so abrupt at their last meeting. Regret left a hollow space in his heart.

"When did you last see her?"

"She left my cabin late, cutting through the woods to return…here. Or so I thought."

"And you let her walk—alone at night—in the cold and rain? What the hell were you thinking?"

Heat warmed Chulah's neck. "Guess I wasn't."

At Steven's continued glare, he tried to defend his actions. "I thought she'd revert to fairy form and be fine."

"It's possible she was spotted walking alone and called to report to the Council."

"Can you check? Go…fly…or whatever it is you do."

"At once. Wait here."

Chulah stared, curious as to how he'd leave. In a puff of smoke?

"Turn around," Steven commanded. "I'll do nothing in front of a human."

Chulah sighed. Best to humor the little man and let him go on his way to search for April. A sizzle sounded from behind. Chulah turned, but Steven had vanished.

"Neat trick," he murmured into empty air. Now what? He couldn't just mope around here, imagining the worst. At the very least, he could walk the trail in the woods, in case she had met some mishap.

Chulah hurried back to his truck, raced through the empty streets of town and parked his vehicle at the woods' entrance. The ground slushed under his boots, and although the rain had stopped, water dripped down from the tree branches and quickly soaked his flannel jacket. What if April had been out for hours with only his thin shirt for warmth?

The constant, steady drip of water on fallen leaves was

like a constant tap on the shoulder, reminding Chulah what a jerk he'd been. He should have told Joanna that her crisis could wait until morning and then given April a ride home.

On he went, cautious not to miss any sign that she had been this way. With each step, his concern and self-recrimination grew. He imagined increasingly bad scenarios, including one in which Hoklonote had captured her.

Dejected, he turned to retrace his path in the woods when a flash of silver and white caught the corner of his eye. Through the darkness, he searched and found a figure of a woman in a long white skirt and with pale hair trailing about her hips.

April.

She sat on his back porch steps, hugging her knees to her chest, head leaning against a wood post.

She was okay. She'd come back to him.

Chulah sprinted across the cold, moonlit field. April didn't look up until he was within a few yards. She started to rise, startled, then sank back down on the step when she recognized him.

"What happened?" he asked. He sat beside April and wrapped his arms around her thin body. Shudders racked her, and he ran a hand up and down her wet shirt.

"I—I went to see C-C-Council," she stuttered through chilled lips.

"Never mind. You can tell me inside."

He scooped her in his arms, surprised at her feather-lightness. Misery shone in her blue-purple eyes. Unthinking, Chulah lowered his head and tenderly kissed the tip of her delicate nose. Her cheeks were wet, whether from crying, the rain or both, he couldn't tell.

"Shhh," he murmured soothingly. "Everything's going to be okay."

To hell with the never-ending shadow battles and the nefarious fairy world that would cast out someone as special as April. Chulah headed straight for the bathroom, April still in his arms. Unceremoniously, he sat her on the commode and turned on the bathwater. As hot as he thought her skin could stand.

"Wh-what are you doing?" she asked.

"Getting you warmed up." The blue tinge at her lips and her uncontrollable shaking scared the crap out of him. A hot bath and a cup of hot tea were in order. If she was still shaking after all that, he'd call Annie over. No doubt Annie would have some vile—but effective—herbal concoction.

"Out of those wet clothes," he ordered matter-of-factly.

"Gladly."

Chulah silently applauded her lack of modesty as she slipped off shoes and socks with shaking hands. She stood, and her body tilted to the left.

He caught April in his arms and steadied her. "I'll help you." With one hand wrapped around her waist, Chulah pulled down her white skirt. Only thin lavender panties covered her hips and mons. He sucked in his breath.

"Now your shirt," he said huskily. "Can you stand on your own for a minute?"

She nodded and he peeled off the two layers of shirts. His own hands trembled as much as hers. Only his was from desire, not cold.

Her nipples were hardened and he wanted nothing more than to taste each one. For God's sake, the woman might be near hypothermia and all he could think about was ravaging her body?

Disgusted, Chulah pointed to the tub. "Get in."

April's eyes warmed. She kept her gaze pinned on his as she hooked her thumbs on the corners of her panties and slowly pulled them down to her ankles.

Chulah abruptly turned away. "I'm going to make some

hot tea." He didn't—couldn't—look back as he heard her slip into the tub.

In the kitchen, he poured water in a teakettle and put a tea bag in a mug. Everyday things, to help return some steadiness and routine. The profound relief of finding April, coupled with his strong desire to claim her body, unnerved Chulah. *Don't get in too deep with this woman. Keep it simple and uncomplicated.*

That was getting harder to do.

The teakettle whistled and he startled. He should probably call Steven. And he absolutely would, if he had his number. But for all he knew, Steven might show up any moment in a puff of smoke.

Damn, he hoped not. Not just yet.

Chulah poured boiling water in the mug and added a spoonful of sugar, stirring absently, thinking of April's naked body. Her glorious, perfect, naked body.

He wanted to possess her. Desperately.

No. You live in different worlds. It will never work.

Chulah threw the spoon in the sink. He was sick of being the Good Guy, the Sensible Guy, the schmuck who always did his duty and approached everything with caution. To hell with that. Didn't he deserve some measure of joy? Some crazy fling to remember in his old age?

Yes, he did. Tonight was his night. And her night. Because he would make it special for her, too. Would love her body like he'd never see her again. Tonight had taught him how frail time was, how tenuous relationships were. For all he knew, April could disappear at any moment and there wasn't a damn thing he could do about it.

But at least he would have no regrets about tonight. He'd apologize for his behavior earlier, end everything on a good note.

That decided, Chulah carried the mug to the bathroom.

Pure notes of music, a crystal clear alto voice, sang an enchanting song he'd never heard. She had the most beautiful voice. Chulah leaned in the doorway, listening. Occasionally, he picked up the sound of a washcloth being dipped in water, then drizzled over skin. He felt like a gauche teenager, awed and paralyzed at a woman's beauty.

Black tea splashed his fingers, bringing him out of his reveries, and he cursed.

"Are you okay?" April called.

He took a deep breath and entered, determined to act like the experienced man he was. "Fine." Chulah set the tea on the counter before looking her way. "I added…"

Mounds of bubbles spilled from the tub, completely covering his view. Damn it. "Where did you find bubble bath?"

She picked up his shampoo bottle. "I partly washed my hair in it and discovered it made all these little bubbles." She scooped up some in her hand and blew on them. April had knotted her hair on top of her head and grinned. "I feel soooo much better. Hot baths are now my favorite human thing, except for your kisses."

You can experience both at the same time. Chulah bit back the words. "You look…back to normal. But drink this for safe measure." He handed her the mug.

April took a delicate sip, then another. "That tastes marvelous." A delicate hiccup escaped her lips and her body jumped in the tub.

A nipple peeked out of the white bubble.

His throat went dry. "Be in the next room if you need me. I'll leave you some dry clothes on my bed. They'll be way too big, but they'll be warm."

"Can't you stay and talk to me?" April took a long swallow of tea and hiccuped. Her body levitated a few inches out of the tub.

Extraordinary. "What the hell?"

"Nothing to worry about," she said cheerily. "Seems to be a glamour glitch. Whenever I drink, it gives me a little lift. Suppose it messes with earth's gravitational field or something."

"I see." He cleared his throat. "Listen. About earlier tonight… I shouldn't have let you wander alone in the woods like that. If something had happened to you…"

April cocked her head to the side and eyed him quizzically. "Wander alone in the woods? I don't understand why that concerned you. It's what I do. I'm a fairy, remember?"

She hiccuped and this time her body rose a foot in the tub. Unnerving. A reminder she wasn't an ordinary human woman. He arched a brow. "Hard to forget that fact when you keep levitating every time you drink."

April giggled. "And to think just a few hours ago I was ready to quit."

"Quit?" He frowned. "Quit your mission?"

The mirth in her eyes extinguished. "Quit everything. I told the Council I was a failure and they should send someone else."

His worst fear was confirmed. As quick as a passing breeze through the treetops, April could disappear. Forever. And that had come oh so close to happening.

Careful, his inner voice screamed. *Warning—don't get too involved.*

Chulah took a deep breath. If Hoklonote released Nalusa, the shadow hunters would be in peril. So would the Fae, according to April. And even if they did capture Hoklonote and the Fae found the spirit of the betraying elder—even then, April would return to her kind and he would be left alone.

Always alone.

Slow down.

He grabbed a towel and placed it on the sink counter. "I'll let you finish up while I cook us some breakfast."

"Okay. I always forget to eat and drink unless you or Steven remind me."

She stood.

His breath caught. Creamy skin glistened and shimmered. The pink buds on her breasts peeked through the white bubbles.

The curtain of bubbles slowly, slowly slipped down, exposing more peach-toned skin. The womanly curve of hips, the soft mound of stomach, the pale curls at the apex of her thighs.

Chulah couldn't move. Not for all the money in Alabama.

A Mona Lisa smile hovered on her lips and her eyes darkened. She either felt the same or recognized his desire.

One exquisite leg stepped out of the tub, then another. April came to him, as inevitable as the eternal ebb and flow of the tide. Her arms wrapped around his neck, and her warm, wet body pressed against his.

His hands glided down the damp surface of her back.

Silk.

She pressed her lips to his own.

Careful... The hell with that. Chulah cupped her ass and squeezed the soft orbs of flesh. His erection was swift and painful, aching for release. April wiggled against him, her sex naked and wet.

"I want you," she moaned.

The words roared in his head like a tropical hurricane. She wanted *him*. To hell with future repercussions. All that mattered was this moment between man and wom— "Hey, wait a sec." How to word this? "Can a...um, fairy have sex?"

April moved his hand from her ass to her breast. "Doesn't this feel real to you?" She guided his hand lower. "And what about this?"

The soft folds of her core were slick with a dampness

different from the rest of her skin. A heated liquid that revealed she desired him as much as he did her. Chulah inserted a finger and she moaned again.

"You're so damn tight," he muttered. "I don't want to hurt you." Another thought stopped him cold and he withdrew his hand. "Are you a virgin, then?"

"Only in this realm," she breathed.

He released a strangled sound—somewhere between a chuckle and a moan. Leaning his forehead against hers, he tried to steady his harsh breath. In his world, a virgin was a virgin. No shades of gray there. "Is that supposed to reassure me? I don't know what to make of it."

She put a finger under his chin and lifted it so that he looked directly into her pools of blue eyes. Another mysterious, feminine smile lit her Cupid's-bow lips. "It means I'm emotionally ready. With the added physical benefit of being delightfully...taut."

"I won't hurt you," he promised.

"Maybe I want you to. A little."

She was going to be the death of him. Chulah grabbed the towel and gently patted down the rivulets of water that streamed down her perfect body. He also rubbed her scalp and long hair until it was no longer dripping wet. "Ready?" he whispered, flinging the towel to the floor.

"Been ready."

He gathered her into his arms and lifted her. April's delicate pixie body was lightweight. So light that a flutter of anxiety twisted his gut.

"You're not going to break me." She ran an index finger over his lips. "Trust me."

In this, he had no choice. There was no denying himself the pleasure of possessing April. He had to have her.

At once.

Chulah carried her into the bedroom and carefully laid

April on his huge four-poster bed. She looked so small that he again hesitated.

April took his hand and beckoned him to lie beside her. Quickly, he tossed off his T-shirt and made short work of unzipping his jeans and pulling them off, along with his boxers. She licked her lips.

"Having second thoughts?"

She shook her head. "It's just…you're so big. I wonder if it will, you know, work."

"Don't worry. We'll take it slow." It might kill him, but he'd do it. Chulah lay beside her and stroked the delicate curve of her jaw and neck. Again, the electrical magic stirred between them. If touching her did this, what would it feel like to actually be inside April?

His hands roamed to her breasts and he caressed the tight buds. April groaned, reaching down to stroke his erection.

Chulah took a shaky breath.

Slow, he reminded himself. *Go slow.*

He placed his mouth over one of her nipples and April writhed against him.

"For queen's sake," she cried brokenly. "It feels so good."

Chulah raised his head. "We're just getting started."

"The hell." April cupped his balls and a wild current of desire ripped through his reserve.

Slow, slow, slow. She made it damned hard. Chulah again sucked a nipple and inserted a finger into her hot core, picking up where he'd left off in the bathroom.

"I want you now," she demanded.

She was ready for him. More than ready, as was he. "Next time, more foreplay," he promised.

"Are you trying to kill me?"

Her echo of his exact thoughts made him smile. It would be good between them. More than good. The chemistry was amazing.

Chulah entered her, careful to take it as slow and easy as her tight passage allowed. She gasped and her hands dug into his shoulders. He stopped. "Did I hurt you?"

"I'm not sure." She wiggled her hips beneath him. "I think it's okay."

Chulah didn't move as she adjusted to the new sensation. Sweat broke out on his forehead, but he commanded his body to obey his promise. Years of training as a shadow hunter had taught him restraint and patience.

She moved against him. "Keep going."

"You sure? Because if—"

"Move," she whispered. "If it hurts, I'll tell you."

Move he did. Over and over until she joined him in each thrust, as seemingly desperate for release as he.

He knew the moment April came apart in his arms. Only then did he allow himself to fully give way to the explosive need that raged in his body.

The world could have split in two, but all he was conscious of was the euphoria of releasing himself in April.

Ah, shit, that reminded him… "I forgot to use a condom." Regret harshened his voice.

"It's okay," she reassured him. "It's not like you would pick up any kind of STD from a sort-of fairy virgin."

He snorted. "But I don't want to get you sort-of pregnant."

She raised up on an elbow and regarded him soberly. "Really, you don't need to worry. The odds are in our favor."

"It only takes one time," he noted drily. "That's a fact of human biology."

"Then let me give you a fact of fairy biology. We can conceive. I'm evidence of that, but it's rare."

"You sure?"

April sat up, pulling a sheet over her body. "Positive.

The pure Fae frown on human liaisons, especially when it leads to a baby, but a minority have pointed out that it should actually be encouraged since we can't propagate our own species."

Chulah tugged at the sheet. "You going shy on me?"

April blushed, but released her hold on his bed linen. "This is serious," she said with a mock frown. "I'm trying to explain why pregnancy shouldn't scare you."

Okay, that was at least three times in this conversation the word *pregnancy* had been batted about, a definite killer of after-sex glow. Chulah sighed and sat up. "You haven't explained anything except that fairies can't reproduce fairies. Interesting, but it's all apples and oranges."

"I'm getting to that part." She slapped his arm playfully. "Anyway, female fairies can conceive but it often takes years or months of trying. Even then, the odds of producing a healthy child are slim."

"Good. But even so, next time we take precautions."

"Agreed. Although…" She paused a heartbeat. "If I had children, I would want them with you."

Whoa. This was happening too fast. *Way* too fast. His world didn't move at warp speed like this. His existence was orderly, neat and quiet. At least it had been ever since he'd been old enough to leave home and his passel of noisy half siblings and needling stepmother.

"April," he drawled, fumbling for the right words. "This is too—"

"—fast," she supplied. "I get it. I've known you for years but you're only beginning to know me. It's okay. I understand."

"Really?" He searched her face, but her gaze was steadfast and patient.

"Really."

He wanted to jump up and shout "hallelujah" but he had

enough sense to realize that was pushing his luck on her understanding nature.

She quirked an eyebrow. "Now, about that breakfast?"

Permission granted to leave the bed. Still, Chulah took his time getting up and donning his tossed shirt and jeans. "I have one specialty. Biscuits with sausage gravy."

April shrugged. "No offense, but it all tastes the same to me."

He stared as she put on one of his old cotton shirts and a pair of long johns he wore during freezing winter hunting nights. Her silver-and-purple hair tumbled in ringlets down to her hips. Damn, she looked sexy as hell.

Breakfast could wait.

He went to April, drawing her lithe body into a bear hug and whispering in her ear. "We could go again, you know. Unless you're too tender?"

A loud, insistent rapping sounded at the front door. Somebody in the heavens must hate him.

April grinned. "Better see who that is."

As if it could be anyone but Joanna with yet another problem to dump on him. Chulah strode through the hall and into the kitchen. The knocking grew even louder, cracking the dawn's silence like a gunshot. "Coming," he yelled above the din. His stepmother better have a damn good reason for this rudeness. He jerked open the door.

It was not Joanna.

Chapter 11

Steven's face was red and he breathed air hotter than a dragon. Licks of his carrot-top hair flamed like an out-of-control fire.

"She's here, isn't she?" He pushed his way inside. "You couldn't have let me know?"

Chulah shut the door behind Steven. "I don't know how to get in touch with you. Do you even have a phone?"

"Um, no," he admitted. "I should check into that." He frowned again. "You still could have run over to tell me."

The little man had a lot of nerve barging into his house and scolding him like he was a misbehaving child. But Chulah bit back his annoyance. Steven was only concerned about April, and she needed a champion. More than one.

"Now you know she's safe, feel free to leave."

Steven folded his arms. "I'm not going anywhere. I have bad news."

"What's wrong?" April stood in the hall doorway, his clothes dwarfing her small frame. She looked thoroughly *his*. In every way.

Steven tossed a quick, irritated glance at him over his shoulder.

Chulah smirked. Served him right for busting up their round two. The morning had been going so well until he dropped in.

"We should talk," Steven said, hurrying to her side. "Alone."

"Whatever it is, you can say it in front of Chulah."

He couldn't help smirking again at Steven's loud har-rumph. "It's Fae business. None of his concern."

"If we're going to work with the shadow hunters, they need be in on whatever's going on. That's only fair, Steven."

He ran a hand through his hair. "All right. But I don't like it."

So April had the same problems with Steven as he did with his own friends. Both sides too stubborn and mis-trustful to cooperate.

"So what's the news?" April pressed. "I just visited the Council and queen an hour or so ago, so it can't be too se-rious."

"You're dead wrong." Steven drew a deep breath. "Our queen has been captured."

April swayed. Such a thing was unheard-of. "Impos-sible," she whispered.

"It's true. All is chaos. They sent a messenger to tell me. Seems they couldn't enter the cabin to contact you—what with all the salt surrounding the borders."

"Was it Hoklonote?" Had to be. Who else would dare attempt such a crime? Or have the knowledge to do it.

Steven ran a hand through his rumpled hair. "No one else could have infiltrated our realm but Hoklonote. And all because of that damned traitor. When we find him…"

Chulah's brow furrowed and he raced to the front door.

"What is it?" April asked.

"I smell smoke."

He threw open the front door and she and Steven followed him outside.

Across the road and a mile farther down, a single thin column of smoke wafted from a neighbor's cotton field.

"I didn't see that when I flew here," Steven said, puzzled. "Must have just happened." He turned to April. "Chulah can call the fire department. We need to return to our own realm."

Red-and-black flames burst upward, spreading rapidly to the cotton plants. Mature white blooms crackled as a wave of fire swept the land. The field of white was transformed to a sea of orange. It writhed and hissed like a giant snake.

Steven pulled at her arm. "Let's *go*. That's not our problem. We have more important matters to handle."

"That's no ordinary fire," Chulah said tersely.

Steven dropped her arm. "What do you mean?"

"It's spreading too fast." He hustled back in the cabin and grabbed the cell phone on the kitchen counter, deftly pressing numbers. "And there's no logical explanation for a fire in the middle of nowhere. Not like we've had lightning storms or campers in the area."

"Arson?" April suggested.

"I know Jeb. He'll lose his ass on this cotton crop. And hard to imagine he has enemies… Hello? I'm reporting a fire at—"

"I don't like this." Steven frowned. "We should leave."

"You go. I'm staying with Chulah."

"Your place is with our own kind. They need us."

When it suits them. But now wasn't the time to argue. She listened as Chulah called Tombi, alerting him to gather the hunters. If there was ever a moment to convince Chulah's friends to help the Fae, this was the opportunity.

Steven jerked at her arm. "You're coming with me."

"Stop it. I said no."

"If Hoklonote is truly behind this, it's too dangerous for you to go near the fire."

Her anger at Steven dissipated under his concern.

"I'll be with her." Chulah tucked his phone in his back jeans pocket.

"Thanks, but that's hardly any consolation."

How rude. April poked Steven's side.

"The lady said no," Chulah said firmly. "Be right back."

He entered the house, no doubt to grab his weapons.

April spoke quickly. "Think," she said. "He called the other hunters. It's my chance to convince them to work with us. I can help more here than in Fairy. You go and see how bad the damage is there and if you can help them on that end."

"I don't like it." He folded his arms and glared, looking like a disgruntled leprechaun.

"You know I'm right. So go and stop wasting time. I'm safe with Chulah."

Steven sighed theatrically. "If you're sure…" He touched the fairy's cross pendant at his neck.

"Not here." She glanced around. Nobody had shown up yet, but fire trucks blared in the distance. "Walk around to the back of the cabin in case anyone's watching."

"All right. Damn it." He stomped toward the backyard and she held a hand to her mouth to hide a smile.

"Something funny?" Chulah asked.

April dropped her hand, chastised. "No. Wait for me to get on shoes and dress in something more appropriate."

Chulah's eyes focused on the fire and his lips tightened in a grim line. "Hurry."

April hustled inside, slipped on shoes and found one of

Chulah's flannel shirts that would cover her more modestly. It was the best she could do.

"I'm ready," she announced, bursting out the front door.

Chulah took her hand. "Stay by me unless I'm in danger. I can't worry about you while I'm investigating."

"I wouldn't leave you—"

He placed a finger on her lips. "Promise me."

Her throat went dry at the smoldering concern in Chulah's deep brown eyes. Heat flushed her skin as she remembered those same eyes devouring her naked body such a short time ago.

She nodded. After all, he didn't say she couldn't remain with him in Fae form. One way or another, she'd be by his side. Like always.

Together, they ran to the spreading fire. From ten feet back, a wall of heat stopped them in their tracks. April lifted her hair from the back of her sweaty neck. "What are you looking for exactly?"

"Footprints, scents…the usual."

She opened her mouth to argue there was nothing to be smelled but acrid smoke, but the wind shifted and blew it in her face. Her eyes watered and she coughed. Silently, she followed him as he paced around the circle of fire.

Wait.

April glanced over her shoulder, drawn to a clump of bare ground encircled with mushrooms. Dread slowed her progress but she arrived at the edge of the fairy ring circle. Their magic tree, the portal to the Fae realm, had been here the night before. Chulah was right—this was no ordinary fire.

Hoklonote knew where to find them. If the fire had burned their tree, their kind would die. The Fae would be extinct, gone the way of the dinosaurs. April squeezed her eyes shut. Had any fairies been killed by the smoke alone?

They might put on airs, and they could be vain and petty and selfish, but half their genetics made up her being. She was raised in the realm.

It was home.

Somehow, she had to convince all the shadow hunters to help them. Otherwise they were doomed.

Uniformed men ran to the conflagration, dragging a heavy hose. Orders were shouted. People milled everywhere on the outskirts of the fire. She could hear them through the smoke, even if she couldn't see them. Water sprayed over the flames, creating a boiling steam.

Chulah was lost to her in the mayhem. Panic pounded a drumbeat in her ears, loud and insistent, drowning out the sounds of the firefighters and the crackling destruction of cotton. She had to find him. She squinted through her streaming tears, unsure what hurt worse, the heat and smoke irritating her eyes, or her parched lungs inhaling air thick with ash.

Find him. Find him. Find him. April walked blindly closer to the center of the heat. A muscled arm pushed her back, and she stumbled to the hot ground.

"Get back," the man dressed in firefighter red ordered. "You're in our way."

High-pitched squeals erupted from behind. An undeniable sound of an animal in pain or terror or both. She rubbed her eyes, searching the gray hell for the source.

Four baby rabbits were trapped under a fallen tree limb. Their mother opened her mouth and screamed, ears pinned back, a desperate cry for help. April crawled forward cautiously. "Don't you dare bite me, Mama," she muttered. "I'm trying to help you."

The raucous screaming grew even louder, more chilling. The rabbit thumped one of her hind legs on the ground. April knew nothing of rabbits other than their infamous proclivity to birth a bunch of other rabbits, but she recognized that thumping as an attack signal. Damn it, she didn't have time to lie here and slowly try to win Mama's trust. Chulah was out there somewhere, possibly hurt or at least worried where she had run off to.

Sometimes, a fairy had to do what a fairy must do. April closed her eyes and breathed deeply, finding a calm, silent center within herself. She opened her eyes again and stared down the mama rabbit. Again, she breathed deeply, weaving in magic and enchantment. Keeping her eyes on the screaming mama, she exhaled long and hard, directing her magic.

The screams stopped. Mama's nose and whiskers twitched. Her tensed muscles relaxed and her ears unfurled.

The magic was working.

April crawled forward slowly. A mother's love was a powerful thing, as powerful as any magic. Not that *she* had ever been the recipient of such love. She reached the large limb where the bunnies shivered and chattered rapidly. Poor things. Another quick glance at the immobilized, but tense, mama and April lifted the limb.

A whole inch.

Of *course* it weighed a freaking ton. Ignoring the popping of raining embers, she took a deep breath, directing magic to her arms and hands. Again, she gripped the limb and lifted, throwing it off the scared rabbits.

Off they hopped, mama close in tow with nary a backward glance. So much for gratitude. Still, April smiled at the white cottontails racing for the shelter of the woods.

"That was a good thing you did."

Chulah!

Strong arms lifted her from the ground and she leaned against his hard frame. Relief jellied her knees in a whoosh and she melted against him, secure she was safe. In this moment, in a hellish inferno, she had no fear.

Pain blistered her right forearm and she yelped, swatting at a burning ember. Chulah took her hand, guiding her away from the crowd. The air cooled a good ten degrees and the noise level was tolerable.

"It was Hoklonote," Chulah said. "I found his footprints and picked up his scent. Can't be a coincidence that he was nearby and this fire erupted soon after. I just can't figure out *why*. Why here?"

"Because he was trying to burn down our magical tree."

Chulah looked around. "It's here?"

"Not anymore. It's moved again."

"Seems like your kind would keep it more to the middle of the woods."

Her kind. Always, he reminded her of the gulf between them.

"Our safety is in moving it constantly. A foolproof method, or so we thought. Hoklonote could have only found our location from Grady."

"And how do you know the tree was here recently?"

"I'll show you." April guided him to the edge of the woods where the large mushroom ring flourished. "It's what we leave behind to help us remember we've been and not to return anytime soon."

Chulah gave a low whistle. "How much damage would have been done if the tree burned?"

"We would no longer exist."

"I'll do my best to keep that from happening."

The quiet authority in his deep voice impressed April. She raised a brow. "Didn't think you'd particularly care. You've been quite clear on your opinion of us. Not that I can blame you." The usual stab of guilt washed through her.

"It's wrong. It goes against the entire spiritual order of

the universe. Anytime a race or spirit—or even an animal, plant or tree—becomes extinct, all of us are the worse for the loss."

"Even if you don't know of their existence?"

"Especially then."

April took his hand and squeezed it. She'd never loved him more than at this moment. He had every reason to despise her and the magic that ran through her being. Yet he would defend their right to live.

"Hey!"

Tombi, Tallulah and a dozen other shadow hunters hurried to where they stood.

"Got here quick as we could," Tombi said breathlessly. "Appears they're starting to get things under control."

More smoke than flames now fanned the air. And yet April watched Tallulah and sneaked covert glances at Chulah to see his reaction to her presence. April had never been with them together before. In the midst of chaos, jealousy squirmed and pinched inside like an unruly two-year-old denied attention.

Tombi peered at them intently. "Y'all okay? You look like hell." He swiped an index finger down Chulah's arm and held up a blackened fingertip. "Your skin and clothes are smeared with soot."

Chulah ignored the question. "Hoklonote started it to wipe out the fairy realm."

"So what?" Tallulah interrupted, tossing her sheen of black hair. "I feel sorry for Jeb and his family. This loss might bankrupt them. But why should we give a damn about fairies?" She fixed her gaze on April.

As if I were to blame for the fire. Her tongue felt thick in her dry mouth. Again, guilt reared its ugly head. Logically, she realized she wasn't to blame. But the guilt reflex was as swift and unpredictable as a flooded river on the rise, snaking a course over all boundaries.

"Because their world affects our world," Chulah said, sparing her the need to defend her realm. He waved a hand over the scorched field. "The fire could have been worse. At least no one was killed." He slowly took in each of the hunters' faces. "This time."

"You're missing my point," Tallulah said. Anger flushed her cheeks. "Let Hoklonote have them and be done with the whole thing. We never even knew they existed until *she* suddenly showed up out of nowhere."

What a bitch. Outrage trumped April's intimidation. "Don't be stupid. Besides the fact that we're talking about the death of an entire race of sentient beings, there's a *reason* Hoklonote wants us. Ever think about that?"

One of the hunters spoke up. "If he wants to capture the fairies, your kind must be able to assist him in some way. Otherwise he'd have no use for you."

"That's what I've tried to tell you all along," Chulah said.

"So *she* says," Tallulah sniffed. "But she hasn't explained exactly how they can help."

"My name's April. And you haven't really given me a chance."

An earthy scent of peat moss and pine wafted through the air, temporarily refreshing the burned odor of cotton. April's shoulders sagged. Backup had arrived.

Steven wiggled his way between her and Chulah. His already-wan face was even more haggard. "Have you convinced them yet?" he asked.

"No. Maybe you can, though. They want to know how we can all work together." April waved her arm in the air, searching for the right words. "You know, what we bring to the table that will help them defeat Hoklonote."

"Our senses are even better honed than yours and we can cloak our presence more than you hunters. While you directly attack will-o'-the-wisps, we fly in from behind to kill them and release trapped spirits. What's more, we can identify and communicate with the released spirits."

"I know this," Tombi interrupted. "But you were looking for a particular spirit and when you found it you were going to trap it."

Murmurs of discontent spread through the hunters.

"We won't do such a thing. It's an abomination," one of them said. The other shadow hunters glanced at one another in silent agreement.

"Doesn't matter anymore," Steven said grimly. "Grady, the traitor who brought Hoklonote to the very throne of our realm, is no longer. I heard that when Hoklonote captured our queen, he killed Grady and destroyed his spirit."

April could hardly feel it in her heart to feel sorry for the former Council member. Because of his compulsion for power, he'd put their entire race at risk. She touched Steven's arm. "How bad is it at home?"

"It's bad. I've never seen such despair. We knew the danger, but none of us ever thought it would come to this. If Hoklonote had arrived even a minute earlier…"

April nodded, swallowing hard. "Do you think the queen is dead?"

"No. He sent a message through the Ishkitini. We have one week to bow to his demands."

"Which are?" Chulah prompted.

Steven's face grew tauter. "To join him in battle at the next full moon. He would force us to use our magic against the shadow hunters in an attempt to free Nalusa Falaya. Your defeat would be certain."

"And you expect us to believe this preposterous story?"

Tallulah snorted. "How the hell can you get messages from a freaking bird?"

Steven lifted his chin. "Like the Ishkitini, we are creatures of the sky and the wind and the land."

"Give it a rest, Tallulah." Tombi cast her an exasperated glance. "I say we can't take a chance that he isn't being truthful. Chulah?"

"My position hasn't changed. I'm in favor of an alliance."

Tallulah walked to him, much too close for April's comfort. She laid a hand on his shoulder and spoke softly. "Chulah, she's a trickster. You can't believe anything she says."

He almost imperceptibly inched back from her touch. "My mind is set."

April, just barely, stopped from smirking at the overconfident Tallulah.

Tombi raised a hand. "I pledge my support to help the Fae. Who all is with me?"

A chorus of assent followed. Only Tallulah abstained. They all stared pointedly at her. "Fine," she said, throwing up her hands. "You need someone with skepticism to keep an eye on the Fae."

The woman didn't have a speck of graciousness. Whatever had Chulah seen in her—past the obvious good looks? April bit the inside of her lip, realizing her error. He might *still* find her attractive. He might even love her. It wasn't that long ago he'd proposed.

"I'm going back," Steven announced.

He turned to leave, and April put out a hand to stop him. "Wouldn't it be better to stay here and fight with us?"

"My place is in the realm. I was only here briefly to ease you into this new world. You've succeeded and now I must return."

You've succeeded. The simple words warmed something

cold deep in April's soul. He didn't have to, but Steven left the group before disappearing behind a tall oak. The hunters exchanged astonished glances at their first glimpse of Fae magic.

Tombi clapped his hands together for attention. "Let's strategize. I say we capture Hoklonote and force a prisoner exchange. His life will be spared if he allows the fairy queen to return to her kingdom."

"We can't let him live on. He'll start causing trouble again," Tallulah pointed out.

Tombi cut her short. "We defeated Nalusa, who is greater in power and strength. Hoklonote may live, but we'll restrain him another time from ever again roaming the bayou."

"In the meantime, April and I can try to track where Hoklonote is hiding out. If we're lucky, we'll spot the hostage with him and try to steal the fairy queen from under his nose." Chulah paused. "If not, we have a battle the next full moon."

Chapter 12

"Well, what did they say?" Chulah pressed.

"They've agreed to help in the upcoming battle."

No need to fill him with the details of the panicked, yet still obdurate Council members. After all she'd done for them, and after the news that the shadow hunters would help their realm, the Council still sniffed their noses at her and the humans.

"You're just like your mother," they'd sniped. "Undependable. Nothing but a human-lover."

She still fumed at the insults. And was even more filled with resolve to prove them wrong. To restore her family's honor.

"Meaning they will jump in the fray and risk their lives like we are risking ours?"

"It took some persuasion, but yes, they will." As she'd pointed out, what choice did they have? Their queen was gone and the balance of power in the universe had tipped to the bayou's shadow spirits.

They headed out to the woods. The night air was chilly

and still held a hint of burned cotton from yesterday. A reminder of the serious threat they faced.

They wandered off the beaten paths, searching for signs of Hoklonote or the Fae queen—a scent, a soft cry for help, a released spirit with information. The odds of them encountering such a spirit in the vast acreage was slim. But they had to try. They needed any edge they could find to prepare for the full-moon battle.

They lapsed into silence. No point hunting if they continued talking. April followed Chulah dispiritedly, dragging her feet and paying little attention to the landscape. Instead, she replayed the Council members' words in her mind like an evil mantra. *Not good enough. Useless. Just like her mother.*

Numbly, she kept her feet moving. Chulah stopped abruptly and she plowed into his hard back. He turned and held a finger to his lips. Shhh. April nodded to show she understood. He pulled her arm until they were crouched under the cover of a saw palmetto.

April gazed ahead, curious as to where they were. Less than twenty feet ahead was a small, circular clearing and an ancient oak draped in Spanish moss. The Choctaw's sacred land and tree.

He leaned in, and with the barest sound of a whisper in her ear, he said, "Nalusa is trapped in that tree."

Her stomach flipped and she clasped his hand. His strong warmth pressed the trembling out of her. Chulah wouldn't have brought her so close to Nalusa if he didn't believe he could protect her.

"Your queen?" he asked, pointing to the tree.

Ah, so that was why he'd brought her to the sacred land. As a human, even with a shadow hunter's abilities, he couldn't sense the old, wily queen.

But she could.

April concentrated, tuning out superfluous noise and smells. Creating a silent abyss on land and attuning to another plane of existence.

She waited. Straining with all her essence.

A squeak. Then another. And another. A pattern of squeaks. April centered her magic, deciphering the pattern into vowels and syllables.

Help. Please help. Over here.

The queen, *her queen*, cried from inside the Choctaw tree.

April clamped a hand over her mouth to keep from gasping. How awful to be trapped with Nalusa. Chulah arched a brow and she pointed to the tree, mouthing, "She's there."

He nodded matter-of-factly, indicating he'd already surmised that much. April had to admit it was the perfect prison. No one wanted to be near Nalusa. And Nalusa would guard the queen well from any escape attempt. After all, she was his ticket out of hell.

A rattle, quiet yet deadly, emanated from inside the oak. Chills chased up and down her spine. Nalusa was in snake form. A viper ready to strike. She couldn't tear her eyes from the tree, expecting a giant rattlesnake to slither out from inside the trunk. The queen must be terrified to be trapped with such a beast. She'd die of fright after the first minute alone with the evilest of the shadow creatures.

A stench of rot and decay assaulted them. Hoklonote was nearby.

Chulah grabbed her hand and they rose. Nothing to be gained waiting for the shadow spirit to check on his hostage.

April followed Chulah's lead and stayed crouched as they beat a hasty exit. About twenty yards away from the sacred ground, Chulah motioned her to rise and they walked briskly toward his cabin while casting quick looks back.

Hoklonote had apparently not seen them.

"Do you think they'll kill the queen before the full moon?" she asked.

He didn't answer immediately. "Hopefully, she's worth more to them alive than dead."

She wanted to ask if he believed the queen was being tortured. But she already knew the answer. It was there in the high-pitched wailing inside the tree. Chulah squeezed her hand, as if guessing the direction of her thoughts.

To the right, from a distance, came a flickering teal glow.

"Might as well take care of that wisp while we're out here," he said. "If you're up to it."

"Sure. Anything we can do to help kill off their army." Action was the antidote to worry.

They switched directions. Another light flickered. Two of them. But no need to worry—she was with the tribe's most accurate hunter, and she had her own defensive and offensive moves. In a matter of under a hundred steps they were upon the wisps. Chulah stealthily loaded a slingshot and sent a rock flying. A puff of acrid smoke curled into the treetops.

One down.

In seconds, he'd reloaded and shot before the remaining wisp registered what had happened to its companion.

Another puff of smoke.

Chulah stuffed the slingshot in his backpack and turned away.

"No, wait. I want to see who's been freed."

His brow furrowed. "Why? Your betrayer has already been annihilated."

"Don't you have any curiosity?" She couldn't tell him she was always looking for her mother with every released wisp. How pathetic was that? April rubbed her arms self-consciously, hardly daring to admit the secret desire even to herself.

Looking for Mother had once proved deadly.

Yet she hurried toward the smoke, anxious to arrive as soon as the spirit broke free and rose to the heavens.

She arrived seconds too late for the first spirit.

Just her luck. April quickly turned to the second spirit. A pure white ball of light emerged from the sulfurous smoke. April immediately sensed it was Fae. A female. *Don't get your hopes up yet. It's never been her before.*

The light danced and bobbed either in joy or from otherworldly music no one on the earthly plane could hear.

Who are you? April pushed the thought to the spirit. It stilled.

Fawn.

Shivers doused her from scalp to toes. Not a common name, not by a long shot. *Slow down, girl.* Could be a Native American female trapped for centuries.

April? Is that you, darling?

April's feet rooted to soil like morning glory to brick. Shallow breathing whooshed the air. Hers. This was a cruel mirage. She refused to believe.

The white orb lowered, drew closer, almost blinding. She squinted. *Who are you really? Did Hoklonote send you to trick me?*

No trick, sweetheart. You are my daughter. My baby girl all grown up.

A sudden gust of wind blew like a mini cyclone, a warning to move on.

And still April could not speak. No words could convey the loneliness of childhood, the years of grief over an unknown mother. Feeling like an orphan, abandoned. She'd envisioned this moment all her life. Yet here she stood.

Mute.

It's okay. You are going to be fine.

Exactly what she needed to hear. Somehow, Mother knew.

I never abandoned you, April. The betrayer killed me and David, your father.

The wind picked up, the orb elongated to an almost flat oval, about to be carried away to the After Life. April found her voice. *Love you, Mama!*

Her mother's spirit was sucked into the cyclone and lifted upward. Hot tears slid down April's pale, cold cheeks and her body was racked with trembling.

"What's wrong? April? Talk to me." Chulah's voice seemed to come from the bottom of a deep well. "Can you hear me?"

She reached out a hand, eyes blind from tears and bright light. A warm, strong calloused hand grasped hers and held tight. She wasn't alone.

Her body was pulled toward his strong center, a gravitational force of power. An anchor in the swirling maelstrom. She had no idea how long they held each other. But the trembling ceased, her wet cheeks dried, and her breath calmed to an easy in-and-out rhythm. Chulah ran a hand through her hair and brushed the chill from her cheeks. "Can you talk about what happened?"

"You didn't hear?"

"No." He bestowed a kiss on her forehead. "Your lips moved but no sound came out. It looked as if you talked to the released spirit before it left for the heavens. Was it someone you knew?"

"My mother."

He gathered her into his broad chest and stroked her back. He understood the pain. No words were necessary. Familiar shame twisted her stomach. How much worse for him when his father died. She'd never known her mother, but he'd had fifteen years of companionship with his father before he died. Surely his pain had been fifteen times worse.

"Come to my cabin," he said at last. "We're done for the night."

"Drink this."

April cupped the warm mug of tea in her palms, already comforted. "Thanks." She sipped experimentally and decided she liked hot tea. Between the heat of the fireplace and the tea warming her inside, the tension eased, if not the sadness.

Chulah sprawled across from her in the recliner, a coffee cup in hand. "So tell me exactly what happened out there."

"I finally found my mother." April closed her eyes, collecting her grief. "I never knew her. Didn't know if she was dead or alive. Now I do." She shook her head. "I shouldn't be so upset. It's not like she raised me. I don't know her at all."

"Hey, kid. Give yourself a break. It was your mother, for Pete's sake. There will always be a bond between the two of you, no matter the circumstances."

April traced the rim of the cup with an index finger, not looking up. "I don't have the right. It doesn't compare to the grief you must have felt when your father died."

Ceramic thudded against wood as Chulah carefully put down his cup on the coffee table. He rose and sat next to her, the sofa sinking with his weight. An arm rested on her shoulder, inviting her to snuggle against his side.

"You have the right to feel any way you want," he said fiercely. "It's okay."

The words rumbled out of his chest like thunder and echoed through her body. April wept. Not quietly as in the woods, but loud, strangled sobs that had a will of their own and would not be silenced. Through it all, she absorbed his strength. His sympathy.

And—as she liked to hope—his love.

Once the storm of tears subsided, she felt worn, as tired as she'd ever been.

"Stay with me tonight," Chulah said. He lifted her in his arms and carried her to the bedroom. Gently, he placed her on the bed and lay beside her. She curled into his heat and sank into the peaceful oblivion of sleep.

Chulah softly ran his hands through April's silver-and-purple hair, careful not to wake her. As she slept, he could watch her unobserved, take in her delicate features and otherworldly beauty without fear of looking like a love-starved teenager.

Despite their deep and obvious differences, they were each alone and something of outcasts. He'd been wrong to think of her as a bit shallow. She'd endured hardship, probably more than him. At least he had his close friends. April, apparently, had grown up friendless and without love.

Somehow, her hard life hadn't destroyed her optimism and faith. She was sunshine and music and gentle in nature. A wry smile split the taut muscles of his face. Only a few weeks ago, he'd been such a fool thinking he wanted Tallulah as a wife.

And while he was being honest…he was relieved rather than disappointed—now the initial embarrassment had passed—that she had refused him. Tallulah had been, perhaps, a little too convenient. They'd grown up together, had shared similar gifts and had fought alongside each other. Their families were close. She'd been his secret crush in high school, and with Bo gone, it was only natural he'd drifted to her familiar, comfortable presence.

Chulah found he preferred the light, delicate, mysterious April over the dark warrior Tallulah.

And that scared the hell out of him. Could he trust his feelings for April now? So much had happened, so quickly. Time would test them, but he hoped their foundation was now solid.

Chapter 13

Annie opened the door before April even raised her hand to knock.

"About time you came for a visit." She opened the door and April walked into the cozy cabin, looking nervously for Tombi.

"He's not here," Annie said with a knowing smile. "He's installing kitchen cabinets for a client today."

Disconcerting how Annie read her thoughts.

"Sorry, dear. I don't mean to alarm you."

Further proof she was a mind reader. She followed Annie into the den and they sat across from each other.

"Would you like something to drink?"

"No, thank you." April stared down at her intertwined hands on her lap, suddenly shy.

Annie briefly touched her knee. "Let me make this easy for you. You came to talk about Chulah."

"Yes," April said gratefully. "I hope you don't mind. I realize you don't know me well, but—"

"I don't have to know a person a long time to get a feel

for their character. It's a gift passed down to me from my grandmother."

"Tia Henrietta. I've heard of her powers."

A smile of delight spread on Annie's face. "Even among the fairies? She'll be so pleased to hear that."

"The thing is…" April swallowed past the lump in her throat. "Well, I love him. I loved him from afar for over a decade, and now that I've been with him in flesh and blood, I love him even more."

"Anyone can tell you love him. It's written all over your face when you look at Chulah."

"That obvious, huh?"

"And you're good for him. I see his eyes soften when he looks at you, the way he totally focuses on you when you're around. His entire energy changes."

April lifted her fingers to her eyes and pinched them shut. She should be happy…and yet her secret shame couldn't let her accept if he could love her. If he knew how selfish she'd been, that she had caused the death of his father, he'd never forgive her sin.

"You love him and he cares for you. So what's the problem?" Annie asked, soft and yet direct.

The need to unburden her secret, one she'd carried alone for years, burst upon her like a waterfall. "The problem is…I killed his father."

Annie paled. "You did what?"

"Oh, not directly. Although that hardly matters. Dead is dead." She couldn't bear Annie's dismay and shock. Caught her by surprise that time.

"Start from the beginning." Annie's tone was deep and her eyes grave.

At least she wasn't looking at her with outright disgust, though she deserved it.

"I was sixteen years old. Young, but old enough to have had more sense. I was rebellious and selfish and—"

"Stop the self-recrimination and just tell me what happened."

April bit her lip and nodded. "Right. Well, at age sixteen I was angry over the way I was treated, so I ran away from the Fae realm. A huge no-no in our world. One that can get you cast out forever.

"It was a risk I was willing to take. I'd been told my mother deserted me for her human lover and I was taunted over my impure Fae status. One day, it was all too much and I ran away, determined to find my mother and make her explain. Ask her to take me away from all the jeers and contempt. So I ran. And there came Chulah. Running through the woods like a silent giant, his long black hair fluttering in the breeze, his bronzed chest bare and rippling muscle. And that face. That perfectly sculpted face. So intent. I'd never felt it before. A shot of pure lust and desire.

"I wondered if he could help me. Maybe he knew of some strange woman with a mysterious past in the bayou. I gathered all my magic, took a deep breath, put my hand to my mouth and blew, directing everything I had at him.

"He stopped, looked around, lines wrinkling his brow. I walked up and questioned him. But he was dazed and barely coherent. I realized then I had used way too much magic. I'd never tried to enchant a human before. I'd overdone it and I didn't know how to undo the magic. He sank to the ground, burying his face in his hands."

April closed her eyes, remembering. She'd whispered *I'm sorry* beside Chulah, for all the good that had done. A buzzing had whistled past her ear. The fairies were close; they'd spotted her, alerted to the magic energy she'd released. There would be hell to pay but it would be easier if she returned on her own without an escort. She had stared again at the immobile, handsome giant. He'd be okay, eventually. Confused, but okay.

April opened her eyes. "So I—I left him."

April expected to see reproach on Annie's face. Now she knew the kind of being she really was.

"Poor Chulah," Annie said. "And poor you."

"I found out later that he'd been running for help to save his father."

"Who had been bitten by a snake," Annie said. "I've heard the tale, but it was long before I knew Chulah."

"Because of me, Chulah was out cold for nearly two hours. By the time he returned to the woods with help, his father was dead. Now you know the truth. My rashness and selfishness cost a life. And it was all for nothing. I didn't even have a coherent plan to find my mother. I just had an overwhelming urge to escape Fairy."

"You were young."

"Old enough to know better. Over the years, I kept returning to see Chulah in fairy form. I owed him. So I did what I could, helped him in shadow-spirit battles and eased his pain when possible. All invisible, of course."

"Wait a minute. Do you love Chulah, or have you gotten wrapped up in his life because of a childhood mistake?"

Her breath caught. Could there be any truth in that? His image flashed in her mind, the feel of his body next to hers, the passion of their lovemaking.

"It's love," she said firmly. "He's a good man. A kind, loyal, brave man who suffered because of me."

"Are you sure you're not fooling yourself? Trying to atone for your mistake?"

April shook her head.

Annie got up, sat beside her and gave her a hug. "Hang in there. Chulah needs you."

"Not if he finds out I'm the one responsible for his dad's death. There's no getting past that."

Heat and chills alternated in pulsing cycles, as if Chulah's skin had been dipped in acid and then plunged into ice water. He'd just come in from talking with Tombi, and although he hadn't meant to eavesdrop, he'd wanted to surprise April. He'd wanted to see her eyes light at the sight of him and wink at her, a secret sharing of their intimacy.

"Explain," he now demanded harshly. How he managed to grind out the one word past the boa-like constriction of his throat was a miracle.

"I knew it," Tombi said, throwing his backpack on the sofa. "We never should have trusted you."

Annie hurried to her husband. "Don't make things worse. Let's leave them to work this out."

"There's no working it out," Chulah said bitterly, eyes fastened on April. "As you said, there's no getting past this."

"Chulah, I'm so sorry. I can explain—"

"Hell yeah, you're going to explain. Then I never want to see you again."

He was aware of Tombi and Annie leaving the room, closing a door behind them to allow him privacy.

Tears poured from those lovely eyes. His heart squeezed, but he hardened the softness. She wouldn't play him for a fool a second time.

"I was sixteen. I'd run away from Fairy to try and find my mother. The first person I saw was you. You were running through the woods and I..." Her shaky voice wound down and she took a deep breath. "I used my magic to stop you and ask if you could help in my search."

"Why did you have to do that? You couldn't have just asked?"

"You were in a hurry and I was afraid you'd brush me off."

"Of course I would have blown you off. I was trying to get help for Dad. He'd been bitten by a snake."

"I—I didn't know that."

"Because you didn't care about anything but yourself."

"I was young. I didn't know better. It doesn't excuse—"

He didn't want to hear it. There was no justification. "Get on with your story."

She swallowed hard. "I must have overdone it. I'd only practiced magic on flowers and small animals."

Just his damn luck he was in the wrong place at the wrong time. "What happened to me?"

"You fell down and passed out."

His missing two hours. Two hours that had cost him everything. His dad. Years of doubt about his sanity and character. Years of waiting on Joanna and his half siblings, trying to atone for failing their husband and father.

His legs felt cut from underneath. Back stiff, he slowly walked to a chair and sat, careful to keep his face stoic.

"I thought I had panicked. Had totally lost it when the person I most respected needed me. Now I find out you put me in some kind of fugue state."

Bits and pieces of dreams realigned into a pattern. The scent of violets, the musical voice, the silver hair—he'd experienced them all before in snatches of dreams upon awakening. But he'd never suspected they were clues to the missing hours.

He would never, ever let that happen again. Since his dad died, he'd kept a tight rein on his emotions, careful to do his duty with little complaint. Determined to live the rest of his life doing the right thing and never again let down family or friends.

April sat at his feet and laid her head in his lap. "I'm so sorry. Please forgive me."

Chulah gently took her shoulders and pulled her away. "Do you have any idea what I've been through because of you? Bad enough my father died, but to believe I failed him as he lay dying? I can never forgive you."

"When I found out later what I had done, I was devastated. I tried to make it up to you over the years. Helped you in battle, comforted you if I saw you were upset."

He laughed bitterly. "Are you expecting a thank-you?"

"No." April stood and straightened her blouse. "I don't blame you for hating me now." She paused, but he didn't respond. She hung her head. "I know it doesn't change anything but I'm really sorry. I love you, Chulah."

"You don't know what love is," he scoffed.

"Yes, I do." She reached out a hand as if to touch him, but he glared and she dropped it by her side. "Are we still… you know…working together?"

Of course that was her first concern. She needed him. *They* needed the shadow hunters to save their race.

"Don't have much choice in that. Seeing as we both want the same thing."

She backed away and grabbed her jacket from the back of a chair. "Thank you."

"Wouldn't want you to lose any prestige among your kind."

"I don't care about that anymore."

"So you say."

She didn't try to defend herself again. "Goodbye, Chulah."

He tried to find a spiteful comfort in her obvious misery, but his heart was bruised along with hers. He turned away and stared at Tombi's bookcase as she left, softly closing the door behind her.

The gentle door closure vibrated like a bullet to his heart. A million times worse than Tallulah's rejection.

Tombi entered and cuffed his shoulder. "Sorry about that, buddy. Now we know fairies can't be trusted."

"Right."

"Don't let it get you down. It would never have worked out between you and April anyway. Two different worlds."

"You heard her. If not for April, I might have saved my dad."

"The coroner said the delay probably didn't matter," Tombi reminded him. "He had a bad heart."

"We'll never know for sure, will we?"

"Don't torture yourself."

"Too late. I've been doing it for too many years to stop now." He slapped his hands on his thighs, eager for a distraction. Anything to escape the sting in his heart. "Ready to get to work? We can get organized while we wait on the others to arrive."

"If you're sure you're up to it," Tombi said doubtfully.

"I'm fine."

What a lie. But the full moon would rise in two nights and there was work to be done.

Joanna's heels clacked smartly on the linoleum as she strode into the Pixie Land shop. April put down the inventory paperwork and eyed her warily. The determined frown on her face did not bode well. "Welcome. May I help you, Mrs. Rivers?"

Chulah's stepmother slapped her hands on the counter and glared. "What have you done to my boy?"

So now he was *her boy*. As if she treated him the same as any of her own children. April's trepidation vanished. "Glad to hear you're concerned for his well-being."

"Of course I am. Now answer my question. What did

you do to him? He's as tight-lipped as I've ever seen him and he's always been a man of few words."

She merely wanted to pry. Protect her moneymaking machine. "If Chulah's not talking, I'm not sure I should either."

Joanna drummed her blunt-tipped fingers on the glass counter. This woman was used to having her way. April took a perverse satisfaction in thwarting her will. A small penance for the way she'd mistreated Chulah over the years.

"One of you needs to talk so I can fix it."

"There's nothing you can do to fix it, Joanna. As a matter of fact, I'd say this is none of your business."

Her frown deepened. "I'm making it my business. Chulah's grouchy as a bear. 'Bout snapped my head off when I told him my car's transmission is busted."

"Doesn't one of your other sons have mechanical skills?"

"Not really. And Chulah can fix it. He even has his own shop."

"For motorcycles, not cars."

"Whatever," Joanna said airily.

"My point is that you have other adult children to help with all your various crises. Yet you always ask Chulah for help."

Her jaw dropped an inch before she snapped it shut. "How dare you? You only met him a few weeks ago. You don't know what you're talking about."

"The hell I don't. Admit it. You're always asking him for help."

"Because he's reliable."

"And none of your other sons are? Maybe you should ask yourself why."

Joanna looked as if she'd been immobilized by a thunderbolt. She blinked rapidly, opening and then closing her mouth, evidently at a loss for words.

April bit her lip. When the woman found her tongue, she was in for a lashing.

"Why is it that people with no children think they have all the answers?" Joanna's mouth trembled and her eyes watered.

Not the reaction April had anticipated. Remorse crept in. "I don't know what I'm talking about. Sorry. Now I'm stepping in your business when I have no right."

Joanna angrily swiped at her eyes. "You certainly don't. You have no idea what it's like to have your husband die and raise four small children by yourself."

Guilt slapped her across the face and April leaned on the counter for support. She was responsible for the death of Joanna's husband. Chulah wasn't the only one who suffered for her mistake. Joanna and her children had suffered as well. She'd known this, of course, but it was another thing to see the hurt up close.

It was horrible to witness the steely woman dissolve into tears.

"Please, don't cry. I'm truly sorry." April searched the shelves and found a box of tissues. "Here, take one."

Joanna sniffed, but accepted the tissue and dabbed her face. "There's some truth in what you not-so-subtly implied. I did my best. At least I had Chulah to rely on."

"Have you ever told Chulah how much you appreciate him?" April gently probed.

Her eyes widened. "He has to know."

So she hadn't. "I think it would mean a lot to him if you did."

Joanna nodded and pulled herself together. "I appreciate that we can be frank with each other. Now. About the two of you—"

April groaned.

"Can't you go over and apologize for whatever fool thing you did?"

"Who said the breakup is my fault?"

"This is worse than I imagined. I'd hoped it was a mere lovers' quarrel, not a split."

April plucked a tissue from the box, feeling weepy herself. And she had done so well this morning keeping busy so as not to think of Chulah. So much for that.

"Yeah, it's pretty bad," she admitted. "There's no coming back from it."

"This is most unfortunate. Suppose he's still pining over that hothead, Tallulah."

"You know he proposed to her?"

She arched a brow. "No. Only that he's moped about her since they were teenagers. So he finally got up the nerve to propose, huh? Poor boy."

"Tallulah's an idiot."

Joanna laughed. "Agreed."

Understanding dawned. "You really do love him, don't you?"

Joanna made an exasperated tsking noise and stuffed the tissue in her oversize pocketbook. "What a ridiculous question. He's my boy."

She couldn't help grinning, recalling Chulah's height and sexy, lean muscles. Hardly a boy.

"You find that amusing?" Joanna asked haughtily.

"No, no. Not at all. I'm glad you feel that way." April screwed up her nerve one last time. "You might want to tell him so every now and then."

Joanna adjusted the pocketbook straps on her shoulders. "We're not a family given much to demonstration."

"Just a suggestion."

"Well, here's one for you. Don't give up on my boy. Whatever the problem is, I could tell he was happy with you."

April brightened. Her first shot of hope since Chulah had dismissed her last night. "Honestly? You think so?"

"I can tolerate anyone but Tallulah Silver." Joanna lifted her chin defiantly. "If she ends up as my daughter-in-law, I will chase you down and haunt you."

Joanna being Joanna, this was a positive sign of endorsement. Perhaps even affection.

"We can't let that happen," April agreed. She stuck out her hand, a human tradition for cementing agreements.

Joanna gave a rusty laugh and shook it. "Deal."

Chapter 14

Chulah dropped the monkey wrench on the hard cement, and the sound echoed loudly in the shop. "Damn it. Son of a—"

"Problem, boss?" J.B. picked up the fallen wrench and handed it to Chulah.

He snatched it from J.B.'s hand and returned to viciously tightening bolts on the Harley engine. Everything at work had been a pain in the ass, all freaking day long. Misplaced files, impatient clients, workers out sick, late shipment of parts—you name it, it had gone wrong. Slowly, he became aware that J.B. hovered above him. "What do you want?" he snapped.

"You put the fuel filter in backward."

Chulah stared at it a moment. "Son of a—" He broke off at the sound of a chuckle and whirled around. "You think that's funny?"

"It's just that you never make mistakes. What's eating you today?"

"Nothing," he huffed, removing the filter.

"Uh-huh. If you say so. By the way, Joanna's in your office."

Chulah dropped the pliers to his side and momentarily laid his forehead on the black-and-orange-striped gasoline tank. "Of course she is. What's next? A visit from an IRS auditor?"

"Don't jinx yourself." J.B. stepped next to him. "I'll finish this up while you talk to her."

Chulah fleetingly considered slipping out the back door and jumping on his Harley for a long, solitary ride. But with his luck today, he'd probably crash. He went to the washroom sink and scrubbed off his greasy hands as best he could, remembering all her countless lectures on cleanliness.

Chulah stepped into his small office, where Joanna sat, all prim-and-proper decorum amid the chaos of paperwork on top of his banged-up steel desk. At least there weren't any dirty coffee cups or fast-food wrappers overflowing from the garbage can. His mood was too foul today to even have an appetite.

Might as well get right down to it. Chulah pulled up a folding chair next to his stepmother. "What brings you here?"

"Can't I just drop by to say hello?"

Didn't he wish. "Hello. Now, what's the problem?"

"No problem."

Chulah stared, waiting her out. She shifted uncomfortably in the cheap seat.

"Had a little chat with your girl this morning."

"Who are you talking about?" he asked coolly. "I don't have a girl."

"That pretty little blonde, April."

Even the mention of her name was a sucker punch to his heart. He stood and walked to the window, quick to hide his expression. A couple of deep breaths and he turned back to Joanna, his composure restored. He sat at his desk and motioned at the paper pile. "Got lots of work to do. If you don't need anything…"

"Nope, not a thing." She stood leisurely and patted her hair. "Have a nice day, son."

Son? She hadn't called him by that moniker in years. Chulah's composure slipped and he felt his jaw slacken. Must be some kind of trick. Be nice to the sucker now and then stick it to him later.

"I'm making your favorite dinner tonight. Roast beef and mashed potatoes. Come by around six if you can."

His mouth watered. He hadn't eaten all day and Joanna's roast was legendary. Even if it was a trick to soften him up for help, he couldn't resist the home-cooked meal. And to tell the truth, he was more than a little curious about her conversation with April. He'd quiz her tonight. "I'll be there."

"Excellent." She absently straightened clumps of paper clips and staples. Always straightening and correcting. Joanna ran a finger down a clear strip on his desk, frowning at the dust that collected on her fingertip. Irritation buzzed in his gut. This was a damn bike repair shop, not the Hilton. What did she expect? She discreetly wiped her finger on a napkin left over from some fast-food joint. "See you later. And don't be late."

Damnation. He couldn't wait until dinner to ask. "What did you and April talk about?"

"Oh, this and that." She gave a maddeningly vague smile. "I like her."

Joanna was dropping the equivalent of f-bomb shockers in his office. She had never liked any of his past girlfriends. Or any of his friends, for that matter. Not that he cared.

"As for what we talked about…you can ask her yourself tonight. She's invited for dinner, too."

With that final bombshell, Joanna walked out, leaving him staring speechlessly at the door. What the hell was happening to the world as he knew it?

He hated her.

April wandered through the swamp, feeling as desolate and gray as the November sky. She should probably be relieved the worst was over. The truth was out. No more holding her breath, waiting for the bombshell to drop. Yet she'd never felt so alone. So bereft.

The earlier optimism of the day had faded. Joanna could try to play matchmaker all she liked, but the truth was that Chulah didn't appear too fond of his stepmother. Her opinion would hold no sway with him. It could even be more harmful than helpful.

She picked up a withered, dead stick and idly twirled it through her cold fingers like a baton. It snapped in two, and she tossed the broken sticks on the frosty soil. Chulah couldn't hate her any more than she hated herself. She was selfish, secretive, impulsive, flighty—

The smell of old-fashioned peat blew in the breeze. Perhaps someone was burning leaves nearby? April circled, scanning the skies, but there were no smoke columns rising in the wind. Odd. Unless… That was exactly how Grady smelled. April shivered, not from cold, but from fear.

But Grady was dead. Steven said that even his spirit had been annihilated in Hoklonote's fire. Uneasy, April turned back to her apartment. The closed-in room was a bit claustrophobic—she was used to living outdoors—but it was safe.

The smell grew stronger, assaulting her nose—then her lungs. She coughed and draped the scarf over the lower half of her face. She walked faster, the aerobic pumping of her heart driving up her fear until she ran down the path. The only noises were the rustle of dead leaves and the sound of her trapped breath in the woolen scarf. Another half mile and she'd be home.

A crash exploded from behind. She jumped and turned, then realized it was only a tree limb that had broken and fallen to the ground. *Get a grip.* She slowed her pace to a quick walk, all senses remaining on high alert. She picked up the sound of every squirrel scurrying through the underbrush, every caw of the crow and the constant whistle of the wind through the trees. And each step drew her closer to safety.

Until it didn't.

Icy fingers ran roughly through her hair, leaving a trail of burn that brought tears to her eyes. They tugged at her long locks.

"Where are you running off to, little girl?"

Grady's voice, all right. Breathy. Girlie. Affected. She'd never liked him. While on the Council, he'd always sat with a smug smile on his fat face. That smile only grew wider when it came to disciplinary matters. With no expression of emotion, he'd offer the harshest punishment possible with a calm, gentlemanly veneer. Only the slight twitching of his beefy hands gave away his secret pleasure.

No one dared cross him. Even the queen acquiesced to his "recommendations."

The tug strengthened to a pull that set every scalp follicle writhing. April raised her hands, uselessly trying to bat away his grip.

He let go and she fell to the ground, smacking her right hip on the hard earth. Instinctively, April rolled out of kicking range.

"I remember you," he drawled, as if delighted to see her again. "The precious halfling who tried to run away from Fairy, looking for her mommy."

On hands and knees, April faced him. He was the same.

Tall, heavy. Huge purple wings so ostentatious they were ugly. A smooth white luster to his form that was too pretty for his sex, too delicate and fair.

"Grady. I remember you, too." The fat bastard had ostracized her for a year. A year in which no one was allowed to speak to her or acknowledge her presence. A year in hell.

"*Sir* Grady," he corrected, smile slipping. "You seem to have forgotten your manners."

She stood on shaky feet, determined not to show fear. Grady thrived on that. Hungered for it. "I was told Hoklonote killed you the night of the fire."

"A little fire won't kill me."

What would? April wondered.

"Nothing that you could do."

He'd read her mind. No, it was rumored Hoklonote had the ability, but Grady was a fairy, same as her.

"That's right, little girl. I can hear what you're thinking. But you insult me by comparing yourself to me."

She lifted her chin. "Lucky guess. And my name's April."

"I know who you are. I also know what you are about here on land. Helping the shadow hunters." His lips curled sardonically. "You're even in love with one of them. Just like your mother."

No sense denying it if he could read her mind. "So what if I am? Why should you care?"

Grady dropped all pretense of civility. The pristine whiteness of his aura began swirling with red streaks. The odor of peat grew more burned, an acrid fume that suffocated. "Because we should stay a pure race, untainted by vulgar human blood."

"If we're so wonderful, so pure, why are you selling our secrets to Hoklonote?"

"Because together we can rule Fairy. Once he kills the queen, of course."

His casual mention of murdering their monarch stunned April. He was crazy. Most likely had been for years. "You're a monster. How could you even think of doing such a thing? And it will all be for nothing. Hoklonote won't let you rule anything."

"You comprehend nothing, little girl." A sly note crept into his voice. "If you join us, we'll not only spare your life—we'll grant you a position on our new Council. Wouldn't you love to sit in judgment of all the people from your past who slighted you?"

Unbidden, an image arose of Larkin, her special tormentor during adolescence. Around the other Fae, he called her names and ridiculed her half-Fae status, but when he caught her alone it was far worse. More than once, it had been a near thing escaping his unwanted advances. April tamped down the unpleasant memories.

"Aha… I heard your thoughts. You could ostracize Larkin for the rest of his existence if you so desired."

"I have to admit it's a little tempting. But no—I would never hurt someone the way I was punished. The way *you* sentenced me to ostracism."

"Your human side makes you weak."

"Compassion is a strength, not a weakness."

"So said Fawn, your dear mother. Uncanny."

Her breath caught. "You knew her?"

He chuckled, an oily rumble that held no mirth. "Not as well as I wanted to. She preferred that base human over me."

Dread prickled her scalp. Grady had been her mother's Larkin. Her breath caught. "You killed her."

He chuckled again. "Had to. One of my finest works,"

he sneered. "Convinced all the fairies that a wisp killed her as she was running away to her lover, leaving you behind."

"She never meant to leave me behind. She loved me."

"Did she ever. Begged me to let her live so that she could return to you."

Bastard. "You hate me because you see my father when you look at me. You failed where he succeeded."

"Don't presume you can read *my* mind," he shouted above the roaring wind. "I hate you as much as any other bastardized halfling."

"There's nothing more you can do to hurt me."

"There's a great deal I can do."

"Like what? Kill me like you did my mother?" If Chulah didn't love her, if the fairy kingdom was to be usurped by the dark shadow spirits, her life didn't count for much anyway. April turned her back and continued down the path.

"Wait. What do you think you're doing?" Grady floated in front of her, flapping his hideous purple wings.

"Walking away."

"You can't walk away from me, you…you…" he blustered, more red clouds spiraling in his white aura.

"Impure halfling? Tainted half-breed? I've heard the insults all my life. No words can offend me. You already killed my mother. There's nothing to threaten me with."

The red smoke settled at his feet and a smile curved his lips. "Chulah."

April tamped down the panic swirling in her mind. "He means nothing to me."

"Liar. You think you love him."

She tried to think of something—anything—other than Chulah. Tried and failed.

"You would do anything to save him, wouldn't you? Stop helping the shadow hunters kill the wisps and the

Ishkitini, and all will be forgiven." He paused for effect. "Or else."

She ignored the threat. "Why do you care so much what I do? I'm a mere halfling. Not important enough to concern yourself with."

"Weellll...you do have the power to roam in human form for extended periods of time. An ability we could spin to our advantage. Infiltrate yourself with Chulah and the others. Enchant him and report back to us his plans."

"No."

"Do it or I'll kill Chulah."

"He'll sense you before you see him. Sniff you out at a hundred yards. You stink now, Grady, in case you didn't know. Stink to the After Life like peat burning rot."

He sniffed delicately and frowned. "I smell nothing, but your thoughts confirm what your mouth is speaking." He glanced upward for a moment, then blinked at her in excitement. "I've got it. I'll keep you with me. When he seeks you, I'll demand his cooperation in exchange for your life."

"There's a huge flaw in your plan."

"What?"

"Chulah hates me now. He doesn't give a damn about my well-being. He wouldn't sacrifice his principles on a lying nobody like me."

"So you say."

April felt a probing inside her thoughts, a heavy finger that pushed and illuminated what she would keep secret, the light burning out the thoughts she'd rather keep hidden in the dark recesses of her mind and heart.

"You were telling the truth," Grady said in surprise.

"So you see, there's nothing you can do to me." April shoved off. "Now get out of my way. I'm going home."

Grady didn't move. "There is one thing."

April ignored him, walked around his fat, fiery form

and kept going. He morphed back in front of her on the path. "Untethering."

The blood rushed from her face and dread rooted her like an anchor. This was worse than ostracizing or death. "You wouldn't. You can't. Only the queen—"

"The queen granted me this power long ago."

"You have to have a reason. You can't do this just because you don't like me."

"Silence." Blackness washed over his aura. "I do what I want. No one can stop me. Especially not a halfling like you."

April sank to her knees, as if she'd been sucker punched. "Please. No." She hated the desperation in her voice, wanted to be strong and clever. Tallulah, Chulah's real love, would never sink to begging. Nothing would scare that woman. No doubt, it was one of the many things Chulah loved about her.

Grady laughed, pleased with her suffering, her pleas for mercy. Sick bastard loved the control of holding her life and happiness on his own shifting whims. Felt most alive when demonstrating his power.

"Give me a reason I shouldn't purge you of every Fae power."

Because it might reduce her to madness. Because it would leave her with no ties to any world. Untethered. Because her life would be meaningless. A giant, purposeless void.

"I care nothing about your feelings," he sneered.

Her mind scrambled, searching for a way to appease Grady, to buy a little time. "Maybe I could be of use to you?"

"Now you're talking." His form turned back to pure white. "You can help me capture the shadow hunters."

No! "I would if I could," she lied. "But it's over. Chulah would never trust me again. I can't help—"

"Stop with your lies. I hear your thoughts. Remember?"

"But I'm telling the truth about them not trusting me now."

"Use your fairy enchantment to gain his trust and affection again."

April took a deep breath. She had to make Grady believe she would do this. Had to block him from her mind.

Yes, I'll do it. My only hope is to enchant Chulah. Yes, yes and hell yes.

She concentrated, repeating the phrase like a mantra.

Grady hissed, a sibilant sound that slithered down her spine. "You can't fool me, little girl. Cooperate, or live alone, tethered to the earth, siphoned away from Fairy with no magic."

It wasn't the stripping of power per se that terrified her. The tales in Fairy painted a dismal story of those untethered from the realm. They wandered human land, broken and confused and pining to return home.

"I can't do it. I won't betray Chulah."

She'd hurt him enough. And now he would never know how much she truly loved him. That stung like a jagged dagger plunged in her soul. Her own kind wouldn't even be aware of the noble sacrifice to save them.

Grady puffed into a shining ball of fire that burned black at its core. "Last chance."

Heat singed her tender human flesh. Death by fire would be most gruesome.

"Not as gruesome as the untethering. So what's your answer? Yes or no?"

"No." Her whisper roared through the swamp and she trembled uncontrollably, despite the heat from Grady's incendiary form. She tried to be noble and brave, face down disaster like a shadow hunter. But her terror was too great and untrained for confronting evil. She had no weapon or ability to fight off her attacker.

"So be it."

A roaring exploded in her mind. The sounds of grinding metal gears, wails of torment, whistles and moans and chanting and fire crackling. Hell. She crumbled, as if her spine was yanked from her skeletal frame, leaving her without support. She was rolling, faster and faster, as if racing to a cliff's edge. The earth and grass and leaves were scorched, and pine needles pricked exposed flesh. Desperately, she clutched the fairy cross stone around her neck, invoking magic to change from human to fairy.

Nothing. It was merely a pretty, useless rock.

Weakness left her dizzy. She'd rumble downhill forever, or until she reached the void of a dead end. Even if she found the strength to resist the fall, she'd lost control of her body's function. Inexplicably, everything stopped.

"That's merely a taste, little one," Grady said. She heard the smile in his voice. "Changed your mind? I won't ask again."

"No. Not ever."

"Stupid, foolish halfling. Good riddance." The stink of Grady vanished.

Fever blistered her body, scorched her lungs. Yet the torture centered her scattered thoughts. Pain purified, cleansed, fused mind and body as one to combat the origin's source. April crawled toward an oak. The giant tree trunk wobbled from left to right and everything around it in a circular blizzard. Her vision jumbled like a snow globe—bits and pieces swirling haphazardly. Needles dug in her raw kneecaps. Something viciously scratched her palms like a nest of nettles.

Good.

It meant she was alive. Capable of still feeling. Anything was better than the frozen void of madness. Untethered Fae were rare, but legend had it that their eyes were as vacant and soulless as a zombie. No stinky, rotten flesh for the Fae, though. Even in the worst desecration, they were beautiful beings. Flickering forms, not quite human or fairy, they roamed the night with unseeing eyes that seemed to search for their lost souls. Occasionally they wailed. Humans once called them banshees.

Rough bark dug into her fingertips and she wanted to weep in gratitude. Eagerly, she wrapped her arms around the trunk, willing the tree to infuse her with its ancient life force.

Again, nothing. The magic was forever lost.

But the will to survive was strong. Stronger than she'd ever imagined. April gathered her shattered body together and gripped the tree with everything left. Bark sliced her arms and she laid a cheek against the beautiful, jagged texture. Alive. Still alive. The muscles of her arms screamed as she pulled to a standing position. Heavy breathing pillowed into wisps of fog. She leaned against the tree, willing her legs to steady and strengthen on their own.

Cold chilled her spine, made more extreme from the earlier intense heat. Salty wind whipped her flesh and hair. She ran numbed fingers down her stomach. What had happened to her jacket and jeans? Only a flimsy white cotton slip protected her from the elements. It looked like a shroud from days of old. *Stop it. Move.*

April took a tentative step from the tree. Her knees wobbled, but held. *Keep moving*, that was the ticket. If she gave in to the cold and the aching fatigue, all was over. Head bent, arms rubbing arms, torso bunched forward, she walked. Step by step, she fought the near-overwhelming desire to burrow into a bed of leaves, curl into a ball and sleep into oblivion.

Cursed. You're forever cursed.

April shoved the terrible mind whisperings away, the miasma of misery that surrounded her on all sides. She concentrated on the rhythm of her steps, the pattern of her breathing. Left foot forward. *Chu.* Right foot forward. *Lah. Chu-lah. Chu-lah.*

It was all for him. Her penance for the sin she'd committed so long ago. A walking purgatory of shame. *Chu-lah. Chu-lah.*

Forever and ever he'd haunt her heart.

Chapter 15

She didn't show.

Chulah stuffed down the roast and potatoes without the usual enjoyment.

"April must have a good reason," Joanna said for the dozenth time. "She seemed so eager to see you tonight."

"Forget about it," Chulah muttered. "I have."

Joanna frowned at Brenda. "It's rude to look at your cell phone during dinner."

"Just checking to see if April got my message."

"You have her phone number?" Seemed his little sister was more connected to April than he was.

"The number at her store. No one's answering it, though."

He wanted to ask for the number, but he wouldn't need it now. April was off-limits. Whenever he saw her beautiful face, all he'd remember was that she might have kept him from saving his father.

He shrugged as if he couldn't care less. But being stood up stung, even if the whole arrangement had been thrust on him.

Brenda's familiar scowl was back in place. "How can you be mad at someone like April? She's pretty and kind and—"

Joanna cut her a kill-it motion with her hand, shaking her head slightly.

The hero worship was getting a little old. Had April used some magic pixie dust on Brenda? The girl believed April was perfect. Bet she'd do a three-sixty if she knew April might have caused her father's death.

But that little secret was between him and April. No need for his family to be dragged into the past with all its what-ifs and if-onlys. It would only cause them more pain. Despite his strained relationship with them, they were blood kin. No choice but to have them a part of his life.

April was optional.

"Pie, anyone?" Joanna rose from the table. "I made pecan. Your favorite, Chulah."

Okay, that did it. She was buttering him up for something. Cooking his favorite meal, calling him "son" and visiting him at work this morning. He'd been flattered and sucked in at her attentions, but time for the show to end.

"Everything okay with the boys?" he asked.

"I told you they were fine." She went into the kitchen and returned with the pie and clean plates.

Chulah's mouth watered. Pecan pie made everything a little bit better. Joanna carved him a generous slice and he bit into the sugary, crunchy warmth. Heaven.

Chulah dug into the back pocket of his jeans and pulled out his wallet.

"What are you doing?" his stepmother asked with narrowed eyes.

"Figured you might need some money." He riffled through a wad of bills. "How much?"

"We don't need your money."

That was a first. "You sure?"

"Not at the moment."

Which meant she was going to spring some future expense on him. He waited.

"Pie's getting cold," she noted.

Had he misjudged her? Chulah stuffed his wallet back into his jeans pocket and resumed eating.

The "Sweet Home Alabama" ringtone blasted on Brenda's phone and they all froze and stared. Brenda grabbed it and glanced at the screen. "It's April."

Heat diffused on his neck. Would she lie about the true nature of their split and make him appear even more a fool? Bad enough she'd stood him up in front of his family. Not that it was a date or anything. He was done with her.

Brenda's brows drew together. "Oh? We haven't seen her either. She told Mom she'd be here for dinner."

A knot of worry tied in his gut. *She's fine. Not my responsibility.* He had enough duty and burdens without adding a deceitful fairy to the mix. He was well rid—

"Okay." Brenda handed him the phone. "It's Steven."

Chulah took it and sighed. "What's up?"

"I think April's in trouble," he began without preamble. "She was supposed to report to the Council hours ago and didn't show."

He tamped down the jolt of concern. "So she blew them off."

Steven laughed, a guttural, bitter rumble. "You don't *blow off* the Council. Especially not in an emergency."

"Or else…what?"

"Trust me, there's a whole range of consequences. None of them good."

Heartburn seared his chest and he pushed away the rest of the uneaten pie. *Be logical.* This might be a ploy by April to draw him back to her. Maybe she was foolishly running away again, as she had as a teenager. Rebelling from her duties.

Brenda tugged at his arm. He frowned, but the sight of her young face, drawn up in worry, stopped him short. The heavy eye makeup and dark lipstick only emphasized the smooth, unlined planes of her face, the innocence in her eyes. She was so very young. And yet April had been about this same age when she'd acted so foolishly.

Youth could be forgiven many things.

Chulah awkwardly patted her arm and left the room to avoid their questioning glances. "Can't the Fae find her?" he asked in a low voice. He strode down the hallway to his childhood bedroom and shut the door.

"No. None of us can pick up a trace of her or her magic."

Despite his growing alarm, Chulah was curious. "How do you trace Fae magic?"

"Same way you can track dark spirits, I imagine…a certain scent, a familiar energy pattern, faint sounds. Look, are you going to help us or not?" he snapped. "I know you two had some kind of falling-out, but you need her."

"You mean the fairies need her," Chulah corrected.

"We both need April. So get your ass over here and help me search."

The order didn't sit well with Chulah. "Now, see here—"

"Please."

The magic word. And if he didn't go, he'd spend the evening imagining all sorts of horrible scenarios. This didn't mean he forgave April; he'd do this for anyone in possible danger. "I'll meet you in the woods by the abandoned hunters' lodge. You know where that is?"

"Of course." A heartbeat of silence. "And thank you."

"You can thank me if I find her. Be there in twenty." He turned off the phone and gazed blankly at the walls. His old stickball medals still hung above the corner desk. Without thinking, he walked over and ran his calloused palms over the shiny medallions. A smile hovered on his lips. Good times. The ancient Choctaw sport had been an outlet during his tumultuous teen years. Sweat therapy.

Surprising that Joanna had kept them.

A soft knock at the door interrupted his reverie and he dropped the medals. "Come in."

Joanna and Brenda both entered, Brenda tense with worry, while Joanna pinned him with a hard stare. "Everything all right?" his stepmother asked.

"Should be. A friend of April's is concerned she missed an appointment and no one has seen her. I told him I'd help search for her."

"She's in trouble. I just know it," Brenda burst out, worrying her bottom lip. "April wouldn't not show up. She's… my friend."

Oh, hell. Now he had to worry about his sister's feelings when April returned to her own world. One day April would disappear without explanation and Brenda would be hurt. The reminder that April would be here only a short time almost took his breath.

The sooner the better. Before he lost his head over the tiny slip of a woman.

Joanna abruptly left the room. Figured. She wasn't one for participating in emotional scenes.

"I'm glad you have a friend like April," Chulah said at last, remembering all Brenda's questionable friends with their sullen airs and an odor of pot that wrapped around them like a cloak. His sister was a good kid, actually. He had high hopes she'd make it out of high school with no juvie record and no pregnancy. Their brothers had put everyone through enough grief with their shenanigans.

To his surprise, Brenda came to him and squeezed him

in a bear hug. "Go find her," she mumbled into his chest. "We both know you love her."

Love? No. Before he could deny it, Brenda pulled away. "Call me later and let me know everything's okay."

"Sure." The idea was novel. He wasn't used to checking in with people, except his fellow shadow hunters while they roamed the bayou. He was his own boss and lived alone. Independent and content. Had been since he was eighteen years old.

Brenda nodded and he followed her out of the room, eager to leave. The sooner they found April, the sooner he could go home and put this evening out of his mind. Quickly, he left the house and climbed into his old pickup, gunning the motor. Joanna ran down the porch steps, holding something in her arms.

He rolled down the driver's-side window and a blast of cold air swept through the truck. "What?"

She stopped, breathing heavy, and thrust a warm dish, covered in aluminum foil, through the window. "Weren't you going to say goodbye?"

Chulah gripped the steering wheel in annoyance. The last thing he wanted right now was a lecture on manners. "Sorry," he muttered. "Thanks for dinner."

"You're welcome." She straightened and nodded at the dish. "Enjoy the pie later. I hope everything's all right with April. Call me later."

Another request to keep in touch? He didn't think Joanna cared about anyone but herself and her own blood children. Had he judged her unfairly all these years? "Okay," he said with a nod. "Got to run."

"Don't be careless on the roads," she scolded. "There's a frost warning tonight."

Terrific. They got one of these cold nights about twice a winter. Today was cursed in every way. He drove through the dark, empty streets, his alarm growing as strong gusts rocked the truck and shook the trees. Chulah turned up the heater. If April was out in this weather, she'd freeze.

Stop it. April's a fairy. She's used to the outdoors. No reason for her to traipse the woods in human flesh. Still, the knot of worry in his gut grew. He kept recalling her stricken face as he'd told her goodbye. Did he want that to be her last memory of him before she returned to the Fae realm?

No. Damn it. Despite his cautious nature, he'd started to care for her. She hadn't meant to hurt his father. Chulah slapped his hand on the dashboard. His feelings didn't matter. First order of business was to find her, and then they'd have to work together to handle Hoklonote. Keep it polite. Civil and distant. No distractions as they faced their common enemy.

It seemed an hour, but Chulah was home in fifteen minutes. Quickly, he pulled on a heavier coat and grabbed his slingshot before heading to the clearing. His cell phone was right where he'd left it on the kitchen table. Half the time he forgot to carry it once he got home from work.

The stars glittered brightly above in the night's cold, indifferent beauty. The wind whipped across the open space and he shivered. He hoped she wasn't out here. Best-case scenario, she was delayed getting to the Fae realm, but had arrived safely.

He flipped out his cell phone and called Steven. "Any word yet?" Chulah asked when Steven answered.

"None. I'm about to head to the lodge."

"Same here. Once I enter the woods, my signal dies. But I'll be there shortly."

"Ditto."

Chulah stuffed the phone in his camouflage coat and stepped onto the path. The close clusters of trees and shrubs

cut down the windchill. But the temperature was dropping, and if April was out here all night without shelter, she
would be at risk for hypothermia. She had to know about
the deserted hunters' lodge. If somehow she was hurt or
stuck out here, she'd know to find the place.

The thought cheered him. She would be there.

Chulah smacked his forehead. Damn it to hell. He should
have called Tombi to round up the troops. If she wasn't
huddled inside the lodge, he'd have Steven go for help.

The cold numbed his fingers and toes, even as he jogged
a good fifteen minutes. An elliptical beam of light pierced
the darkness for an instant, then turned off. Chulah approached the building cautiously. Could be April, could
be Steven.

Could be an intruder. No whiff of Hoklonote or a wisp.
Here was a possibility he hadn't considered earlier. April
could have met trouble in the form of a human derelict.
Stealthily, he readied his slingshot and approached, crouching behind bushes as he advanced. Thorns and brambles
pulled at his hair. Should have taken time to braid it. Too
late now.

Heavy footsteps sounded within. Not April. Whoever was
in there wasn't concerned about being overheard. Quickly,
he crept to a broken window and peeked inside. A short pale
form with a red beard walked across broken glass, cursing
under his breath.

"Steven?"

He jumped and looked toward the window. "Chulah?
She's not here."

What a hell of a night. Chulah pushed aside the door
swinging on one hinge and entered the lodge.

"Did you call your friends?" Steven asked.

"No," he admitted. "Why don't you go back to town and
call? I'll give you their numbers."

"I have everyone's."

He hadn't thought about it before, but it struck him as odd. "How did you get my sister's number?"

"She left a message at the shop."

So much for his theory of a magical phone that had access to everyone's information.

"Did you travel here in Fae form?" he asked curiously.

"Why do you ask?"

The little man was always so defensive about questions. Chulah shrugged. "Just wondered if you had better search abilities to find another fairy when you are on the same plane as them."

"Ah, okay. I did arrive that way, but didn't see or hear a thing."

Dread chilled Chulah more than the cold. "Get a move on, then, while I search."

Steven shuffled toward the door.

"Wait," Chulah called. "Do you think April will be in fairy or human form?"

"I'm not sure. We're forbidden to show our Fae nature in front of humans. That's why I shape-shifted once I got in the lodge." Steven scratched his beard. "If she had a choice, I suspect April would stay in Fae form."

"What do you mean *if* she had a choice? Could the Council force her to be one form or the other? That must be what's happened," Chulah reasoned aloud. "For whatever reason, April was in the woods and the Council found her and forced her to shape-shift and reenter their world."

Steven shook his head. "She never showed up."

"Maybe she has since you last checked."

"I would know immediately."

"How would you know— Oh, never mind. You won't tell me. Does April know anyone else in the bayou? Is there somewhere she might have gone?"

"There's no one. I'm afraid—" Steven snapped his mouth shut.

"Go on. You're afraid of what? I need any information that can help me find April."

"It's highly unusual, but we have a punishment called untethering, which can strip a fairy of all their magic."

Harsh. He couldn't imagine being siphoned of his trekking powers. It would almost be like losing his sense of taste or touch. "Permanently?"

"Permanently. Usually it results in madness or death, although some fairies have survived. Depends on whether the untethering was partial or complete."

"No wonder you've been so worried," Chulah ground out past the knot in his chest.

"It's not likely," Steven hastened to explain. "And if the Council did it—and it goes against their best interest—they wouldn't have ordered I find April and bring her to them."

"Then who could have done it?"

"Some lawless fairy. Even though it's forbidden by anyone but a Council member, it happens every decade or so. A jealous lover, a greedy relative…"

"But April doesn't have any such enemy. Not that I'm aware of." He raised a questioning brow.

"Not that I know of either. To do this… This would be over-the-top cruelty. And if they were caught doing such a taboo act, the consequence would be permanent expulsion from Fairy."

"Interesting, but you'll have to fill me in later. I have a better idea what I'm dealing with. Go get help. Quick as you can." Madness and murder. "Tell Tombi to bring Annie along. We may need her if April's hurt."

He held up his flashlight. "You need this?"

"I've got one. Go."

Steven left, tripping over strewn garbage left scattered

on the floor by vagrants. Chulah stood at the window, staring out, opening his senses. *Where are you, April?*

As if in answer, an orange luminescence appeared a few feet ahead. It flickered brilliantly, like a fallen star, before it collapsed. In the darkness, Steven kept walking. Disappointment washed over Chulah. Just once, couldn't life give him an easy solution?

No sense staying in the lodge. Chulah fastened the top coat button at his throat, taking care as he stepped down the cracked concrete entrance steps. First he'd stay on the main path. If he didn't find her, he'd widen out the search area. Hopefully, help would arrive soon and they could cover the woods' entire perimeter.

Outside the vacant building, he again expanded his senses. No unusual sounds or smells. It was as if it were too cold for even the Ishkitini to venture from their warm nests.

Chulah walked slowly, gazing at every inch of ground and even above to the treetops. After all, April could fly.

"Are you there, April?" he called out every few minutes. "It's me. Chulah."

But the Gulf breeze only howled forlornly through the oaks and cypresses. It seemed hopeless. If he didn't know better, he'd think a wisp had invaded his mind, preying on his emotions. The parasitic creatures loved to feed on human misery. Once they entered your mind, they attached to a person's sorrow until it turned to unbearable grief. A consuming grief that led one to long for death. A kind of madness.

Had something like this happened to April? He kept going, concentrating on the night instead of the pointless worry. Almost near the edge of the woods, he heard a low moan. He stilled, straining to hear it again. "April?" he called out. "Where are you?"

Another small groan. He headed southwest off the beaten path. A few broken twigs were ahead, approximately every eight inches or so, in the pattern of a foot. Either April in human form or another person had walked here recently. He dared not speak aloud again, in case another person lay in wait.

A whiff of something sweet, like cotton candy, stopped him in his tracks. No, not cotton candy.

Violets.

His pulse thudded and he drew a deep breath. It was April. She was hurt. He wanted to run down the trail, but couldn't until he knew April was alone. At a steady but cautious clip, Chulah forged through thick underbrush and increasingly muddy soil. At least he didn't have to worry about snakes this time of year.

And Nalusa Falaya, who could shape-shift into a rattlesnake, was contained. He'd do whatever it took to make sure the dark spirit stayed safely entrapped.

The violet scent intensified until the underlying note of moss was discernible. She was near.

Chulah hardly dared breathe, afraid to disrupt his senses and break the fragile connection. A pool of silver waterfalled amid a large pile of dry leaves. Uncaring, Chulah broke through the underbrush.

"April!"

He ran to her and dropped to his knees on the cold frost. Gently, he reached through the blanket of leaves and turned her over.

Her eyes were closed and unseeing.

Chapter 16

April felt like the cold would never leave. Her human bones must be frozen solid. Her heart beat slow and erratic and the blood coursed through her like icy sludge, too thick to properly circulate. Too bad her brain hadn't slowed. Her thoughts raced and circled and nipped at her like an angry pit bull. Of all the calamities, she'd never expected Grady to appear and mete out an untethering. Death would have been kinder. Another day out in this weather, and it was inevitable.

She tossed under the pile of leaves on top of her body and the bed of pine needles underneath. She'd fashioned this makeshift shelter when her limbs grew too heavy and numb to function. Not that it had provided much warmth or shelter. Somewhere out there was a vacant building, but damn if she could find it. She'd kept endlessly circling the same path, unable to determine her location.

Lost.

The irony of being a fairy lost in the forest didn't elude her. In Fae form, she'd wandered this area her entire life, recognized every small clearing and nest of trees. Now everything appeared the same. Dead, brown, lifeless.

How fitting that she should die out here alone in the woods like Chulah's father had died so many years ago. At least she knew not to expect help from Chulah. Her fate was clear. If a will-o'-the-wisp didn't attack and entrap her, the elements would destroy her vulnerable human body.

April curled even tighter into a fetal position, shivering in cold misery. If only she could fall back asleep, pass into the After Life without these tormenting thoughts. Energy seeped from her body to the hard ground. She was too tired and weak to even shiver now. Silence roared in her ears and the night grew a shade darker.

All systems failing.

Fine. If she couldn't sleep, she'd think about Chulah. Remember their one night of passion when he'd been hers so completely, had stared at her so intently as he entered her core. His gaze had been so long, so passionate, as if she were his world. Almost as wonderful was the memory of the safe warmth of curling next to his naked body in bed, drifting to sleep and waking up with him beside her. Strong, handsome and brave.

Hot pressure jostled her body. Had the wisps found her? April groaned but couldn't even find the strength to open her eyes. Her lids felt like they weighed a ton.

"It's okay. You're going to be fine, my love." The words rumbled inside her. Her heart quickened at the familiar voice.

Not a wisp, then. This was the slow, slow sinking into the After Life. But if Chulah was there in her memories whispering sweet words like this, she'd found bliss.

He wouldn't let anyone carry April but him. Steven tried to help, but Chulah told him to have the others waiting for April at his cabin.

He ran through the forest, uncaring of the weight and the fatigue. He'd found her. Half-dead, but he wouldn't let her die. Chulah had covered her near-naked body with his coat and ran. She needed warmth first. Then Annie could examine her and make some herbal remedy. All would be fine.

He wouldn't allow his mind to dwell on how he'd found April. Covered in mud, her skin blue and rigid with cold. He'd located the faint pulse on her neck and had gathered her close to him, willing his warmth and life to seep into her body.

As he broke through to the clearing, the headlight beams from Tombi's car illuminated the field.

Home had never looked so welcoming. Chulah ran in the light's path. *Hold on, April. Almost there. I'll take good care of you.*

"Is she alive?" Tombi shouted.

Chulah was aware of at least a dozen people huddled by the car.

"Barely. Open the back door." He didn't want to waste precious seconds fumbling for house keys while April froze to death in his arms.

He ran past the crowd and up the porch steps where Tombi held open the door.

Once inside, Chulah laid her across the sofa and wrapped her in every blanket he could find. She groaned a few more times, but never opened her eyes.

Steven tried to shake her awake. "Who did this to you?"

No response.

Chulah squeezed his eyes shut. April was forever changed. He faced Steven. "Someone did that thing you mentioned— an untethering?"

"No doubt. Her aura's been drained. There's nothing left but a grayness. Same as any other human."

That made no sense. "I only saw her aura when she was in Fae form."

"We always have an aura, even shape-shifted as humans. It's faded, but only another Fae can detect it."

Steven rubbed a hand over his face. "Poor girl is useless to us now. Too bad." He glanced at Chulah sheepishly. "You know, I even had a thing for April once. Such a shame." He pulled a wool hat out of his coat and donned it, shaking his head.

Arrogant prick. "She's still the same woman, fairy or not," Chulah said between clenched teeth.

"Sure. Whatever. I must get back to the Council at once with the news. I'll return later. April needs to provide the attacker's name if she ever wakes up. They'll be suitably punished."

Chulah's hands fisted at his sides. *He* would be the one to mete out justice to this fairy. He—or she—would pay for what they'd done. Steven slipped out of the room and Chulah sought Annie in the crowd. "Can you help April or do I call an ambulance?"

Annie immediately sat beside him and took April's cold hands in her own, rubbing them briskly. "No frostbite. A good sign." Then she bent her head over April's mouth, listening to her breath and feeling the side of her neck.

"Her pulse is strong. Give me five minutes alone with her. We'll take it from there."

Joanna stepped out of the crowd of shadow hunters. "Girl, do you know what you're doing?" she asked sharply. "'Cause if she dies—"

Brenda stepped in front of her. "C'mon, Mom. Let's fix coffee for everyone while Annie does her healing work."

Chulah shot his sister a silent thank-you as she rounded up Joanna and the others to the kitchen.

"I'm not leaving April," he warned Annie. "Do what you have to do."

She nodded. "Bring me candles and matches."

"Anything else?"

Annie pointed to a black bag lying in a chair. "I'll need that as well."

Chulah brought her the bag and hurried to his bedroom, returning with several candles and a book of matches.

Annie held April's hand, chanting soft words that sounded like something between a prayer and a spell. A form of hoodoo passed down from her grandmother, the infamous Tia Henrietta, who'd been credited with saving many a soul. Tia was too old and feeble now for house calls, but Annie went wherever she was summoned. Tombi had found a good woman in her.

His anxiety eased a touch under the music of Annie's voice. Chulah lit the candles and placed them on the coffee table. Annie glanced up and nodded.

The blue tinge of April's skin and lips faded. She was still unnaturally pale, but appeared to have turned a corner. Chulah sat on the sofa's armrest and ran his fingers through April's muddy, tousled hair. There was no electric magic in their touch. It was as if a switch had been turned off. But it didn't matter as long as she lived past whatever had happened to her this evening.

She was beautiful to him.

April wore a filthy, flimsy nightgown that was torn and bloody where she had walked or crawled through underbrush.

A new worry assailed Chulah. What if she lived, but never recovered her mind? No. Annie could help her. She'd already performed a miracle.

He hated to interrupt the chant, but he had to ask. "Is she okay?" he whispered. "Can you tell what she's…thinking?"

Annie kept her eyes on April. "Too early to tell. Everything feels jumbled."

April groaned. "Chulah," she muttered.

The sound of his name on her lips filled him with hope. "I'm here."

Annie nodded and patted April's hand. "I'll leave you alone with her a minute."

Chulah leaned into April and kissed her forehead. "Come back to me. You're safe, I promise."

She licked her lips. Surely a good sign. Her eyes flickered open, unfocused and confused. "It's me," he said, stroking her arm. "You're safe."

Her purple-blue eyes focused on his. "Is this the After Life?" she asked weakly.

He laughed and almost wept with relief. "No, you're in my cabin. I found you in the woods."

Her eyes grew dark and her lips trembled.

"Don't think about it," Chulah urged. "We'll talk about it later. For now, you need to warm up and rest. Do you think you can eat and drink a bit?"

"I already have something for her," Annie said, returning to the room and holding a cup. "Can you sit her up?"

Chulah maneuvered his body on the sofa so that April's back leaned against his chest. "How's this?"

"That works." Annie patiently brought the cup to her patient's lip. "Take a little sip for me," she cooed.

April did. Then sputtered and coughed. "That's nasty."

Annie winked at him. "Nobody appreciates my tonics."

"I do," Chulah said in a rush. "I've seen what they can do."

"She's going to be fine." Annie smiled. "I prescribe a long, hot bath after she finishes drinking this. And lots of sleep."

"You got it, doc."

Joanna spoke from the kitchen. "Does this mean we don't call for an ambulance?"

"No, we're good," Chulah assured her.

"I'm all right." April's voice was so low, he didn't think anyone heard it but him and Annie.

His friends came over. "We can stay if you need us," Poloma said. The rest mumbled their agreement.

"No, go on home. April needs rest. It's been a long day for all of us."

The sound of sobs from the kitchen tore at him. He followed the noise and caught Brenda at the kitchen table, head in her arms, shoulders shaking. Chulah put an arm around her shoulders. "Don't cry. Your friend is going to make it."

Brenda looked up, mascara streaming down her blotchy face. "I was so w-worried."

"I know. So was I. But everything's fine now. Why don't you go home and rest? I'm sure April will want to see you first thing in the morning."

Brenda nodded and swiped her cheeks. She smiled wanly. "Mom and I will get out of your hair."

"Thanks, sis."

Now he knew April was safe, he wanted to take care of her, and he couldn't do that properly with everyone gawking.

Tallulah in particular.

She stood alone in a corner, not speaking with anyone, but he was aware of her watching his every move. A dark presence, a reminder of past failures, a childhood friendship ruined.

The shadow hunters filed out the door and Tombi clamped a hand on his shoulder. "Call if you need us. Anytime."

Chulah extended his hand and they shook. "Thanks, man."

Nothing else needed to be spoken. All was understood in the firm handshake. They'd been friends all their lives and would die for each other if needed.

Annie pulled a packet out of her black bag and handed it to him. "Stew a tablespoon of these herbs in a cup of boiling water and make sure she drinks it at least three times a day."

He accepted the bag and eyed it with distaste. "I'll see she does. Can I speak with you alone for a minute?"

Chulah guided her into the hallway. "I see her physical health will be fine, but I'm worried about…" He tapped a temple on the side of his head. "The Fae have this thing where they can punish another fairy by stripping them of their powers. Apparently, one of the consequences is that the fairy loses their sanity. Got anything in your little black bag for that?"

"No. I'm sorry. There are herbs that can help calm agitation, but they can't restore a broken mind." She placed a hand on his arm, eyes full of gentle sympathy. "Pray for her. When I get home, I'll light a candle and do the same."

They returned to the den, where Joanna shoved a cup of coffee in his hand. "Drink up. You look exhausted. You never take care of yourself like you should."

Bossy woman. He sighed, but took a grateful sip. Perhaps she meant well, in her own way.

Joanna gave a sharp nod. "We'll be on our way, then."

Chulah walked to the door and breathed a sigh of relief they were all gone.

"Are you in love with her?"

He whirled around at the familiar voice, almost spilling his coffee. Damn it, Tallulah had hung back from the exiting crowd. He must be exhausted not to have noticed she'd remained.

"Why are you still here?" he countered. He took a long swallow of coffee and set his cup on the table.

Tallulah shoved off from the wall and came toward him, dark eyes full of challenge. "Only a few weeks ago, you asked me to marry you."

Chulah's eyes darted to April's still form but her eyes were closed. At least the steady rise and fall of her chest reassured him she was sleeping normally. He faced Tallulah again. "Why are you bringing this up now?"

Her eyes turned sly. "What if I told you I've reconsidered?"

"You're lying," he said flatly, although her mood was hard to decipher. Even knowing her since she'd been in kindergarten, he could never be sure of Tallulah's thoughts.

"Are you sure?" Her full lips lifted at the corners, teasing him. She reached a hand up and stroked the side of his neck.

Chulah stepped back. "Stop."

"So you do love her." She cocked her head to one side, studying him.

"None of your business." Chulah went to the door and held it open. "Thanks for stopping by."

She chuckled but picked her coat up from a chair and shrugged into it. "Hint taken." At the door, she sidled up to him. "A kiss good-night?" Before he guessed her intention, Tallulah had her lips on his, her arms around his neck.

For a moment, he responded, placing his hands on her lower back.

Nice, but no cigar. Nothing like the magic of touching April. Chulah gently pulled away. "Things have changed."

"You really must be in love."

He kept his features neutral. He'd give away nothing to Tallulah, just as she gave away nothing of her real feelings to him. And he'd accused April of deception. Next to Tallulah, she was an open book. A woman unafraid to show honest emotion.

"Good night, Tallulah."

He went straight to April, unwilling to engage in Tallulah's game. The door shut softly and he was alone with April at last.

Chulah gazed down at her still form. He'd almost lost her. Love? He couldn't say.

April's eyes shot open. "Is Tallulah finally gone?"

His jaw slackened. "How long have you been conscious?"

"Long enough to see you kissing her."

"Did you also see that I stopped it?"

"Not right away." Her eyes dulled with misery. "I can't blame you, though. She's everything you want in a woman. Strong, direct. A real fighter."

"Maybe I prefer blondes to brunettes," he said lightly. "How are you feeling?"

"Honestly? Like I'll never be warm again."

"Annie said a hot bath would do wonders."

She rose unsteadily on one elbow and glanced down. "Wh-what happened to me? I only remember..." She drew a deep breath. "Grady hurting me. After that..."

"Don't worry about it now. I'm sure it'll come back to you later." He supported her arm and helped April rise to her feet.

"I'll feel a million times better once I'm clean. And warm."

They made slow progress to the bathroom. Once inside, Chulah quickly drew the hot water, and the small room filled with steam. Gently, he helped April out of his camo jacket that she still wore.

"I've got it from here." She wrapped her arms around her waist.

"Shy? I've seen you naked before. I've even bathed you before."

"I know. But I...look so horrible."

"Who cares what you look like? You've been through a traumatic ordeal. Now, let me help you with that nightgown or whatever it is you're wearing."

"I don't think I was wearing this before I encountered Grady."

Chulah eased the torn and dirty nightgown over her head. "In the tub you go," he said matter-of-factly, even as his body responded to hers.

Carefully, he eased her into the bathtub, and she leaned back and sighed. "I never want this bath to end."

"Glad it's helping." Chulah picked up a bar of soap and lathered one of her arms. Her smooth skin was like stroking liquid satin.

"Why are you being so nice to me?" April asked suddenly. "You said you didn't want to ever see me again." She gulped. "You acted like you hated me."

Chulah winced. "So you remember."

"I don't blame you. What I did was unforgivable—"

He squirmed with a tinge of guilt. The doctor had told them his father probably died within ten minutes of being bitten. His heart had been bad for many years. If that was true, the lost time from April didn't matter. Clearly, she didn't know this. Yet he had suffered for years, wondering about his character, wondering if the doctors had said what they did merely to appease the family. "Let's drop it for now, okay?"

She nodded. "Deal."

Slowly, methodically, Chulah washed her back, arms and legs. Skin against skin, slippery and oh so tantalizing. *Damn it, she's hurt. Get yourself together.* He didn't dare face her, knowing she'd instantly read the passion in his eyes. His breathing grew heavy.

Chulah wet a washcloth and wiped mud, blood and tears from her face. He wanted to kill that Grady fairy. Ditching the washcloth, he splashed water onto her neck and upper chest. Chulah lathered his hands with soap and dipped lower. His rough palms glided over soft, rounded breasts that peaked with hard buds.

April groaned and sank an inch farther in the water.

"Did I hurt you?" he asked quickly.

"No. It feels amazing." She closed her eyes. "More, please."

"I aim to make you happy." He couldn't stop the goofy grin that plastered his face. April was alive, mind apparently intact, and moaning with pleasure under his touch. His hands roamed lower, past the slight swell of her abdomen and flare of hips. He remembered taking her before, the electric, erotic sensation of skin on skin. He cupped her core and she arched against his palm. With one finger, he parted her folds and entered.

April's breath grew as heavy and jagged as his own. She gripped the edges of the tub, knuckles white with tension. "Harder," she whispered.

Always a gentleman, he complied.

April's body twisted and tightened until her thighs locked and her head tilted back. He watched her come to release, the most beautiful sight he'd ever witnessed. She opened her eyes and gutted him with a sensual, soulful jolt of their shared pleasure. Because she couldn't have enjoyed it more than he'd enjoyed watching her.

"Your turn." She playfully tugged his arm, inviting him to bathe with her.

"Not yet. We aren't finished here."

Her brows lifted. "What—"

Chulah turned on the faucet and adjusted the temperature. "We need to get the mud out of your hair. I'll be your
shampoo boy."

April giggled and got on all fours, sticking her head in
the running water. Chulah poured out a handful of shampoo
and set to work, massaging her scalp. A clean, fresh scent
enveloped them in the steamy warmth, a cocoon of comfort. He tried to concentrate on the job at hand, but his attention roamed to her firm, rounded ass delightfully arched
upward, exposed for his viewing pleasure.

One shampoo-laden hand slid down her spine and cupped
her cheeks.

April gasped and raised her head, bumping it on the
faucet. "Oomph."

"Sorry, my fault." He rinsed the soap from her long silver-
purple hair, eager to get her in his bed.

"It felt good," she said with a laugh. "Just wasn't expecting it."

"All done."

April sat up and flipped her wet hair down her back.
Damn if she wasn't the most sensuous woman he'd ever seen.
Her pale flesh still bore a few scratches, but those didn't mar
the pearly perfection of her skin.

She looked whole. Unscathed from the night's terror,
although the true scars were inside. Time would tell how
deep the untethering had scarred her soul.

Chulah grabbed one towel and wrapped her hair. She
climbed out of the tub and he dried off her body with another towel, appreciating every exposed inch. His erection
bulged painfully against his jeans. April delicately traced
its outline with her fingers and pulled away.

"Time for bed. Didn't Annie prescribe lots of rest?"

"That's not what I had in mind."

She pointedly glanced down at his erection. "So I noticed."

He followed her into the bedroom, hastily discarding his clothes and slipping under the heavy blanket where she awaited. He tenderly covered her exposed shoulders. "Still cold?"

"I'm hot, on fire for you."

It was all the encouragement he needed. Chulah sucked on her nipples and she writhed against him. His passion couldn't wait any longer. He entered her core and thrust, pounding out his need. She matched him and their rhythm grew fast and furious, focused on the sweet relief of orgasm.

And at the crest of the climax, Chulah realized he couldn't live without April's sweet passion. She may have been stripped of her Fae essence, but their lovemaking would always be this way.

Magical.

Chapter 17

Damn it, damn it, DAMN it!

Mounds of soapy bubbles kept rushing out of the metal monster contraption Chulah called a washing machine.

He'd reluctantly left for work this morning—a motorcycle repair scheduled to be completed. Evidently, bikers weren't too happy when their wheels weren't ready on time.

April ran to the bathroom, grabbed a handful of towels and raced back to the utility room, throwing them on the soggy floor. They barely made a dent in the gathering pool of water. What the hell? She'd turned that knob to Off and yet water still poured out of the stupid thing.

Prior to this morning, this wouldn't be a problem. Abracadabra and she'd command the water to return to its source. But today?

Ah, she could get Steven over here pronto to fix this... situation. April punched his number in the cell phone. Now, there was a human invention she could get behind.

No answer. Surprising. She'd tried to call him all morning with no luck. Usually, he was forever keeping tabs on her and being a bit of a pest. A prickle of unease chased down her spine. Was he hurt or in some kind of trouble? The gurgle of gushing water called her attention to the disaster at hand. She'd worry about Steven later.

Back in the utility room, she gasped at the rising water level on the floor. No hope for it but to interrupt Chulah at work. He'd been so kind last night, even after learning of her culpability in his father's death. When he'd left this morning, she found herself inexplicably crabby and at loose ends, so she'd decided to clean house and cook as a thank-you.

Should have stayed in bed.

Burned toast stank up the kitchen, and most likely his flooring was ruined. April shut the door on the disaster. As if that would make it go away.

The doorbell rang and she perked up. If it was Steven, they'd have this fixed in no time. Quickly, she went to the front door and opened it.

Tallulah pinned her with her typically haughty gaze. "Appears you managed just fine last night," she said drily, staring at April's bare legs poking out from beneath one of Chulah's old flannel shirts.

The last person she wanted to witness her disastrous day. "Chulah's at his shop," she said stiffly, shutting the door.

Tallulah blocked her attempt and pushed against the door, squeezing herself in. "I came to see you."

"I'm kind of busy right now." April ran a hand over the shirt. She'd picked it out of the closet and thrown away the tattered nightgown from last night. It covered her only to midthigh and she self-consciously crossed her legs at the ankle. To top it off, her hair was a tangled mess from sleeping on it wet. Not her best look. By contrast, Tallulah was poised and fresh in her jeans and a black top that emphasized a silver necklace with large turquoise nuggets.

Matching chandelier earrings highlighted the blue-black smoothness of her long hair. Very stylish.

Tallulah sniffed. "What's that smell?"

"I don't smell anything," April lied.

"This place reeks of burned food."

"What did you come over to tell me?" She had to get Tallulah out of here and take care of that water. She'd call Joanna for help. If she was lucky, they could get it cleaned up and Chulah wouldn't have to know what an idiot she was.

"That if you ever…" Tallulah's brow furrowed. "What's that noise?"

"Nothing. Like I told you, I'm kinda busy here." April opened the door wider but Tallulah ignored her and walked down the hallway. Damn her supernatural hearing.

"What the hell? There's water all over the place!"

April came up behind her. "You're right. I hadn't noticed. I wonder what it could be?"

Tallulah headed unerringly to the closed utility-room door. She jerked it open. "The damn hose is broken. You have to turn off the faucet behind the machine."

"Oh."

The silence stretched between them.

"I didn't know that," she added.

Tallulah was acting strange. Her mouth twitched and her shoulders shook. Finally, she slapped a hand on the machine, threw her head back and laughed. Deep, full-throated chuckles until her eyes ran and she hunched forward, clutching her stomach.

"It's not *that* funny."

Tallulah straightened and swiped at her eyes. "Right. The hardwood in the hall will get damaged if we don't clean it up right away."

Hard to believe Tallulah was helping. Probably helping

merely to save Chulah's floor—not April's pride. "There's no more towels. Should I get the bedspread?"

"Good idea. I'll run out to the garage and get Chulah's wet vac."

April grabbed the bedspread, noting Tallulah's familiarity with Chulah's house. Did Chulah still have feelings for her? He hadn't immediately pushed Tallulah away when she'd kissed him last night at the door. There had been a good five seconds before the kiss stopped. Five seconds of agony.

Forty minutes later, April sat at the table and watched Tallulah expertly make them tea, looking right at home in Chulah's kitchen. April rubbed her sore temples, feeling cranky and out of sorts again. Which was ridiculous considering Chulah's kindness last night and then receiving unexpected help from the person she would have least expected it from.

Tallulah set two steaming cups on the table. "Lucky you, the herbal crap from Annie is all yours. It might help your headache, but I'd suggest at least two spoonfuls of sugar to make it palatable."

"You really think it can help?" she asked, stirring in the sugar.

"Couldn't hurt. You're bound to feel some aftereffects from the untethering."

She could only hope the effects weren't permanent. She'd felt more than fine last night in Chulah's arms, but now the hurt was kicking in. Adjustment to this new life would be tricky. Her throat closed up; would she ever fly again? Ever see the beauty of the Fae realm once more? She couldn't, wouldn't, dwell on that now with Tallulah here.

"So you overheard everything?" she asked, sipping the herbal brew.

"I try to stay aware of everything that happens around

me. It's part of being a shadow hunter. You notice the smallest details. A skill that could save your life one night."

April played with the frayed edge of the tablecloth. It had been awfully kind of Tallulah to help, but she was bone-tired and wanted nothing more than to crawl back into bed. Or a hot bath. Her face warmed remembering last night's bath and Chulah's lovemaking.

"I can guess where your mind's wandering."

April sputtered midswallow. She coughed and took another long sip of tea. At least there was no hiccup, no slight levitation as before. "So why did you come today in the first place? You said you had something to say."

Tallulah drummed her nails on the table, apparently considering her words. "I've seen the way Chulah acts around you. How worried he was about you last night. I don't want you to hurt him."

"The way you did when he asked you to marry him?"

Tallulah flinched. "Have to admit I didn't see the proposal coming. I thought we were…close friends."

"Friends? Is that what you call it when you exchange long goodbye kisses with a man? I saw you wrap yourself around him at the door last night. If you want Chulah, tell him. Don't keep giving him mixed messages. That isn't fair."

"You're right."

April opened her mouth to argue and then snapped it shut. Tallulah actually agreed with her.

"I have to admit I was a little jealous when I saw Chulah fawning over you." She held up a hand. "Yes, it was stupid of me. It's just… I've always known Chulah was there for me. No matter what the problem. After Bo died—"

"Who's Bo?"

"The love of my life. Always was, always will be. Nalusa

Falaya killed him." Her voice was clipped, but April heard
the pain that lay beneath the words.

"Chulah helped me through some of the worst. He's the
best friend I ever had."

"Only a friend? Wait. Don't answer that. It's none of
my business."

"I wish it were more than that, but the spark wasn't
there for me. I don't think it was for Chulah either, only he
didn't realize it until you came along. He's a good man—
attractive, brave, everything a woman could wish for. But
he isn't Bo. No one will ever be as dear to me as him."

Who knew? Tallulah had a soft side, a womanly side capable of great love. "I'm sorry for your loss," she said softly.

Tallulah took a long swallow of tea and set the cup down,
shoulders back and chin high. "Don't pity me. I hate that."

"Pity you?" April snorted. "No way. I'm jealous of you."

Tallulah's eyes narrowed. "Because I kissed Chulah last
night?"

"Why did you do that?" She drew a ragged breath, curious but hurting.

"Vanity." Tallulah took a long sip of tea. "Condemn
me all you want. I was curious whether or not Chulah still
desired me."

April sighed. "And he did."

Tallulah shook her head, earrings dancing in the black
curtain of her hair. "No. He was testing the waters, same
as me. The spark was gone."

A heaviness lifted from her chest; she felt light enough
to fly again. "Thanks for telling me that."

Tallulah stood and gathered their cups. "I'll put up the
wet vac. If you're up to it, I'll drive you to your place to
pick up some clothes."

April stood as well. Whether it was the herbal tea, Tallulah's kindness or some combination of both, her headache

was tolerable. "A change of clothes would be awesome." She hesitated. "Are you going to tell Chulah I almost ruined his cabin the moment he left me alone in it?"

Tallulah winked. "It's our secret."

"Awesome. I'll try to see if there's some pants of his I can wear to cover my legs." April bounced out of the room, but stuck her head out around the corner. "Hey, did I ever satisfy you that I won't hurt Chulah?"

"Yes. Just had to make sure your heart was in the right place. Hurry up and let's go. You don't want his stepmom and little sister to drop by and find you roaming the cabin semi-naked."

Despite the dozens of people crowded into Tombi and Annie's cabin, the mood was solemn and quiet. April, Joanna and Annie busied themselves cleaning the kitchen. It had taken hours of cooking and serving, but everyone had feasted on a traditional meal of hunter's stew, corn fritters and colorful dumplings made from grape juice. The shadow hunters would need their strength for the long night ahead.

From the den came a murmur of deep voices as the hunters strategized for battle. April tried to take comfort in the strength and number of their voices, but her nerves were frayed. What if Chulah were injured...or killed? A dish slipped through her hand and crashed to the floor.

"Sorry." She slipped Annie an apologetic look.

"No problem. I'll sweep up the pieces."

"Here, let me take over." Joanna handed her a kitchen towel. "You can wipe down the table and counters and I'll finish drying the dishes."

She set to work, trying to eavesdrop on the conversation of the hunters, but could decipher only a few words here and there. Joanna and Annie calmly went about their normal household chores. Only the pinched lines of their mouths and absent look in their eyes betrayed their concern.

April twisted the towel in her hands. "How can you take this so calmly? Chulah and Tombi are preparing to confront Hoklonote. I'm worried sick. Do you ever get used to this?"

"Never," Joanna said. "My Nita was a hunter all his life. I dreaded every full moon. That's why I made my own sons vow to never join the shadow hunters. Chulah didn't listen, though. That one is headstrong."

Sounded like her other sons were cowards, but April bit her tongue.

"I worry, too," Annie said. "But it's part of who Tombi is and I wouldn't change a thing about him." She finished sweeping up the broken bits of china and emptied them into the waste bin. "Besides, I know he's a formidable opponent and I'm confident in his fighting ability. That helps."

April stared out the window at the full moon, swollen and potent and beckoning the hunters to battle. "Your husband's name was Nita?" she asked Joanna.

"Yes. It's Choctaw for *bear*." Her sharp face softened in reverie and her hands slowed as she dried a plate. "He was like a bear, too. Big and strong and fearless."

Guilt lanced through April. "You still miss him."

"Yes. But at least his death was merciful."

"Merciful?" The man had been left alone for hours to die from a rattlesnake bite. A slow dying that she was responsible for.

"He went quickly. A freak accident in the woods."

"Quickly?" Her brain spun as she tried to grasp the implications of the news.

Joanna pursed her lips. "Feeling bad again? Sit down. We're about done with everything."

She sank into a chair, light-headed with shock. All these years she'd blamed herself for his death. Wasted years of guilt and shame. "I thought… Chulah said…he should have gotten medical attention quicker."

"Wouldn't have made a bit of difference. Nita had a bad heart and was on borrowed time. Chulah always takes too much upon himself. He's not to blame."

And neither am I. She felt the blood drain from her face.

"Have you been drinking the tonic I left you?" Annie asked. "You're so pale. Let me brew you a cup. Better make it two cups. It's going to be a long night."

Chulah should have told her. He knew she blamed herself, had been tormented about it for years. Yet instead of telling her the truth, he'd been angry when he discovered she was the cause of the delay in the woods. Had let her keep believing the worst.

It's not my fault. April put her head in her hands, letting the truth seep into her mind and heart. Relief, anger, regret—a dizzy swirl of conflicting emotions.

"Take this." Annie placed a cup of herbal tea in front of her. "It will make you feel better."

Dutifully, she took a long sip. Yes, she needed fortification to give Chulah a piece of her mind. Anger stiffened her spine and she rose from the table, aware that Joanna and Annie exchanged looks.

She strode into the den, where all the men—and Tallulah—ceased their conversation and regarded her curiously. Her eyes immediately settled on Chulah. "May I speak with you a moment?"

Without waiting for his answer, she marched outside and went on the porch. The screen door creaked open.

"Something wrong?" he asked.

She whirled around. "Your dad would have died whether or not I enchanted you that day. Joanna said he died almost instantly."

Chulah didn't deny it, nor did he defend himself. Instead, he met the challenge of her stare head-on.

"Well?" she demanded. "Why didn't you say so? You knew how bad I felt about the whole thing."

"Because the doctor who reported that was an old family friend. He might have told Joanna Dad died quickly merely to pacify her and ease her suffering."

"He had a bad heart, Chulah. You didn't mention that either."

"So?"

"Damn. Why are you so stubborn? I don't believe a doctor would lie to ease anyone's suffering. And with your dad's bad heart, the snake's venom was too much for his body."

His jaw clenched. "So everyone says."

"And you're still determined to believe the worst. To make me suffer...hell, to make yourself suffer as well. And for no good reason."

"I have every reason to be bitter," he said tersely. "I lost two hours of my life that day. Do you know what that feels like? I convinced myself I was either crazy or, worse, a coward."

"And do you know what it felt like for me? Every day I lived in shame, convinced a man died because of me."

"What do you want me to say? That you win? That you suffered more than me?"

"Nobody wins at this. It's not a game," she said softly. And after all, she was the one who had set it all in motion with her selfishness. "Is this something we can ever get past?" she asked. "Or will the memory of that day always stand between us?"

He leaned against the porch railing and stared into the inky black night. "I can't honestly say. I'd like to say it won't, but I'd be lying."

April put her hand in his. "I'm sorry. I'm the one at fault. Can you ever forgive me?"

"I realize you didn't set out to harm anyone." He squeezed her hand.

It wasn't a real declaration of forgiveness, but she'd take it. The night reeked of danger and soon they would march into the heart of the evil. Other, kinder, words should be spoken on a night such as this one. "I love you, Chulah," she whispered.

He swiftly gathered her in his arms and held her tight. Kissing her until nothing else existed but the safe haven of their entwined bodies.

A discreet cough interrupted them.

"Shall we get on with tonight's business?" Steven bounded up the steps. "I've brought an army of Fae like we agreed upon."

April searched the woods. Sure enough, dozens of fairy lights ringed the treetops. "Guess Hoklonote's fire convinced them they needed to get their hands dirty in battle."

Steven avoided her gaze. "We can discuss the specifics inside."

Suspicion flared. If this was a giant ruse, it wouldn't be the first time the Fae were guilty of deception. "Are they really on board with helping the hunters, or is the light show a trick?"

"Of course we're on board." Steven addressed his answer to Chulah. "Let's get on with it."

Heat fanned her cheeks. "Why won't you look at me?"

He continued to ignore her. "We can scout ahead and—"

"The lady asked you a question," Chulah interrupted. "Answer her."

Steven flicked her the barest of glances. "There's no trick." He faced Chulah again. "We're ready to go."

"Too bad. We aren't. We haven't even started our pre-battle ritual." He put an arm around April and gestured to the door. "Go on in. If you're hungry, we have stew and corn bread."

The weight of Chulah's arm, the show of his support, eased her embarrassment. Steven gave a terse nod and left them alone.

"He sure was acting strange," she muttered. "Like he was mad at me. Although I can't imagine why."

"Men react to pressure in different ways. Some turn outward and want to hang out and talk with friends, a few will have a drink to take the edge off, and some like Steven withdraw into themselves and even act like jerks."

It felt like something more was missing in the explanation, but what did she know about fighting battles? Sure, she'd intervened a few times to save Chulah from a will-o'-the-wisp or one of the birds of the night—but it wasn't *expected* of her, and she'd never deliberately set out to confront a shadow spirit.

He opened the door and she entered the den. "If you say so. I'd kind of like a drink myself, but I remember how alcohol made me loopy the day we met. I'll need my wits."

"Need your wits for what?" he asked, shutting the door.

"For the battle tonight," she called over her shoulder. She smiled warmly at the men as she passed into the kitchen. They sure had gotten quiet all of a sudden. Acted a bit stunned, too. Perhaps Steven's sour mood had infected the hunters.

In the kitchen, Annie was silently laughing, hand covering her mouth. Joanna shook her head, mouth twitching in some secret amusement.

"What?" April asked. "Have I missed a joke?"

Annie pulled herself together. "Let's go in the bedroom where we can talk without being interrupted."

Miffed, April followed them down the hall and to a

spare bedroom. Annie shut the door behind her and sat on the bed, patting the mattress, while Joanna sat in a rocking chair.

"Here's what you need to know. Our men are old-school. Extremely protective. They don't want us fighting alongside them."

"But that's so...so archaic."

"True. Believe me, I agree. And I'm working to change Tombi's attitude."

"Tallulah is one of them," she pointed out. "If she can, I can."

"Tallulah was born with shadow-hunting ability and trained along with Tombi."

"I have abilities, too..." No, actually she had none. Grady had royally screwed her out of her Fae birthright. "Scratch that. But there has to be another way I can help. I won't be left behind to wait and wonder."

Joanna spoke up. "The shadow hunters' wives aren't shrinking-violet sort of women. We aren't good at waiting and wondering."

April glanced back and forth between the women. "Then how...?"

"There are other ways," Annie said in her quiet fashion. "Sneakier ways."

"Such as?"

Annie shrugged. "We follow behind them on nights we know there is high danger. Like tonight."

"But...don't they hear you?"

Joanna rocked, looking calm enough to be discussing the menu for dinner. "I've been caught a time or two over the years. Each time, I told Nita I'd never do it again."

"That's great. But they generally go their separate ways in the woods to scope different prearranged perimeters."

"Chulah told you all this?" Joanna asked. "They're usually tight-lipped about their methods."

April squirmed. Joanna couldn't know she'd observed them firsthand. "Uh-hum," she muttered noncommittally. "But my question is—when the men scatter, how can you find them?"

"Easy," Annie broke in. "They end up in the same place every time. If something major goes down, you can bet they'll wind up on their sacred ground. There's an ancient tree there, and inside of it, Nalusa Falaya is forcibly contained. You've heard of him, right?"

"Of course. He's the worst bayou shadow spirit, the one Hoklonote wants to free."

A red flicker of light strobed in from the front window. Annie rose from the bed and motioned them to the window.

Outside, a bonfire roared in the yard. The hunters gathered around it, their faces set with deadly intent. By the tree line, where field met forest, dozens of fairies hovered. A drum sounded.

"It won't be long now," Annie said softly.

Chapter 18

The drumbeat echoed in his gut like the roar of the ocean on the sea breeze. Hoyopahihla, their ancient war dance, set his hunter senses soaring. His legs and feet automatically shuffled. Back and forth, side to side, left right, right left right. Slowly, every hunter moved around the bonfire's circle until each had returned to his original position.

The drum ceased its beating at once.

Chulah stared into the fire, hypnotized by the crackling embers, the licking flames leaping higher in the night sky, the blue core dancing to its own living rhythm. Tombi started the chanting. Old war songs, hoyopa-taloah, that their ancestors had sung through the ages. He sensed the connection to them, an unbroken link.

His father was nearby, with him in spirit. Not as clear as when his dad appeared and spoke to him on a vision quest. But in these ceremonies, his father's spirit manifested as a warm, settled presence deep in Chulah's heart.

Silence abruptly descended again. Their energy quickened with anticipation. Waiting.

Tombi opened his mouth.

Chulah knew what was coming. They all did. And yet that didn't lessen the startling impact of the nightmarish war whoop. The hoyopa tasaha that signaled time for battle.

They each joined in, a chilling chorus of deadly intent.

The ritual was over. He was ready. From here out, the hunters would maintain as profound a silence as possible— gliding through the gloomy depths of the bayou like warriors of old.

Chulah stared at the trees that shielded the good and the evil within its borders. For years, all he had known was the evil side, the Ishkitini, will-o'-the-wisps, Hoklonote and Nalusa Falaya. But April had come into his life. And there was a beauty he'd never suspected that lived in the heart of the woods. A fairy realm.

Perhaps not "good" according to mankind's ethical compass, but a different dimension with their own rules, filled with beings capable of much beauty and much cruelty.

Just like humans.

Tombi raised his arm and stepped out of the circle. Chulah fell into step behind him and the others aligned in their place with military precision. A single line, marching in the same footsteps of the preceding hunter.

Steven walked outside the line, muttering, "There's no room for me. What the hell am I supposed—"

Chulah frowned and raised an index finger to his lips. Damn it, he'd told the little man to stand at the end of the line after the ritual ceased. Either Steven was insulted at being last, or he had a memory as small as the no-see-um insects that plagued the bayou in summer. Hard to have respect for someone who mistreated April. Once he'd discovered she'd lost her Fae essence, he had no use for her. Steven was as big an elitist as the other Fae who scorned him as a halfling. Actually, he was even worse. A hypocrite. He despised the Fae for their denunciation, but executed the same attitude at the now-powerless April.

Impatiently, he motioned Steven to cut ahead of him in line. At least this way, he could keep an eye on the little man. It was in the Fae's best interest not to cross the hunters, but Chulah had a healthy skepticism toward all not part of the hunter brotherhood. Besides, even innocent errors in judgment could be fatal.

Now as one, they filed across the field, away from the warmth of the dying fire and toward the dark, hidden core of the woods. With every step, Chulah sank deeper into relying on his hunter instincts. Each noise and smell increased in significance. The crunch of frost beneath them, the lone howl of a coyote, the Gulf wind cutting tunnels of chill in the swamp. The scent of moonlight and water and soil as familiar to him as his own heartbeat.

They walked the main path, headed due west. As arranged, the small, glowing fairy lights streaked ahead and then blinked out to blend in the dark. First sight of a wisp or owl, they would kill it. Should it be a large cluster, one of them would return to the hunters and communicate the location to Steven.

An illuminating flash of blue and green erupted and then faded, followed by a thin curl of smoke spiraling upward, and at its tip, a clear white spirit ascending to the After Life.

Score one for the fairies.

The silence weighed on Chulah. The quieter the night, the fewer attacks along the path, only meant more concentrated evil gathered in one location. It signaled that they awaited the hunters on Choctaw sacred ground by the venerable ancient tree housing the trapped Nalusa Falaya and the kidnapped fairy queen. Waiting, biding their time, ready to strike.

So be it.

The only question remaining was whether the shadow spirits would try to cut down their ranks at the edge of the consecrated ground, or if they would wait until they actually set foot on sacred soil. Hatred burned in Chulah's chest at the creatures' arrogance in desecrating the land.

Nalusa must be writhing in the tree, excited, reveling in the nearby evil power of those who would once again obey his bidding upon release. The old shape-shifter would be twisting and coiling his snake form inside the cramped hollow of the tree. Hissing, its forked tongue flicking in and out of the flat roof of his venomous mouth, testing the environment and priming its poison. Unlike a true rattler, Nalusa's eyes were capable of glowing red. They would shine like banked embers in his black prison, alert for the first opportunity to escape and strike.

Their best chance was to capture Hoklonote before he loosed the monster. Thankfully, Hoklonote was ignorant of the words that held such power. His best chance was to force it from them, killing each hunter one by one until they broke.

Chulah straightened, shoulders back, chin raised.

He would not break. Not ever.

Tombi signaled, pointing both his hands outward in both directions. Silently, they changed tactic, spreading out in a horseshoe formation.

A foreign energy form from above niggled at Chulah's awareness. He poked Steven and pointed a finger at the treetops. Steven nodded and tapped his chest, and pointed upward as well. The fairies were with them. Chulah could only hope that Hoklonote wasn't aware they had joined forces.

Tombi dropped his hands to his sides and the hunters advanced as a single unit, quiet as stalking jaguars.

Evil tainted the air in a malevolent miasma, worse than Chulah had ever encountered. The wisps were responsible for most of it. That was one of their powers, to invade a man's thoughts and smother his hopes, replacing dreams with misery and dread. It could lead to a broken spirit or suicide or betrayal of one's loyalties. As toxic as chlorine gas. The wisps' own version of chemical warfare. Once you got too close to one, you were vulnerable. That was why he and the others shot them from a distance.

Something niggled at the edge of his senses. Chulah glanced around and behind, then looked up. Dozens of Ishkitini swarmed.

A screech pierced the silence. The owl signal to strike. Chulah loaded a stone in his slingshot and waited. The owls needed to come a few yards closer for him to launch his most accurate shot.

Almost there. Another couple of yards. His tight biceps and forearms quivered with tension and anticipation. The Ishkitini kept coming, close enough now to smell the rot and decay they feasted upon.

Chulah drew the slingshot back one more inch and released his shot. A thud and an Ishkitini dropped. Another bird was a foot away, flying directly at him, feet and talons extended, ready to sink its claws in tender flesh. His flesh. Quick as lightning, he loaded another stone and pulled back. In all directions, he heard the whir of rocks speeding through the sky and thudding against Ishkitini as his fellow hunters attacked as well.

And then the unexpected happened.

Pastel lights flickered among the Ishkitini and they dropped from the sky at the hunters' feet. Dead and undangerous. The half a dozen remaining birds flew off, screeching in alarm. That ought to tick off Hoklonote. Nalusa could command every Ishkitini to fight to the death, but

Hoklonote didn't equal Nalusa's power. The moment the Ishkitini caught on to the Fae ambush, the few left had enough self-preservation instinct to get the hell away from the slaughter.

Steven nudged his side, a smirk of pride lighting his ruddy face. Chulah nodded an acknowledgment of a mission well accomplished. The fairy ambush had worked. But he knew better than to celebrate too soon. The owls were only the first line of defense.

Next up, the will-o'-the-wisps.

Sure enough, large columns of flickering orbs appeared, the trapped spirits inside them a pulsing teal glow. The wisps were parasitic, needing their victims' souls to provide a life-giving heartbeat. Once a spirit escaped, the wisp died moments later, extinguished. Again, Chulah quickly loaded his slingshot and began shooting. But they were so outnumbered. The fairies ambushed as best they could from the back and sides, but the wisps had seen them attack the Ishkitini, so the surprise factor was lost.

Teal flares illuminated the woods as a few wisps were killed. But yet they still advanced.

Chulah's eyes watered and his throat constricted. They were getting too close. Way, way too close. They'd all die if they came too much nearer.

The wisps stopped, less than ten yards from where he and the others held their line. Why would they do this?

Ah; he started to slap his forehead. Hoklonote, of course. The shadow spirit had stopped them, was holding them in check as a threat. He still needed the hunters alive in order to free Nalusa Falaya. Rather, he needed Tombi alive.

Torture time.

The column of wisps parted down the middle, like the parting of the Red Sea. The wizened figure of Hoklonote hobbled between them until he stood before the hunters, wisps guarding his back.

Leaning on a hickory cane, he made his way to Tombi. "Say the words that will free Nalusa." His voice was wobbly and weak. To Chulah, he more resembled an old gnome than a shadow spirit.

"I don't know what you're talking about," Tombi said.

"Don't lie to me. As leader of the shadow hunters, you alone know the words to unbind Nalusa from the tree. Do it."

"I will not."

Hoklonote smiled. "Very well. The misery of your hunters will only make the wisps stronger. And amuse me as well."

His heavy-lidded eyes darted to Chulah. "You first."

April bit down on her lower lip to stifle the scream. Annie laid a hand on her arm and shook her head, cautioning silence.

Easy for her to do; it wasn't Tombi facing Hoklonote's wrath at the moment. April glanced at Joanna, who glared unflinchingly at Hoklonote's back.

April parted the underbrush slightly for a better view, never loosening her grip on the black mojo bag Annie gave them before they ventured out after the men. She needed all the supernatural protection she could muster.

"Can't you do anything?" she whispered fiercely to Annie.

Annie squeezed her hand. "Have faith."

Chulah stepped forward. Hoklonote raised his cane; a laser of white-blue light extended from its tip like a lightning bolt. It struck Chulah's left shoulder and the stench of burned flesh had April on her feet and running to Chulah's side. "Stop it! Leave him alone!"

All eyes were upon her. One frozen moment in time. It was all she had. Her eyes lit on Steven. "Call in the fairies!"

He scowled. "They don't need us yet."

Bastard. So the Fae were going to hang back now that the going was tough and Hoklonote's power was concentrated in one place.

April lifted her head and raised her hands skyward. "Grady's alive and working with Hoklonote. Our threat is greater than ever. Intervene now or die!"

"April? What the hell." Chulah awakened from his stunned stupor and whisked her behind his back with his good arm.

Chaos broke out in a boom of sound and color. Lights in every rainbow shade flashed and popped. Shouts and whistles rang like cannon fire and the air became polluted with toxins. Her eyes watered and she swiped at them with the sleeve of her jacket. Burying her head in Chulah's back, she coughed and drew a labored breath. She didn't care if this was the end of the world. Better here, holding Chulah, than hiding behind a bush like a coward and watching him suffer and die.

"Get down," he said with a hiss. "Go back and hide if you can."

April crouched, but no way was she running for cover. Quickly, she gathered handfuls of the smooth river rocks the hunters had stacked in a large duffel bag. They could come in handy later, so she stuffed them in her jacket pockets.

The hunters might still lose, but at least the Fae had entered the battle and she didn't have to sit and watch Chulah being tortured. The Fae struck at the wisps, decimating their ranks from behind, as the hunters loaded and reloaded their slingshots in a volley of attack. But where was Hoklonote?

April peeked from between Chulah's legs. Tombi had

wrestled the little weasel to the ground. His biceps bulged as he tried to force Hoklonote's arms behind his back. The shadow spirit had a surprising physical strength she wouldn't have suspected from his aged, wrinkled face and hunchbacked body. Hoklonote's hand crept forward on the damp, cold ground—fingers outstretched. His cane was a mere six inches from his fingers. Hoklonote muttered some words and the cane began to inch toward his twisted fingers.

April looked around. The other hunters had their eyes forward, preoccupied fighting the wisps. Tombi's concentration centered on tying a rope around Hoklonote's right hand, unmindful of his left.

The cane moved another inch closer. If he got that cane, he'd swing it wide, carving a death arc through the shadow hunters. And Chulah was the closest target.

If anyone could prevent that—she'd have to be the one.

April squeezed through Chulah's calves and ran, crouching and coughing. She dropped to the ground by Hoklonote and grabbed the stick as his fingers began to curl over the hickory handle.

It burned her palm. The cane pulsed and sputtered in her hand like a live electrical wire—yet she tightened her grip, determined to hold on. Hot tingles shot through from hand to arm to shoulder.

She would not let go.

Tombi grabbed Hoklonote's left arm and the spirit screeched—a long, piercing howl of rage. Tombi tied his arms together behind his back.

And still, she held on to the cane, afraid Hoklonote's power was capable of drawing it to him, the rightful owner of such dark magic.

Chulah bent down and wrapped one large hand over the cane, and with the other he pried her fingers from their death grip. "Let go now. I have it."

His face was grim, eyes red and swollen from the toxins in the air. A cloud of pain dimmed them, yet his jaw and lips were firm and unyielding against the agony.

"I'll hold it. You're needed to fight the wisps."

"Do you trust me?" he asked.

"With my life."

"Then let go."

April withdrew her hand and he gave her a slight nod. "Good job."

Chulah stood, flourishing the cane at Hoklonote. "Call off your army."

Hoklonote glared. "My cane will burn your hand in two before I'd agree to your demand."

"You'll burn first." Chulah tapped the cane on Hoklonote's right shoulder, burning a hole through the spirit's shirt. Hoklonote screamed in agony. Chulah raised the cane, ready to strike again. "Call them off," he warned.

"Hell no," Hoklonote muttered between clenched teeth. Beads of perspiration ran down his weathered cheeks, but his eyes burned with hatred.

Again, Chulah lowered the cane, this time striking Hoklonote's left shoulder. April cringed at the sound and smell of singed flesh.

"Stop! I'll do it," he wailed.

Chulah held the hickory cane at his side.

Hoklonote screamed out a series of words and syllables that sounded like gibberish to April.

But it worked.

The explosions of light and smoke ceased, allowing the stiff wind to clear the way to reveal a better picture of the battleground.

Nearly half of the shadow hunters lay on the ground, moaning. Joanna and Annie crawled on the ground between the bodies, tending to the wounds as best they could.

The columns of wisps, reduced to merely a fourth of their previous numbers, retreated backward.

Fairies glowed like lanterns in the black night, ascending from the ground up to the treetops.

Chulah shifted the cane from one hand to the next. He was still in pain.

"The cane's burning Chulah," she shouted at Tombi. "Do something."

Tombi motioned to the shadow hunters who remained standing. "Stand guard around the cane. Chulah, lay it on the ground."

He released the cane only once the other hunters encircled it. It writhed on the ground at their feet like a snake set on fire.

One of the hunters, she believed it was Poloma, raised a dagger and sliced it through the cane, as if it were made of butter instead of hard hickory. The other hunters did the same, cutting the cane into a pile of splinters that were matchbook in size.

Hoklonote wept in fury, kicking his short, spindly legs repeatedly into Tombi's shins. If it hurt, Tombi didn't show it. Two of the hunters hurried to Hoklonote and bound his ankles.

Steven scurried out of a ditch where he'd evidently been observing the fray from a safe position. Brushing mud from his jacket, he strutted to Hoklonote, puffing out his chest as if he'd done something.

A foot out, he jabbed a finger in Hoklonote's face. "Release the queen."

"I don't have your queen."

A swarm of hissing erupted from above. The fairies in the trees buzzed like a hive of angry hornets.

"Liar. She's trapped in the tree with Nalusa Falaya. Release her at once."

Sure. Steven was good at commanding orders when the enemy was bound in front of him and the shadow hunters were at his back. And to think she'd once felt sorry for him when Steven claimed that he cared for her. How quickly his affection had cooled once she'd lost her Fae essence.

Nothing showed a man's true worth like a battle. April glanced at Chulah. Despite the gaping wound in his left shoulder, and burned and blistered hands, he stood tall, silent and regal.

Hoklonote's eyes narrowed. "Perhaps we can make a trade, eh? Release me and I'll release the queen."

"You go first," Steven said, folding his arms across his chest.

Tombi glared at Steven. "If you think you can waltz in here at the last second and take over—after everyone else has fought your battle—then you can think again," he said in disgust.

Steven's face flushed. "What's your plan?"

But Tombi's gaze had flickered past Steven to where Annie and Joanna were bandaging the few remaining hunters who hadn't rejoined their group. "What the hell are you doing here?" he bellowed.

"Tending the wounded," Annie said, nonplussed. She waved a hand in his direction. "Continue on doing your thing."

Several of the hunters snickered and Tombi glared in their direction. "This isn't the first time our women have shown up unannounced," he reminded them. "In fact, I think all of your wives and girlfriends and sisters and such have shown up at some point."

Chulah shook his head slightly at Tombi and pointed to Hoklonote.

"Back to the matter at hand," Tombi muttered.

April held her breath. If the hunters tethered Hoklonote

with Nalusa inside their tree, it would mean they'd never have to fight on such a large scale again. On the other hand, they did promise to help the Fae.

With the notable exception of Steven, the Fae had valiantly assisted the hunters tonight. Without their help, they very well might have lost to Hoklonote.

Yes, the Fae had treated her unkindly most of the time. But the Fae realm was home, they had raised her, and not everything about her life had sucked. There were moments of incredible beauty and magic, the taste of nectar waters, flying by moonlight…

"We always honor our agreements. The Fae will have their queen restored." Tombi forced Hoklonote to turn in the direction of their sacred tree. "Move it."

Hoklonote gave up the fight, a pleased smile hovering on his thin, bluish lips. Still, they progressed the twelve or so yards slowly, everyone else falling in behind. Even the injured hunters who had been lying on the ground stumbled to their feet and limped forward. At the base of the tree, they formed a horseshoe.

Poloma stepped away from the group holding the splintered remains of the hickory cane bundled in his jacket. He dumped the wood in a heap and dropped a match on the pile. It roared to life in an instant, much stronger than a normal fire would have done.

"My cane!" Hoklonote screamed. "You didn't have to burn it."

She could almost feel sorry for him. After all, he was old and could barely walk on those twisted, tiny feet.

"We're not stupid," Chulah said. "This was the only way to kill the black magic you stored inside it."

"You're lucky we aren't throwing you on the fire," Steven said with a growl.

Yep. That fairy could be pretty bold once an opponent was crushed.

"Now release the queen," Tombi ordered.

"You first."

Tombi jerked on the rope binding Hoklonote's hands. "Oh, hell no, little guy."

Hoklonote delivered a withering scowl at Tombi, but began mumbling. Again, April couldn't decipher a word he spoke. Would he release their queen? April shuddered to think of her enclosed inside a tree with Nalusa. What a nightmare.

The cypress tree shook and rattled as if an earthquake had erupted underneath its deep roots. A misty fog enveloped the tree, so thick she could discern only the barest outline of its trunk and branches. The fog cleared.

The queen emerged, disheveled and unable to stand straight. Nevertheless, there was regality in the lift of her chin and an unmistakable dignity in her composed features.

The fairies immediately surrounded her, a flying aura of glittering pixie light.

And then they were no more. April blinked at the sudden darkness. She glanced back over her shoulder. Steven had disappeared with them.

April shook her head. They hadn't so much as said thank you before leaving to return to their world. A tiny ball of hurt lumped her throat. They hadn't even looked at *her*. After all she had done, she was still unworthy in their eyes. She'd never be good enough.

Chulah threw an arm around her shoulders, and she snuggled into his warmth and comfort. From the vantage of his protective strength, she watched as Tombi took out his dagger and unbound Hoklonote. "You're free."

The shadow spirit rubbed his wrists, frowning. "But my cane is destroyed," he complained. "Hardly fair."

Tombi shrugged. "You know what they say—all's fair in love and war."

Hoklonote faced each one of them down with a snarl. "You'll pay for this one day. Every one of you. Mark my words."

"You're full of it," Chulah said with a laugh. "It's over. Without Nalusa and without your cane, your influence over the wisps and Ishkitini is minimal. You're no threat to us."

So the balance of power had shifted.

Weariness washed over her as the adrenaline seeped out of her bones, leaving her cold and so very, very tired.

Hoklonote lifted his chin, obviously trying to hold on to some small shred of dignity. He turned his back on them and headed to the safety of the woods. By the Choctaw sacred tree, he patted the trunk. "Not this time, Nalusa."

"Not ever," Chulah vowed beside her. He kissed the top of her head. "Tired?"

"Extremely." She gazed at him through a fringe of lashes. "Are you angry I followed you out here tonight?"

"How could I be when you saved our ass?" He kissed her again. The small knot of unhappiness from the fairies' snub unraveled. This was where she belonged. Where she wanted to be.

She yawned. "Let's go home."

The men all shook hands and April smiled wanly at Joanna and Annie and gave a little wave. The first lights of dawn rose over the horizon—blue and purple and coral. It had been a long night.

But it was over.

Chulah's left shoulder burned like sin. Should have asked Annie for something. He'd catch her in the morning. For now, he wanted a hot bath, a soft mattress and April lying by his side. Despite the pain and his own tired bones, he kept her propped up, absorbing her weight as much as he could. She was practically sleepwalking.

He smiled down at her silver-lavender hair and inhaled her sweet scent of violets. He'd secretly been afraid that the Fae would whisk her away when all was over, but they hadn't so much as glanced April's way. Did this mean she was staying with him?

The question had been haunting him for some time. Now that the battle had been fought and won, he still didn't have a definitive answer. Chulah squeezed her shoulder. He'd make love to her so passionately tonight she'd never want to leave.

The light from his cabin shone through the clearing. Another ten minutes and they could rest.

A stirring rustled through the dead grass and Chulah stopped, immediately alert. It happened again, louder, closer. That was no deer. He gently shook April. "Run for the house," he whispered in her ear.

April jolted and turned wide eyes on him. "Why? Wh—"

"Just go," he urged. "I'll be along shortly."

The rustling grew to a sound like an oncoming train. Ahead, the grass weighed down as an invisible object bore down upon them.

"Grady!" April cried.

A ball of light materialized from the darkness, morphing into a human form. Chulah drew his dagger from his belt. "Run," he yelled at April, without letting his eyes leave Grady's.

Grady laughed. "How sweet."

"You hurt her," Chulah growled.

"She looks perfectly fine to me," he trilled. His face darkened. "Unfortunately."

"What do you want?" Chulah asked.

"What do I want?" he mimicked with a frown. "You both took everything I wanted. Everything I've dreamed of for years."

"Power?" Chulah guessed. His burned shoulder ached from gripping the dagger upright, but he dared not relax his stance.

"Exactly." He rubbed his jaw, considering. "I think I shall kill April first. Last time I stripped her powers. This time I'll rob her of life."

"Do you think I'd stand by and watch? You'll have to go through me to get to her."

"Chulah, don't," April pleaded. She faced Grady. "Take me and leave him alone."

Fool woman. Brave, but foolish. Chulah stepped in front of April, shielding her with his body. "Like I said. Me first."

"As you wish. This shouldn't take long." Grady snapped his fingers and a golden dagger glowed in his right hand. He lunged forward, slashing the knife in a downward arc. Chulah stepped aside at the last second, avoiding the blow. He raised his own dagger again, but halted, confused, at the empty space by his side.

"Looking for me?" Grady's figure emerged several yards away. The light from his aura flickered red.

Damnation. This was going to be his toughest fight ever. Chulah stole a quick glance over his shoulder, but April was nowhere in sight. Good; hopefully she'd made it to the cabin and would call Tombi for backup. That was her best bet for staying alive and his best shot at surviving this fight.

A whir of air brushed the left side of his head, lifting the hair from the back of his neck. Grady was near. Blindly, Chulah swung the dagger, hoping to make contact.

A laugh sounded from behind and he swung around.

"Close, but not close enough. You missed." Grady's form

lit up. "I'll make it a little fairer for you." He smirked. "See if—"

Chulah raced forward and jammed his dagger into... something. It wasn't firm enough to be skin and guts, but it wasn't the lightness of air either. A gurgling sounded a few yards away. Grady's figure reappeared at the edge of the tree line where he leaned against an oak. "Lucky jab," he said, his voice thin and weak. His glow oscillated from darkness to a pale light.

"More like superior fighting skills. And bravery."

Grady frowned and held up a hand. "You win. Okay? Just let me go. I'll leave you and April alone."

He didn't believe him for a moment. But his father had taught him to temper honor and bravery with mercy for a defeated foe.

Chulah stepped forward cautiously. "Why should I believe you?"

"Because you damn near killed me." Grady's voice was even weaker, the light from his aura dimmer.

Chulah dropped his knife to his side. "Remember that. If I ever catch you anywhere near April, I'll—"

A light blazed, blinding and confusing him. Chulah jumped back, but he was too late. A force knocked him to the ground, shaking the knife loose from his hand. He started to roll, but a heavy weight pinned his back to the ground. The light dimmed and Grady stood above him, grinning, dagger drawn.

This was it. He'd faced death many times in the past, but his luck had run out. He refused to shut his eyes. He'd meet it head-on, unblinking. With honor.

Grady's face crumpled in pain and he screamed once, falling to the ground. April stood before him, long hair blowing in the breeze, a bloody rock palmed in one hand.

His avenging angel.

Chulah hastily rose to his feet. "Are you okay, April?" She appeared to be in shock; her eyes were wide and vacant, her mouth slightly ajar. Before he could draw her into his arms, hundreds of pinpoints of light appeared low in the sky.

Dozens of them flew lower. The lights elongated and transmuted to men and women dressed in long, flowing robes, ostentatiously decorated with gold embroidery. He recognized their queen, still dressed all in black and silver, but looking fit and composed.

The queen held out her hand to April. "Well done," she said in a strong musical voice. "We anticipated the betrayer would seek you out. Now hand me the rock."

Wordlessly, April dropped it in the queen's hand.

The queen gazed down at her feet, where Grady lay motionless, with only the palest of gray light outlining his form.

"As queen of the Fae, I command that what remains of Grady's spirit come forth now, to be captured and bound by this stone. Forever and ever. As I wish, so mote it be."

Grady's form disintegrated into a thin, silver wisp of light that arose from the ground, only to be sucked into the rock. The queen calmly slipped the rock into the pocket of her robe and nodded at the stunned April. "You shall be well rewarded for your work here on earth. Even though you are less than a halfling."

The queen snapped her fingers and the lights went out.

A cool trick there, binding Grady, but Chulah didn't care for the condescending tone she used addressing April. Chulah squinted his eyes at the void before him. Where had she gone? "April?" he called out.

No answer.

"April?" he yelled again, louder.

But he knew. Calling her name over and over was useless. He'd known all along this would happen one day, had tried to prepare himself for the inevitable. And yet now that the moment had arrived, his heart felt flayed and burning.

The silence was deafening and mocked his fate. He was alone again.

He'd lost April forever.

Chapter 19

The queen's eyes drooped closed throughout the celebration feast. Despite just returning from her ordeal, certain customs had to be fulfilled, and a feast, complete with music and dancing, was expected by her subjects.

April could almost feel sorry for her, if not for the presumptuous manner in which she'd been whisked back to the Fae realm, without even asking if she wanted to return. She ached to be with Chulah. Not here among the chatter and glitter and all the court superficiality. She picked at the food on her plate, ignoring the fairies' veiled glances of curiosity that came her way from up and down the long table.

Several times this evening she'd approached the Council to request a return to land, but each time they'd put her off.

The queen raised her wineglass once again for one of the interminable toasts. "And here's to April for murdering the betrayer Grady."

Loud cheers and whistles and much glass clinking followed the remark. April winced. She wasn't proud of what she'd done. But when it came to defending Chulah, she'd stop at nothing.

The queen tapped her crystal glass with a silver spoon. "I am in a particularly gracious mood tonight." She pinned April with her gaze. "So gracious, that I am willing to extend a boon to our little halfling. Or maybe I should say our little *no-ling*."

Surprised murmurs erupted from all around. April stifled irritation at the insulting name. And why not a boon? Steven had received a pouch full of diamonds for his paltry role in rescuing the queen. And she'd done so much more. Yet with no magic power, she was even below the status of halfling in their Fae caste hierarchy.

"What shall it be, April?" the queen asked. "A position as lady-in-waiting in my court? Or perhaps a tiara of opals?"

April stood, breaking protocol. A queen's subject should never draw attention to herself in such a manner. Especially not while the queen was still seated. To hell with all that. All she desired was in an isolated cabin located in remote Bayou La Siryna.

The music stopped and all eyes were upon her.

"I want to go home, if it please you."

The queen's eyes flashed like moonbeams on obsidian. "You *are* home," she snapped.

Careful, April. You can't insult the fairy who has the power to grant your heart's wish.

She feigned modesty. "It's just… I don't belong here anymore. Grady stripped all my magic power. My Fae essence died at the untethering." She hung her head, playing it for all it was worth. "I don't belong with such esteemed company."

"Ah, I see." The queen's face smoothed. "We are pleased to suffer your company because of your noble deed. I believe the lady-in-waiting position is in order." Her voice sharpened. "Now be seated."

She should have asked for the opal tiara.

April sank back into her chair. A few fairies cast her smirks. Everyone knew that the court position was the absolute worst. A glorified maid job. Some honor. Besides, all she wanted, all she needed, was Chulah.

She'd settle for nothing less.

If they weren't willing to release her, she'd sneak out after they were all sleeping off the effects of the huge dinner and dancing. Her heart lifted with the resolve. She'd done it once before; she could do it again. With any luck, she'd be with Chulah before tomorrow's eve.

She nearly choked on the honey confection she'd placed in her mouth as she pictured Chulah. Alone and hurt. A full day in Fairy meant a week in human time. Did he think she'd deserted him?

Never.

She'd escape or die trying.

"It's over. Move on, Chulah."

Never. "Leave me alone. I'm doing fine."

Tallulah shook her head and sank to the ground in front of him, tucking her long legs underneath her. "What's your plan? Camp out here forever? April might not ever come back. Be realistic."

"She will. And when she comes, I'll be here."

"But you said yourself, the fairy tree always changes. How do you know this spot is where she'll come—if she comes?"

It was here he'd gone for his vision quest, and when it was over, April had appeared to him in the dusky dawn, and it was where he'd decided to throw his lot in with her and the Fae. And it was also here where he'd kissed her and because... Well, that was none of Tallulah's business. "Let me worry about that."

"But you've been out here a week."

"Your point?" He could live in the woods year-round if he wanted.

"What about your business?"

"J.B. can handle things at the shop for the time being."

She picked up a stick and poked at the fire in front of his tent. They sat together a spell in silence. But Tallulah being Tallulah, that didn't last long.

"Everybody's talking about you, you know. They're worried you've lost your head over a woman who is gone forever."

He shrugged and took a sip of water from his canteen.

"Don't you have any pride, Chulah?"

Pride didn't warm his bed or soothe his soul. Let them think he was crazy. Perhaps they were right, too. Still didn't matter. April would come back, and when she did he would be here to welcome her home and keep her safe.

Tallulah gave an exasperated sigh and stood. "Listen, I get it. I'm not the heartless bitch everyone seems to think I've become since Bo died. You cared for April. I actually started to warm to her myself. But it's over."

"I could say the same for you. Bo's dead. Get over it."

Tallulah's face paled.

"See? Not so easy, is it? Let me ask you something. If there was a chance Bo could return from the After Life, wouldn't you wait for him—no matter how long it took?"

"I'd wait forever." She brushed off the seat of her jeans with a terse motion. "Point made."

He nodded and screwed the cap back on the canteen. "Wasn't trying to hurt you. But as long as we're being bru-tally honest—Bo isn't coming back. He was my friend and a good man. But if Bo were here, he'd tell *you* to move on with your life."

Tallulah nodded and stared into the distance, her face and thoughts as inscrutable as ever. "Is there anything I can bring you? More food? Water? Blankets? Supposed to get pretty chilly tonight."

"I'm good. Tell everyone I haven't fallen off my rocker too bad," he joked.

She patted his shoulder, about as demonstrative as her personality permitted. "I hope your April returns. She's good for you. Draws you out of your shell in a way that I never could."

He and Tallulah weren't suited for each other at all. He could appreciate that in hindsight.

Tallulah left, leaving him alone with his thoughts. He stared into the fire, lost in memories of April. The first time he'd seen her, standing at the edge of the woods with her long hair blowing like a shimmering halo in the breeze; their first electric kiss; her naked skin brushing against his own; the way she drew out the soft side of Brenda and Joanna; her laughter and musical voice. The way she made him *feel*—protective, tender, passionate and…loved.

It couldn't be over. He refused to believe she was gone for good.

A dash of red fur sped close by. Once again, a fox appeared, a signal of an impending spirit message. His mouth went dry. These messages weren't always good news. The ancestor spirits might bring a number of messages—a blessing, a warning, a bit of guidance or a pronouncement of bad news.

The fire's flames danced and crackled. He stared, mesmerized, allowing himself to sink deep into a plane that existed between now and the past, between the physical and the spiritual, between man and nature. Here was the place he discovered messages from the spirits.

The rolling beat of a drum vibrated in his gut. The unique pattern that meant his father approached.

"You have suffered," his father began, cutting to the heart of the matter. "Listen to me now. Really listen and believe. You are not responsible for my death. No one is."

Chulah opened his mouth to object, then slammed it shut. This was his father, his elder. A man who spoke truth while alive, and in death became a wise spirit who counseled with honesty. He wouldn't lie, not even to soothe his son's feelings. Too bad he'd been so stubborn—or immature—to realize this years ago.

No one is. Meaning April wasn't responsible either. His heart squeezed, remembering that he hadn't truly forgiven her before she returned to the Fae realm. Or maybe he had, but a twisted pride had kept him from acknowledging that truth.

Chulah nodded. "I believe you, Father."

Dad's voice grew sterner. "And it's time I spoke to you about our family. Years ago, I forced a deathbed promise that you take care of Joanna and your brothers and sister."

Oh, hell, he hadn't bailed Chris out of jail this last time. He couldn't bear to be lectured from beyond the grave. "Sorry. I'll post bail next time Johnnie or Chris get in trouble. I've tried to do my best, but sometimes I fall short and—"

"I hereby release you from that vow."

"—then I get angry…" He faltered to a halt. "You do?"

"Your brothers chose their own path, forsaking their shadow-hunter call and getting into trouble with the law. They dishonor the family name."

"They're young." Chulah couldn't believe he was defending them, not after what they put him through. But, after all, they were blood.

"No excuse," his father said shortly. "Let them suffer the consequences and become men."

Chulah nodded. He'd said much the same to Joanna after the last bail request.

"And as far as Joanna…" His father sighed. "She's a good woman. A strong woman. But you have to be equally strong and set boundaries. Live your own life." A smile ghosted his old features. "She'll adapt and grow even stronger."

"Yes, sir."

"But more than old hurts, you suffer for love. You pine the woman-fairy creature."

Chulah's spine stiffened, awaiting a blow. "Her name is April. April Meadows."

"The time will soon come when you have to make a decision. To stay here with your family and your ancestors and the land they have honored forever, or to leave our way of life for another. Choose wisely."

To ask his father which was the wisest choice would be futile. He'd remind him that decisions were for the living. Not for the dead.

The drums faded, receding into the bayou forest. He was alone once more.

Chulah puzzled his father's words about April, unable to decide if the upcoming choice was good or bad news. Good, in that there was hope for a life with April, but disconcerting at the price it would cost.

Could he leave Bayou La Siryna and all his friends and family?

Everything he'd heard about the Fae realm didn't leave him with a favorable impression. Fairies like Steven with his bigotry and hypocrisy. Or their queen. The sly, selfish ways of the Council. Fairies like Grady who killed and mutilated their own kind.

Leaving home meant living with all of that. Forever.

Footsteps alerted him to the presence of two people. One set of footfalls was heavy and labored, the other light and almost as faint as a shadow hunter. Was now the time to decide? Chulah stood, arms crossed, awaiting the people to arrive from the path.

Annie's familiar, kind figure emerged, holding the arm of a large, dark woman wearing a purple turban, a red wool coat and a turquoise scarf. A peacock among the brown autumn landscape. So this must be Annie's grandmother, the infamous Tia Henrietta, known throughout Bayou La Siryna and beyond as a wise and powerful hoodoo practitioner.

Tia huffed and puffed like a dragon about to blow down a tree. "Chulah Rivers," she boomed in a deep, loud voice. "I was given a message to help you."

He frowned. "From who? I don't need any help."

"Where I get all my messages. From the Other Side." She grinned, revealing a golden front tooth. "Hear ya need safe passage to another world."

"Maybe," he conceded. "It's not a done deal."

Tia Henrietta chuckled. A full-throated raspy sound that carried far. Annie helped her settle on a nearby tree stump, where she collapsed with a sigh as loud as the breeze. "Honey, you just keep right on believing that." Tia faced Annie. "He a lot like Tombi, ain't he?"

Annie gave him a gentle smile. "That's a compliment. She loves my husband."

Humph. Chulah wasn't sure what to make of the mysterious Tia Henrietta.

Tia stilled and lifted her nose in the air, studying the

lay of the land. "Some spirit been here a short while ago. You know what I mean?"

"My father." The woman had the Sight. He'd give her that.

She nodded. "A wise soul. You listen to him good, ya hear?" She waved an arm at the blankets below her feet. "Y'all sit down a spell and let's get to work. My old bones cain't take this chill fer too long."

Annie darted a slight, apologetic shrug his way. "I'll take a little hike. Leave y'all some privacy."

"Don't you be gone too long," Tia warned. "I needs to get back inside my warm home."

Annie set off at a brisk pace. "Yes, ma'am."

Chulah sat down, regarding her wearily. "What, exactly, was the message you received this morning?"

"That you be wanting to go to Fairy with yer true love."

Disconcerting that she acted as if she knew his mind better than he did.

"Not yer mind—yer heart," she corrected.

"I'd rather you didn't read my mind," he said, shifting his legs on the blankets.

"It ain't always a picnic for me either." She reached a plump hand in a coat pocket. "Now. I brought yer a little somethin' for the journey."

He didn't bother to correct her again. This was *not* a done deal. No matter how many times Tia Henrietta claimed it was.

She pulled out a purple drawstring bag and tossed it at him. He caught it one-handed and lifted it to his nose. Smelled like a sachet of dried flowers. "What's this for?" He loosened the string and emptied the contents in his hand. A hodgepodge of weird.

"Iron nails to repel any fairy who means you harm. A bit of chain for you to pull between your hands should you need a hasty retreat outta there." Tia held up an identical piece of chain in her own hand. "I'll feel this pull immediately if you are held against your will. But yer best bet is to soften up the ole fairy queen. Flatter her and give her a present."

"Like what?"

"With that mojo bag there. It has a little bit of things she'll love. A doll's silver comb, a couple of shiny marbles, a chip of teal sea glass, a bluebird feather and a book of matches. All of it's sprinkled with lavender, rose and foxglove petals. Just make sure to remove the chain and nails first."

"Matches?" he asked, puzzled.

"It'll be a hit," she assured him. "Strike one of them babies up and they'll be a-oohing and a-aahing all over ya."

He tucked the bag in his jeans pocket. "Anything else I need to know? That is *if* I decide to go."

Tia's good-natured smile slipped. "Don't be a fool. I even gave ya a way out with the chain. Think long and hard what yer life will be like without her."

"Thank you," he said stiffly.

She laughed and slapped her hands on her thighs. "Just callin' it like I sees it, honey child. Yer choice." Tia threw her head back. "Annie? Let's get goin'."

Annie immediately appeared and went to her side, holding her elbow out for Tia to grab on to as she rose slowly.

Chulah stood as well. "How much longer until April comes?"

"Cain't says I know that. The spirits can be mighty tight-lipped when it comes to names and dates and such."

Of course they were. Dad was the same way. Chulah stifled a sigh and extended his hand. Tia drew him into a hearty embrace. "You take care now, ya hear?"

"Tombi and I will come around to see you tonight,"

Annie said, leading her grandmother back to the path. "J.B. says to tell you everything's fine at the shop. Not to worry."

He hadn't even thought about the motorcycle shop, his pride and joy that he'd built up from nothing a few years ago.

Chulah restlessly gathered more branches to feed the fire. April would come tonight. He was sure of it.

Every hair on his scalp suddenly tingled and he slowly turned.

April stood at the edge of the woods, long hair blowing, as miraculously as she'd appeared the day he'd first met her. She'd come into his life and turned everything upside down and sideways.

She ran to him, a joyous smile lighting her face. He held out his arms and she jumped into them. Chulah ran his fingers up and down her back, marveling at the solid weight of her. "How did you manage to escape?"

"Easy, actually. They're so certain they've flattered me by allowing me to be in their pure fairy presence that they have no clue I still wanted to leave." She showered him with kisses.

He could hardly believe his luck. "Does this mean you're back for good? They won't come and take you away again?"

Shadows ghosted across her pale face. "They might."

"I won't let them," he vowed, tightening his hold. "You're mine."

She cocked her head and arched a brow. "Am I?"

For an answer, Chulah kissed her. A long, deep, claiming kiss that left them both breathless and hungry for more. He walked a few steps backward, her legs still wrapped around his waist.

"Where are we going?" she mumbled against his lips.

"Inside my tent."

She threw her head back and laughed, rubbing her hips against his erection. "I can't wait either."

It was all the invitation he needed. Chulah hastily set her feet on the ground and tugged her hand, guiding her inside. Even though she'd been untethered, April filled his tent with her unique scent and glowing presence. This dark prison where he'd camped out for a week was transformed to a cozy den.

"I've missed you." Understatement of his life.

April lightly stroked her fingers down his face. "All I could think about was getting back to you."

He lay down and closed his eyes, savoring her touch. April lay beside him, her lips pressed against his again, fervent and demanding. He clasped her chin in his hand. "Wait. There's a few things that need to be said." And he needed to get them off his chest before passion swept away all reason. "First. You had nothing to do with my father's death. He had heart problems and wouldn't have survived no matter how soon help arrived. I've done nothing but punish us both by insisting otherwise. Can you forgive me?"

Tears rimmed her long lashes. "I forgive you."

Tenderly, he ran his fingers through her hair. "And second, living without you has been hell this last week. I wasn't entirely sure you'd ever come back, or if you were hurt, or in some kind of trouble. Not knowing churned my gut, drove me nearly crazy."

"I love you, too," she whispered.

Was that what this was? Chulah closed his eyes, surrendered to the obvious. It was a novel experience, a total surrender of his heart's control. He opened his eyes and touched a finger to her plump, swollen lips. "You once said you weren't anybody's savior. But you were wrong. You're my savior. My sunshine that lights the hidden shadows."

"Chulah," she breathed.

He sat up, shrugged out of his jacket, his shirt, his jeans. He needed to feel her naked skin against his, needed to show her how much he loved and cherished her.

Her deep blue eyes darkened and she hastily shed her own clothes. Reclining against the blankets, she held out her arms to him. He sank into her soft, silky body, caressing her curves. This time was different. The passion was there, always would be, but tenderness and love were there as well.

He sucked the hardened peaks of her breasts, while his hand cupped her womanly mound.

"I want you now," she moaned. "Please."

He wanted the same. Chulah entered her, his erection tight inside her core. Nothing existed but this dance of love as they sated each other's need. Afterward, he held April close, a profound sense of contentment that soothed his battered heart.

All was well with the world again.

April yawned. Her head rested in the crook where arm met shoulder. "It may have been a week since you last saw me, but for me it's only been one night in Fairy. I'm exhausted."

"Sleep. I'll keep you safe."

Her eyes closed, and he watched the steady rise and fall of her chest in slumber. Chulah drew a blanket over her naked body so the cold wouldn't awaken her. Just a little nap, and then they would return to his cabin. He didn't want to risk being in the woods at dark. They could come again, steal April away forever.

He couldn't—wouldn't—let that happen.

Gently, he disengaged April from his arm and she rolled over, snuggling deep in the blanket. If anyone dared to come around, he should be prepared. Not naked and vulnerable. He quickly donned his clothes.

Outside, the fire was almost banked. Chulah kicked up

dirt over the gray ash, not willing for an ember to fly in the breeze and catch the woods on fire. He gathered his canteen, backpack and camping gear, stuffing them in a large duffel bag. He frowned at the deepening shadows. Much as he hated to wake April, he couldn't take a chance.

He returned to the tent and gently shook her awake. "Sorry, baby, we should go. When we get to my cabin you can sleep for days. Okay?"

She slapped his hand away and mumbled incoherently.

Chulah laughed. "Get dressed, sleepyhead. It's getting dark and we need to get out of here."

April sighed and flung off the blanket. "All right, all right."

Had to be love; even her grumpiness was adorable.

A howling wind shuddered the tent. Something was out there. Chulah lifted a finger to his lips, cautioning April to silence. He picked up his dagger and slowly stepped out.

Chapter 20

Two large fairies, dressed in military red and gold uniforms, glowed liked fallen stars, blinding in their finery. Despite the ostentatious rows of metal pins and braids of their regalia, their expressions were stern and set.

"Why are you here?"

Their glower remained directed at the tent's opening. "Come out at once, April," one of them ordered.

Chulah raised his dagger. "She's with me now. Get off my land."

They stood as stiff and unyielding as giant wooden nutcracker statues come to life. Again, they looked neither to the left nor to the right, but straight ahead.

Were they deaf?

Chulah walked in front of them, waving the dagger. "I said *get off* my property."

The tallest one slowly raised his right hand. A trail of purple light extended from his palm, a current that knocked Chulah's dagger from his clenched fist. His hand burned and then numbed. "What the hell was that?" He shook out his hand, pumping blood back into the deadened fingers.

April rushed out of the tent. "I'll come with you. Just leave him alone."

"No!" He wouldn't go down this easy. Chulah picked up the dagger with his uninjured hand.

April tugged his arm, eyes wide and pleading. "Don't do it. They can direct a beam at your heart that could kill you."

Anger coursed through every cell in his body. His warrior instinct was to protect her at all costs. These fairies must have a weak spot, a vulnerability open to attack. But damn if he knew what it was.

"I have to go with them," April said, her voice choking on the words. "I'll sneak away again one night. This isn't goodbye forever."

He didn't want stolen moments from time to time. Didn't want the uncertainty of knowing whether or not she was safe or even alive. Didn't want to be alone and lonely again. That would never be good enough. He needed April in his life.

The decision was made in an instant. "Then I'll go with you," he vowed.

"But…if you come, they may never let you return home."

"Home is where you are," he said simply. He'd plead his case to let them both return to Bayou La Siryna, but if the queen refused, he'd beg to remain with April in their realm.

The fairies grabbed April, one by an arm, the other by her long hair. Their glow flickered and diminished. They were leaving.

Chulah grabbed April's free hand and held it tight. No matter what, he wouldn't let go. The bottom dropped from beneath his feet and he was falling. A black abyss spun and whirled liked a tornado, his body spiraling down at a furious pace. Weightless. Only darkness passed before his eyes, but the pressure of April's hand remained, even if he couldn't see her. "April," he called.

But there was no answer, only the echo of his voice in the cavernous void. It seemed as if the free fall would never end. Darkness shifted to shades of gray; a distant chiming of bells wafted in the thin air. Images passed before him like the channel changings of an old black-and-white television set—fire ravishing a field, a chorus of singing angels, sun shining through the stained glass of a medieval church, a meadow of bluebells.

His body crashed to the ground and he rolled down a long hill. April's hand was wrenched from his own. At last the hill leveled and he faltered to a stop. Chulah lay on his back and opened his eyes, immediately wishing he hadn't. Everything spun so fast it left him dizzy. His stomach roiled in protest. Noise ricocheted in his brain, a riot of screeches and music and words.

"Chulah? Can you hear me?"

April's voice sounded so far away. He lifted a hand in the air and she clasped it.

They had arrived.

Chulah carefully lifted himself to a sitting position and rubbed his eyes. The world still tilted, but the spinning slowed.

"Close your eyes for a minute," April urged. She ran her fingers through his hair and the contact grounded him. The sun shone warmly on his face and he inhaled the earthy, herbal scent of clover.

Slowly, he opened his eyes again. April's face was before him, searching, concern etching her forehead. "Feel better?" she asked.

"Fine." He struggled to his feet, alert to danger as always. "Where are the guards?"

She pointed to her right. "Over there."

The nutcrackers were wooden as ever, standing at attention.

"What happens now?" he asked, surveying the land with curiosity. Honestly, it didn't look different from any other field at home. He didn't know what he'd expected, but it wasn't this. Even their guards no longer glowed as they had done on earth.

Her teeth worried her lower lip. "Now we're off to see the queen."

Worry clawed his guts. Chulah patted his jeans pocket, relieved to feel Tia Henrietta's mojo bag. Everything depended on winning her favor. He brushed his jeans and straightened his shirt. "Never met royalty before," he joked.

April flicked leaves and bits of grass from his hair. "You're in luck. She happens to love handsome men." She glanced nervously at the guards. "We better go. They're getting antsy."

"How can you tell?"

She smiled, but he could feel her fear.

"I've got some tricks up my sleeve," he said, trying to reassure her. "A few gifts for bribing."

"You're going to need them."

Hands joined, they walked to the guards and followed their stiff gait until they reached a castle of sorts. Its walls were constructed of morning glory vines, rose petals and flowers blooming in every hue. English ivy glued together the patchwork of blossoms and greenery. An open space was carved as a doorway.

"That's the entrance to the fairy court," April explained. "Whatever you do, don't eat or drink anything that's offered. If you do, you'll be stuck here forever."

"Anything else I should know?" he murmured.

"Flatter the queen," she said shortly. "You can't overdo it when it comes to paying her compliments."

He scowled. "I'm not a flowery-talking kind of man."

"You sure swept me off my feet." April squeezed his hand. "Don't speak unless someone addresses you first and be sure to bow when introduced to the queen."

He was already dreading the ordeal with all its rules. But he could deal. After all, April had been subjected to it her whole life.

Long tables with white lace tablecloths were set with elaborate floral centerpieces. Everywhere, fairies, dressed mostly in pastel robes, sipped from crystal glasses and chattered. The head table was composed of obviously more mature fairies. Still beautiful, but with sprinkles of gray in their hair and wrinkles etched around their eyes and into their foreheads.

He knew the queen the moment he set eyes on her again. She was dressed all in black; her robe glittered with celestial designs of stars and crescent moons. Even her hair was raven-colored, with streaks of silver. Unlike most of her pale-skinned, blue-eyed subjects, her skin was as dark as his own, and her eyes were black and shiny as obsidian.

The queen's gaze swept him from head to toe. She regally motioned him to come forward.

The chattering ceased and all eyes were upon him and April. Their evening's entertainment, no doubt. He felt horribly underdressed and on display.

No need for that. He was a shadow hunter, one of the few of his kind, descended from a long line of warriors who fought evil. Nothing to be ashamed of at all. Chulah lifted his chin and marched forward, April at his side.

He'd never been one to back down from a challenge, and he wouldn't start now. Not when everything he wanted was at stake.

Chulah was fearless. Confident. One of the many reasons she loved him. Of course, he hadn't witnessed the queen and Council after they'd been whipped into a fury. Hadn't been the recipient of the Fae's cruelty.

They stood a few feet from the queen. She curtsied and slanted her eyes sideways as Chulah bowed. He did it so gracefully, as if he'd performed it every day of his life. She should have known. When he trekked the forest, his footsteps were as measured and silent as a doe. A natural elegance, although he'd scoff at that description.

"We haven't had a human here in ages," the queen drawled, lifting her nose up an inch. "Except for April, of course. She's nothing but human since that unfortunate encounter with Grady."

"A pleasure to meet you," Chulah said. April nudged him with her elbow. "Your Highness," he added quickly.

"Why did you come? I didn't grant you permission."

"I wanted to be with April. I'd have asked permission but there was no time." He nodded at the guards. "They were insistent on leaving immediately."

A frown creased her forehead. "Why do you want to be with April? There's nothing special about her."

Her face flamed at the insult and she looked down at the ground, lest the anger showed in her eyes.

"Because I love her."

His bold pronouncement warmed her heart and wiped out her anger over the queen's disparagement. April smiled at the shocked faces of the queen and her court. An excited titter broke out at the tables.

"Love?" the queen drawled. "How charming."

Her tone indicated she was anything but charmed at the pronouncement.

"Your Highness," April said quickly, eager to gain her favor. "Chulah didn't have time to ask permission to enter our realm, but he did bring you gifts."

She clapped her hands in delight. "Excellent. What did you bring me? Where is it?"

Chulah withdrew a purple bag from his pocket and undid the drawstring, shaking out a few shiny objects. A few items remained in the bag, but he stuffed it in his pocket so quickly she couldn't tell what he'd kept.

"Let's hope Tia knew what she was doing," Chulah whispered. "Doesn't seem like much to me."

"Quit whispering," the queen scolded. "Come here and show me what you've brought."

He approached the head table and held out his hand. The queen smiled and greedily scooped up the treasures as he stepped back by April's side.

"Well, well. What is this?" she asked, holding up a shiny round object.

"A marble. It doesn't compare to the jewels you wear but—"

"A marble, you say? What's that?" She squinted, rolling it between her fingers.

"A child's toy."

She picked up a glass chip that sparkled with a sea foam–green color. "And this?"

"Sea glass, polished and tumbled by the ocean waves."

"It's lovely," she breathed. "What else do we have here?" She picked through the flower petals. "A miniature silver comb."

"I hope you are pleased," Chulah said.

"What else is in that bag?" she asked sharply.

April held her breath, hoping it was nothing that would get him in trouble. Chulah withdrew the bag once more; his fingers deftly slid some kind of small silver objects in his pants pocket, before he shook out what was left of its contents.

"What's that?" the queen asked. "It's not pretty and shiny."

"It's a book of matches."

"Never heard of it. What's it do?"

"Makes fire."

Her lips twisted, as if skeptical. "Demonstrate, please."

Chulah shrugged slightly and struck a match on the side of the book. A tiny flame burst to light.

She gasped with delight. "Bring it to me."

The queen eagerly grabbed the matches and lit one, watching it burn until it reached her fingertips. She blew it out and lit another. Then another. Until all the matches had been lit and extinguished.

April wanted to smack her forehead. She should have brought the queen matches long ago as a gift. How had Chulah known what gifts would delight the queen? She'd have to ask him later, if there was a *later* for them.

Finished with the fire display, the queen leaned back in her chair and regarded Chulah through hooded eyes. "How long did you want to visit us?"

"That depends."

"On what?"

"On whether you will allow April to return with me to my home, to live with my people, *her* people. She is human now, after all."

The queen drummed her long, spiked fingernails on the table, considering.

April fought to control her shaking. Chulah wrapped an arm around her shoulders, his muscles coiled under his skin. He was as tense as she was, although his face was as impassive as always.

"No," the queen said at last. "Request denied."

His jaw tightened. "Then I'd like permission to live with April in your realm."

Chulah's sacrifice stunned her. A rush of love engulfed her body.

"No. I can't let humans stay here in my kingdom. That just won't do."

Chulah squeezed her shoulder. "May I ask why, Your Highness?"

"I don't have to justify my decisions to you," she said, the coldness returning to her voice.

Chulah looked astonished. And angry. But the sudden mood change of the queen didn't surprise her. She'd seen it over and over through the years. Time to do something—anything—quick.

April stepped forward. "If I may, Your Highness, there's a few things you and the rest of the fairies should know. First, my mother didn't desert the fairy realm. She was on her way back home when Grady intercepted her along the way and killed her."

She let that sink in. She wasn't the unwanted, deserted love child that they had imagined. And her mother had never turned against their kind.

The queen nodded. "Grady met the fate he deserved. Go on."

This was it. She had hoped to have a private audience with the queen for this request, but it hadn't worked out according to plan. April gathered her courage. "Let's talk about justice. I did everything you and the Council asked of me. I convinced the shadow hunters to help protect your kingdom. And I killed Grady, thus preventing any future danger to the realm."

"All as you should have done," the queen said haughtily. "I'd expect no less from any of my subjects."

Bitch. Anger fueled her courage. "Then I'd like to remind Your Highness, and the esteemed Council, of the Fae code on justice and compensation. To quote—an avenging fairy who executes justice on behalf of the Fae realm shall be granted a boon of their choice should they seek recompense."

The queen's eyes darkened and her fingers fisted over the marbles and sea glass in her hand. "You dare—"

"And I choose to leave here and be with Chulah."

Chulah spoke up, placing a warning hand at the small of her back. "Your Highness, if I may. I have nothing but the highest respect for you and this magnificent kingdom. It would please me to live among you the rest of my life."

April fought doing a double take. Since when did Chulah succumb to such flattery, such flowery language?

"But I do understand that my human presence—*our* human presence—would be difficult for you and the rest of the fairies to endure."

The queen's death grip on her new treasures eased and she leaned back in her seat, temper restored. So that was what Chulah was up to—letting the queen save face.

"If you could find it in your hearts to let us return to our humble existence, all of the shadow hunters will be forever in your debt. Allies for eternity."

The queen steepled her fingers together, as if weighing his plea. "I have my subjects to consider." She poured bloodred wine into a goblet and held it out to him. "Shall we drink to a new partnership between the Fae and the shadow hunters?"

Ungrateful, wicked bitch. After all they had done for her, she was trying to trick him into staying trapped here forever, a servant to her bidding. April opened her mouth to protest, but Chulah tugged slightly on her shirt.

"Thank you, but I'm not worthy enough to eat and drink fairy delicacies."

The queen set the goblet down, a reluctant smile twitching her lips. "You are as wise as you are brave, Chulah Rivers. And handsome to boot—for a human."

He bowed low, his long arms sweeping the ground. "You are free to leave."

"Both of us?" April blurted out, hardly daring to believe their luck.

"Yes. Be off with you." She shooed them with a dismissive flick of her wrist.

"Thank you, Your Highness," Chulah said.

April grabbed his hands and turned, eager to leave before the capricious queen had a chance to change her mind. They hadn't taken two steps before she ordered them to a halt.

"One more thing."

April slowly turned around, dread prickling the hairs at the nape of her neck.

"I can't restore what you lost when Grady untethered you, but I can grant you this one gift. Every full moon, should you wish, you may return to the Fae realm for one night, your Fae essence restored. You'll be able to fly and be among us as you once were." The queen's face softened. "Fawn—your mother—was one of my closest friends. I bestow this gift to honor her memory."

Her throat clogged with tears and she was unable to say the words of gratitude. The queen nodded at her in understanding. "Go in peace," she said.

April walked through the crowd, the other fairy faces a blur as tears burned her eyes. She'd been able to restore her mother's good name after all, as she had originally set out to do. But she had so much more. She stole a glance at Chulah. He winked and pulled her close to his side.

They again passed through the open doorway and into the open field. She began running, eager to return to Bayou La Siryna and start a new life. Chulah lifted her in the air with his strong arms and spun her around. "Put me down," she ordered at last. "Let's get out of here before anyone can stop us."

He set her on her feet and his eyes grew serious. "Ready to go home?" he asked. "It will be a different kind of life for you, but I promise to do everything in my power to make you happy."

"You already have," she assured him, marveling that this man—this kind, courageous, handsome man—cherished and adored her. "I have everything I've ever wanted."

Epilogue

"This is the most ridiculous wedding ceremony ever!" Joanna pursed her lips and surveyed the area. "Out in the middle of the woods, in the freezing cold. Whoever heard of such?" She cast her eyes over the decorations and shook her head.

"It's beautiful, Mom!" Brenda clapped her hands and twirled in a circle, taking in the thousand glimmers of light. "It's like a fairy tale."

"You're sixteen—of course you'd think this is romantic," Joanna scoffed.

"You have to admit, it's kinda cool, Mom," Chris said, fiddling with his tie.

Chulah had never seen his half brother in anything remotely formal. Just jeans, T-shirts and shorts.

And prison whites.

Tombi leaned into him. "Relax. I'm guarding the wedding ring," he muttered.

Chulah snorted and Joanna regarded them suspiciously. "What's so funny?"

Annie left Tombi's side and soothingly patted Joanna's arm. "You know how men are. They like to joke around at solemn occasions. Makes them less nervous."

Joanna's eyes widened. "Chulah's never nervous." She turned to him uncertainly. "Are you?"

"Course not," he denied.

Annie laughed. "Sure he is. He's getting married tonight."

Tombi poked his side. "It's okay. I'll admit I was a little nervous when I married Annie." He gave his wife a tender smile. "But it's the best thing I ever did."

Chulah poked Tombi back. "You look besotted, you poor old married man."

Was that how he appeared when he gazed at April? Probably. Chulah inwardly groaned. He wanted to get this whole ordeal over with. And get April in his bed.

Joanna's face softened and she awkwardly patted his shoulder. "April's a wonderful girl. If your father were here—" she blinked and swallowed hard "—he'd be so proud of you. Like I am."

Shock muted his tongue. Had she actually said something kind about him? Joanna enveloped him in a quick hug and he inhaled her familiar powder coupled with the astringent scent of hair spray. She broke away, clearing her throat. "Now, then. Let's go have a seat, Chris."

He thought nothing could again surprise him after learning of the Fae, but Joanna had proved him wrong.

The bayou breeze was a bit chilly, but hardly the freezing cold that Joanna had claimed. The sun set low, beaming coral rays as a farewell to the day. All his friends and family were present.

Hunters stood on either side of the massive oak. Icicles of light cascaded from its branches like a tree chandelier. Lights were everywhere, from candles to lanterns that outlined the processional aisle. Frothy, girlie pink and white material draped the chairs for the small wedding party. Some kind of flower petals decorated the aisle and in front of the trees where they were to say their vows. Brenda stood in front of the cypress wearing a pastel dress and a tiara of flowers and ribbons in her hair. An April touch, no doubt.

A table was set off to one side, laden with cake and punch. Draping the front of it was a sign in fancy calligraphy. Once Upon a Time.

And *that* was a Brenda touch. She took her role as maid of honor seriously, and was responsible for most of the romantic touches that dominated the tableau. A justice of the peace would have suited him just as well, but he couldn't deny letting the ladies in his life enjoy their day. Brenda was almost as excited as April. Joanna even got a kick out of it, though she wouldn't admit it.

There was no music, other than the awakening sounds of nature in spring. But some invisible clue shifted the atmosphere. Everyone took their places.

A patch of pixelated lights burst in two neighboring trees.

Ah, the Fae had arrived.

April stepped from behind the cypress dressed in a deep emerald gown with pearl buttons. Her head was adorned with a tiara of opals, a gift from the fairy queen. She gazed at him with shining eyes and his heart pinched with love. His girl, his fairy, who had loved him before he even knew she existed.

Tombi grinned and waved a hand in front of his face. "Time to get this show on the road. You besotted fool."

Let them laugh. All that mattered was that April was bound to be his forever.

* * * * *

MILLS & BOON®

18 bundles of joy from your favourite authors!

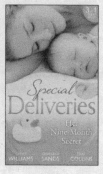

Get 2 books free when you buy the complete collection only at
www.millsandboon.co.uk/greatoffers